Secrets of Number Six Ashby House

JO-ANN PASTERNAK GILBERT

NEWMAN SPRINGS PUBLISHING
320 Broad Street
Red Bank, NJ 07701

First originally published by Newman Springs Publishing 2019

ISBN 978-1-64531-400-4 (Paperback)
ISBN 978-1-64531-401-1 (Digital)

Printed in the United States of America

To family and friends

Everyone has secrets. Some secrets die with us.
And then there are those that never rest…

PROLOGUE

CASSIA MARIE WESTFIELD BURNS was born six weeks early. Six minutes after giving Cassia life, her mother died. Her father took an early flight home from a business trip abroad so he could be with his daughter for her sixth birthday. His plane crashed into the ocean at exactly 6:00 a.m. Cassia lost her own child in the sixth month of her pregnancy. On her sixth wedding anniversary, Cassia found her husband locked in a passionate kiss with his photography assistant.

Cassia never arrives early for appointments. She keeps and follows a daily to-do list. She never schedules anything for 6:00 a.m. or 6:00 p.m. Cassia steers clear of anything involving the number six. With these precautions in place, she finally feels safe.

On June 6, 2006, Cassia learns that she has inherited Number Six Ashby House.

CHAPTER ONE

CASSIA WAVED HER HAND WHEN Mitch came through the doors of the Broadway Diner. He had gotten accustomed to her steadfast rule of not arriving early, so he instinctively arrived a few minutes late. Mitch waved back, displaying that familiar grin. Cassia put her right hand on her stomach attempting to tame what felt like a thousand tiny ladybugs taking flight. It was that silly toothy smile that took her back to the day when Mitch came into her life. He saved the day like the knight in her favorite fairy tale, the *Green Knight*. Cassia preferred the Danish Cinderella-like version over the more traditional *Cinderella* because in the end, the knight and the princess save each other. At their first meeting, Mitch was not decked out in shining armor, but in Cassia's eyes, he may as well have been. He saved the day and possibly her career by sporting a camera and video equipment.

Cassia was coordinating her first wedding without an assistant since being hired by Marcie McCall Wedding Planning Services. She felt confident as she placed a checkmark next to the last item on her pre-wedding checklist. On the way to the bride's Hunt Valley estate where the wedding was taking place, Cassia rehearsed a speech in her head. By the time she reached her destination, Cassia believed that she had formulated the perfect speech even though she had no experience in marriage herself. However, her life experiences taught her to treasure every moment with those you love.

As the hours ticked by, wedding jitters not only swept over the bride-to-be but Cassia could feel her own confidence waning. She tried to convince herself that her onset of nerves was because her boss, Marcie McCall, would be at the wedding observing her first solo event. Marcie was a perfectionist and expected nothing less of her employees. Cassia liked that about Marcie but knew that most weddings never went off without some minor or, once in a while, major hiccup. While Cassia hoped for a hiccup-less day, Cassia's gut told her something more was causing her distress. She brushed it off, smiled at the bride, and announced that it was time to begin.

As they began their procession to the outside, Cassia caught a glimpse of Marcie in the crowd while giving last-minute reminders to the bridesmaids who were now lined up on the grassy area. They were ready and waiting for the proper cue to proceed down the white carpet toward the groom and groomsmen who were standing next to the perfectly constructed archway decorated in white ribbons and red-and-white plumeria flowers flown in from Hawaii that morning. Despite Cassia's misgivings about outdoor weddings, the day was picture-perfect with large puffy white clouds drifting slowly across a backdrop of blue sky and an ever so slight breeze. As the wedding began and with the bride and groom ready and anxiously waiting, Cassia accepted that her bad feeling *had* to be a false alarm.

Cassia waited for a nod from the cameraman to begin the procession. However, instead of a nod, he began wildly flailing his arms. In fact, everyone standing near the flowered covered arch began swatting at the bees who at that moment had decided that they had enough sweet nectar and it was time for a harassing rampage. Two quick-thinking groomsmen pulled the arch out of the soft dirt and threw it far away from the crowd but not before each were stung at least twice. Within a few seconds, it was apparent that the cameraman had been stung too. He was down on the ground. His face was rapidly swelling, and his breathing quickly sounded more labored as the seconds ticked by. Cassia dialed 9-1-1. At the same time that Cassia was dialing for help, Marcie was making her own call from one of the many lists that she always kept in her purse. She got lucky when Mitch, another cameraman in her employ, answered his phone and said he could be there in less than an hour.

By the time the paramedics arrived and stabilized the man's breathing with a shot of epinephrine, Mitch was running across the grassy area with a large camera bag hanging from each shoulder.

Cassia wished that she had asked the paramedics for her own dose of heart-starting medicine as she watched Mitch getting closer and closer. Later, whenever Cassia recalled the story of their first meeting, she always called Mitch her "knight with the camera bags."

Mitch and Cassia could not deny the sparks between them but slowly worked their relationship into a friendship first. Marcie began assigning them weddings together because she too saw their obvious chemistry. It was not until they were assigned a large Greek wedding that their friendship turned into something more. By the time they took on the most expensive wedding that Marcie McCall Wedding Planning Services had ever been contracted to do, Cassia and Mitch had completed over a dozen nearly flawless weddings together. Mitch's confidence boosted Cassia's, so when Mitch said that they would "hit it out of the park," she believed him. And that is just what they did.

When it was time for group pictures for the twenty-six members wedding party, the eight children ages three to ten years old were cranky and uncooperative. Jewel, Mitch's new photography assistant, was no help at all just sitting and filing her nails. But Mitch, so professional and with a natural easiness that made him so likable, stooped down his 6'5" frame to their level. He smiled that toothy grin, and with his Buddy Holly-like dark-rimmed glasses pushed high up onto his nose, had them laughing and lined up in no time. That smile won over the hearts of those little ones as well as Cassia's. They were married six months later, and six years later, they divorced.

Since their divorce, they had not been assigned another wedding together though continued working for the same company. While their work schedules now took them in different directions, they usually managed to get together at least once a month for lunch or dinner. However, the last six months consisted of playing phone tag or a short text message. Cassia worried that Mitch was drifting out of her life. She was relieved when Mitch answered the phone last night and was able to meet her for breakfast.

As Cassia watched his lanky frame make its way to the table, she wondered if Mitch remembered that it was the anniversary of her miscarriage. Five years ago, Cassia lost their baby. That morning, she woke Mitch up after a sleepless night telling him that she had not felt the baby move the day prior and all that night. Cassia was sure something was not right. Mitch believed that she was being paranoid because as soon as she reached her sixth month, Cassia began obsessing that something would go wrong. While she called the doctor, Mitch just blew it off as another one of her superstitions relating to the number six. The sonogram proved otherwise. It did not make any sense to Cassia why their baby's heart just stopped beating at six months gestation. The doctor's last words still echo in Cassia's head almost every day, "This type of thing happens sometimes." A week later, she delivered a baby girl they named Elizabeth. They buried her next to Cassia's mother and father. Cassia decided not to mention anything about her miscarriage during their breakfast because it would only dredge up too many hurtful memories.

CHAPTER TWO

"Hey, Cassie," Mitch said as he bent down to kiss her cheek. Cassia smiled. Some people called her Cass, but she loved the fact that he was the only person who called her Cassie. Mitch sat down across the table from Cassia. "You look great, but I must admit you sounded somewhat crazy on the phone last night. Are you okay?" Mitch knew that Cassia always got a little crazy around the anniversary of losing the baby, but he vowed not to bring it up because that conversation usually ended up in an argument and tears.

Cassia smiled. "I'm fantastic." The waitress placed two waters and straws on the table.

Mitch ordered two coffees.

"So…what's the big news that you have to tell me that can't wait until I get back from my two-week assignment in London, as in London, *England*? Did I tell you I am photographing the royal family?"

"Who do you know, and whose ass did you kiss to get that assignment?" Cassia said while grinning ear to ear.

"You sound a tad jealous, my friend." Mitch ripped off the end of the paper covering the straw and blew the remainder of the paper at Cassia. She held her hand up to deflect it from hitting her face. Cassia was familiar with this little trick, so it came as no surprise.

"Don't you get tired of being so immature?" Cassia said while laughing and remembering the first time the paper hit her eye and how Mitch came across the table and smothered her face with kisses until she forgave him.

"I am not immature. *I* just have a great sense of humor."

"Are you implying that *I* don't?" Cassia kicked his leg under the table. Mitch jumped, causing the items on the table to rattle against each other.

"Ouch. Still a good shot. Okay. You are funny. Ha, ha, ha," Mitch said while moving his legs as far away as he could from Cassia. "Well, the truth is that I'm getting sick and tired of Marcie and her new commission splits. She is making more money than ever since we did that big Greek wedding. She just gets greedier and greedier. Maybe I am sick of the whole wedding business. Anyway, I've been putting my resume out there, and a couple weeks ago, I got a call from *People* offering me this job."

"*People* as in *People magazine*?"

"Yes."

"Damn, you are one lucky bastard."

"And I thought it was my talent that got me the job," Mitch said as he picked up the second straw on the table.

Cassia closed her eyes. "You hit me with that one, and you are paying for this breakfast, and I will order steak and eggs and fifty other things on the menu." Mitch put down the straw. He would be paying for the meal anyway because that was what he did whenever they dined together. Today, Cassia was especially counting on him paying because she had not been paid for her work on the last two weddings. The waitress placed their coffees on the table and took their orders.

"Okay, finish your story. How did you get hooked up with *People*?"

"I snapped a couple pics here and there, sent them in, and they called with a couple small assignments. I guess they liked my work because they gave me this 'cake' job. I will still be doing weddings until I can make enough money with *People*. I have a feeling that my awesome work on this assignment will seal the deal."

"What about Jew-el? Will she be going with you to London?" Cassia tried to pronounce her name like everyone else, but it always came out Jew-el instead of Jule. Mitch gave up correcting her mispronunciation years ago. It was about the same time that Cassia stopped blaming Jewel for their breakup. She had reconciled that it was inevitable that their marriage would have ended with or without that kiss between Mitch and Jewel. Their signatures were nearly written on their divorce degree when Mitch, according to Cassia, seemed relieved when she lost the baby. The affair just dotted the i's and crossed the t's on their names on the document.

"Jewel will be joining me in London for the second week of my trip. Her uncle died last night, and she is staying behind to attend the service and help her aunt for a couple days. Bad luck for that old bastard, but good luck for me. It gives me a few days by myself."

"Is there trouble in *paradise?*" Cassia's eyes widened, and her eyebrows raised.

Looking down at the table, Mitch said, "No, it's just that we moved in together three weeks ago. It's an adjustment living with someone again—a *big* adjustment."

"Well, it's been four years. It's about time. In fact, it's way over-due," Cassia smiled, but Mitch knew it was not an honest smile—not the one he fell in love with. It was not the smile where her green eyes lit up and pulled him in like it did when she told him for the first time that she was in love with him.

Mitch crossed his eyes and pursed his lips. "Now there's Jewel in my face in the morning. Jewel in my face at work. Jewel in my face in the evening. And Jewel in my face even when I take a shit in the bathroom."

Cassia laughed. "Your punishment." Mitch shook his head and burst out laughing too.

The waitress refilled their coffees and took their orders. She smiled. "You two sure are having a good time this morning." Cassia and Mitch could not hold back giggling a little more as the waitress walked away.

Mitch picked up his fork and finally remembered that Cassia had something important to tell him and blurted out, "God, I'm so sorry, Cassia, I'm going on and on about London and forgot about *your* big news you needed to tell me."

"I've inherited a house in Richmond, Virginia. Well, it's more like an estate." Cassia smiled while adding a third creamer to her second cup of coffee.

13

Mitch was relieved. He had thought that Cassia's big news might be that she is seeing someone and maybe even getting serious. Since the divorce, he knew about a few guys she dated, but nothing serious. He felt guilty and selfish that he was glad her announcement was not a new man in her life.

Cassia waited for any reaction from Mitch. She could not understand why he just stared into space. Cassia waved her hand close to Mitch's face. "Earth to Mitch."

Mitch snapped out of his daze and looked up. "What? Sorry, Umm...yeah, did some rich uncle die or something?"

"Exactly." Cassia laughed at his correct response. "Well, he wasn't a biological uncle, just a good friend of my mother and father. I barely remember him. All I know is that Grandma B hated him, and she would never tell my why. The last time I saw him was at my father's funeral."

"Cassie, Catherine Brittle hates *everybody*," Mitch said rolling his eyes.

Shrugging her shoulders, Cassia said, "Grandma B liked you for a little while. Still don't understand that one."

Mitch recalled the day when Catherine Brittle turned on him. It was the day after Cassia told her grandmother that she was pregnant. She was already in her third month. That morning, Catherine called Mitch at work. She wanted him to meet her for lunch at her home without Cassia. She made him promise that he would not tell Cassia. He agreed. Mitch was confused because Catherine never invited him without Cassia before. He thought maybe she wanted to set up a trust fund for the baby as a surprise for Cassia. He thought again and knew that if Grandma B did anything like that, she would make sure the whole world knew. When he arrived at her home, immediately she was curt and unpleasant when Mitch tried to engage in small talk. While she was never a warm person, her frostiness made him wish that he had brought an ice scraper with him that day. He could not understand why she was pissed at him because he was always so careful to not offend her for Cassia's sake. He had gotten used to her offending ways and felt that he had a good handle at staying on her good side.

Catherine took Mitch's coat and placed it on the rack by the door. Forsaking any pleasantries, Catherine got right to the point, "How come I did not hear about you and Cassia wanting a baby until yesterday when she announced that she is already three months pregnant?"

Mitch was unprepared for this questioning. He snapped back, "Because, Catherine, it is none of your business, and you don't make it easy for Cassia to tell you a lot of things."

Catherine's face instantly reddened. "What the hell does that mean?"

"C'mon, Catherine, this pregnancy for example. One would think that you would be happy for your granddaughter. Instead, you are acting like it's all about *you*. This really has nothing to do with you," Mitch said, taking a deep breath.

"It has *everything* to do with me. Cassia is going to die giving birth just like her mother."

Catherine collapsed on a chair. She covered her face with her hands. Mitch's face was red. He screamed while pacing back and forth in front of Catherine, "Don't you *ever* say those words to Cassia."

Catherine got up from the chair and poured herself a cup of tea. She tried to steady her hands, but the teacup rattled against the dish as she began her story, "When I was a young girl, I had an affair with a man named Charles Winchester II. Cassia's mother, Marianne, was the product of that affair. My husband never knew—well, at least he never said anything to me. And I never told Marianne. Years later, Marianne married Michael, and by coincidence or some sick twist of fate, they became friends with a man named Charles Winchester III during a trip to Paris. When Marianne told me about their new friend, I discouraged that relationship. However, just like Cassia, Marianne was strong-willed and refused to listen. I should have told Marianne the truth, Mitch."

"What the hell are you talking about?" Mitch said more puzzled than ever.

Catherine's eyes could no longer hold back the tears. She blurted, "I knew that Michael and Marianne were having trouble conceiving a child, but never in a million years did I think that they would ask Charles Winchester III for help. Marianne was in her fifth month of her pregnancy when she told me that Charles was the biological father of the child she was carrying. I could not tell her that Charles Winchester III was her half brother. Losing Marianne was punishment for my sins, and I will be punished again if Cassia carries this baby because it has Winchester blood. You should have told me that you and Cassia were trying to have a baby."

That was the first time Mitch heard the name *Charles Winchester*. Mitch agreed to keep Catherine's secret because Cassia was too far along in her pregnancy to change anything. He loved Cassia, and it began eating at him—the possibility of losing her. From that day on, even though he fought to hide them, negative feelings about Cassia's pregnancy kept surfacing. Cassia was confused and heartbroken about this sudden change because Mitch was elated when she told him that he was going to be a father. He stopped going to appointments with her and showed little interest in the sonogram pictures she brought home. Cassia tried to talk to Mitch, but he refused to discuss it.

Mitch's attention returned to Cassia. He took a bite of his toast and drank his last sip of coffee. "Don't you think it's kind of weird that he named you the heir to his fortune?"

"Yes, it is weird. I don't know if it is worth anything. It may be one wrecking ball away from demolition. And it gets weirder. I don't have all the details, but according to the brief conversation that I had with Mr. Oates, the executor of the estate, I cannot rightfully own the house until I stay in it for six days. I go there tomorrow, and by Saturday, it's mine. Then I can do with it as I please." Cassia finished in a whisper, "Sounds a little E. A. Poe-ish, doesn't it?"

Cassia had Mitch's attention now. He leaned across the table and whispered back, "Is it haunted or something?" Before Cassia could respond, Mitch jumped up from his seat. From the corner of his eye, he saw a couple enter the restaurant. He had been trying to arrange their engagement photo session without any success. He said, "I'll be right back. I need to talk to that couple over there. I need to let them know that I'll be out of town for the next two weeks. Hold that thought for one minute."

Cassia had many thoughts, and suddenly they were flashing back to that night in the attic with Uncle Charles and the beautiful lady. She tried to remember every detail of what really happened, but it was so long ago, and much of that night had faded from her memory. She was not certain if what she did remember was real, her imagination, or just some remnants of Uncle Charles's wild stories. Over the years she had even convinced herself that it was just a dream. But if it was just a dream, why did Uncle Charles instruct her to tell no one?

Mitch returned to the table. Cassia snapped out of her stupor. Mitch said, "Okay…why this mysterious proviso in the will?" Mitch spoke in a poorly imitated Bela Lugosi voice while waving his fingers in front of Cassia's face. "Do you think the house is haunted?" Cassia pushed his hands away.

"No? Yes? Maybe? I don't know." Cassia was not ready to disclose to Mitch what may have happened in the attic because she was not sure herself. She said, "I really don't remember much about the house except that it was huge. I was so in love with it. Another thing I remember, not about the house but about my uncle, is that he was a great storyteller. His housekeeper would get so mad at him. She once told him to stop his nonsense and stop scaring me with his crazy stories. Her name was Maddie." Cassia's eyes widened. "Oh my god! Maddie! I wonder what happened to her. She was always so nice and funny. Every night before tucking me in, she would say in her thick Southern accent, 'Child, I love you to pieces.'"

"For as long as I've known you, how come you've never mentioned anything about staying there as a kid?"

"When I was about three years old to six years old, I started spending a month with my uncle at Ashby House during the summer while my father met with his London clients. I was at the house when I got the news of my father's accident. You know that I don't like talking about that time of my life. Well, Grandma B put an end to my visits after my father died. She said I would never visit that house again, and I never did."

"Do you want to wait until I get back so I can go with you? Of course, I would sleep on the couch," Mitch said while lowering his head and avoiding eye contact with Cassia.

"Well, if it turns out to be a dump, we both might be sleeping in the tree house, but I don't think that would go over so well with Jew-el. Remember Jew-el?"

Mitch smacked his forehead with the palm of his right hand and crossed his eyes. "Dah, oh yeah Jew-el," mimicking Cassia's smart-ass pronunciation of Jewel's name. Cassia smiled.

"So, when do you get more information from the attorney?"

"He is meeting me at the house tomorrow with the key and some papers. I will put on my big girl pants and do this myself. But first, I am going to visit Grandma B later this evening at the retirement village and tell her that I am now the proud owner of Number Six Ashby House, the estate of Charles Allen Winchester III. She'll probably take her rickety ass out of her favorite chair and do a happy dance at the news of his death."

Mitch's face was pale. "Did you say *Charles Winchester?*"

"Yes. Do you know him?"

"No. No." Mitch jumped up from the table, causing its contents to once again rattle about.

He looked at the check, took twenty dollars out of his wallet, placed it on the table, and in an uncharacteristic stutter, he said, "I...I...have to go and finish packing. E-mail or text me when you can." He kissed Cassia on the forehead and quickly turned away.

Cassia yelled out loud enough that several people in the restaurant turned to see, "Mitch, Mitch, is everything all right?"

He turned back around and waved. "Everything is great." Mitch stepped outside the door.

He checked his watch. He wished that he had enough time to pay Grandma B a visit before leaving for London.

CHAPTER THREE

CASSIA TOOK HER TO-DO LIST from her purse and counted the appointments. She checked the time on her cell phone. No way could she squeeze in a visit with Grandma B. It would have to wait until she got back from Richmond. She had appointments scheduled back-to-back with five potential new clients and needed to pack. With Marcie breathing down her neck to bring in more business because of the recent exodus of two high-dollar wedding planners from the company, it was necessary to keep the appointments, even though preliminary information suggested that they would all be small weddings, which meant small commissions. Mitch was right. Marcie was running her business into the ground. Everyone was leaving because no one was making any money, except Marcie.

Cassia checked the time on her phone again. She *had* to make time to visit Marcie and get her paycheck because she had already written a few checks on that money, and they would do a bouncing trick if she did not get the money in the bank today. This was the first time in Cassia's four years on her own that she was having serious money problems. Cassia hoped that the house in Virginia would be the answer to her debt issues. As the day went by, the more she thought about the condition that Uncle Charles put in his will of making her stay six days, the more annoyed she became. However, considering her financial situation, she felt that she had no choice but to comply. She was tired, hungry, and angry at Uncle Charles. After a few sips of wine and several bites from her dinner of cheese and crackers, Cassia's mood mellowed. She took a page from her notepad and wrote the words "to-do list—June 12" at the top of the page. She stopped and began chewing on the end of her pen and stared straight ahead. She closed her eyes and sighed. "This will all be done in six days." Cassia opened her eyes and wrote the number one at the top of the page.

In order to meet Mr. Oates at ten, Cassia figured that she had to be on the road by at least six thirty. Then she thought about morning rush hour on the 495 near DC and decided to leave by five thirty instead. Cassia picked up her to-do list from the table and changed her start time to five thirty. Cassia scratched the number six off her schedule. She smiled. It was common practice every evening for Cassia to write her agenda for the next day's events. She got teased by everyone in the business that knew about her *famous* to-do lists. Even Mitch laughed when she pulled her list from her purse to make changes throughout the day. Cassia understood that those lists might have made her seem inflexible at times, but she saw herself as organized. Cassia closed her suitcase, removed it from the bed, and thought about her breakfast with Mitch. His strange response to her mentioning Uncle Charles's name baffled her more and more. Cassia got into bed, set the alarm for 4:30 a.m., and turned off the light.

She quickly fell asleep and began having the same dream that she had so many times before, but she was unprepared for the new ending.

Uncle Charles was standing on the front porch of Ashby House arguing with Grandma B.

Words were coming from their mouths, but Cassia could not understand any of them. Grandma B towered at least two feet over Uncle Charles, leaning in more and more while shaking her finger in his face. She looked so poised in an all-black pant suit and a black hat with an attached veil that covered her face. Uncle Charles's cowboy boots had alligator heads attached to the toes of the boots. The alligators suddenly came alive and opened their mouths and eyes. They snapped at Grandma B. She finally backed away.

Uncle Charles was dressed in his usual cowboy attire—white dress shirt tucked into dark-blue jeans and a leather-fringed vest. Uncle Charles always wore a shiny belt buckle with a large cursive W, representing the Winchester name, but in the dream, the belt buckle had a number and letters: #6 AH (Ashby House). It was almost six by six inches. His belly hung slightly over the buckle, and when he exhaled, his flab pushed against the #6 AH like it was trying to escape. He was smoking his favorite pipe. A circle of smoke blotted out his face except for his overgrown mustache. The more he puffed, the more smoke came pouring out along with cherry juice that dripped down his chin and stained his white shirt. His smiling lips were enormous, as if he recently had been given an overdose of a collagen injection.

Maddie was standing on the opposite end of the porch wearing a yellow sundress with a huge ladybug on the front. Cassia told Maddie how pretty she looked. Maddie said, "I love you to pieces, child." Then Maddie hugged Cassia so tight and did not let her go until they both were laughing. The hug made Cassia feel so loved and safe, like she remembered during her visits.

Maddie began a throaty laugh that got louder and louder. Maddie released Cassia. She ran her fingers down the deep three-inch scar on Maddie's left cheek. Maddie sobbed. Behind them, the house began crumbling, and huge black birds filled the sky. Several scooped down and carried Grandma B away. Cassia watched until she could no longer see the birds or Grandma B's legs kicking frantically in the air. She then felt something hugging her body again. This time it was not Maddie but instead the long branches of a weeping willow binding her until its branches and leaves covered her mouth. Maddie and Uncle Charles were now standing side by side with their right index finger on their lips saying, "Shh...shh...shh..." Cassia fought to scream, but the leaves of the weeping willow cut off any sound. Mitch came out of the collapsing house with the beautiful lady from the attic—the one she saw as a child. They were arm in arm smiling at each other. Mitch walked by Uncle Charles, tipped his head in greeting. Uncle Charles did the same in return.

Cassia was trembling when she woke from her dream. Her face was tear soaked. She sat up, grabbed her legs close to her, and began rocking back and forth. Cassia had had that dream before, but this time it was different. Mitch was in the dream this time. And *she* was in the dream—the beautiful lady from the attic with Uncle Charles that night she sneaked a peek at them. Cassia turned on the bedroom lamp by her bed. She wished Mitch was there to hold her like he had before when she had a nightmare. She kept the light on. Before drifting back to sleep, Cassia wondered if it was Jewel in the dream with Mitch and not the lady from the attic. Mitch and Jewel moving in together bothered her more than she admitted.

CHAPTER FOUR

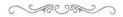

CASSIA WHEELED HER SUITCASE TO the curb. She opened the back of her neatly organized 2005 Toyota Prius and placed the suitcase next to her briefcase. Still half asleep, Cassia jumped from the vibration coming from her purse. She reached into the side pocket for her phone and saw a message. It was from Mitch, "good flight but tired. too expensive to use phone here. email u later. hope u remembered ur computer." Cassia smiled and shook her head while reading Mitch's text. She knew that the time difference would make it difficult for any IM communication with him. Jewel would be the other obstacle next week.

Cassia had a hard time hiding her feelings about Jewel, though she was always fake-friendly the handful of times that they saw each other. On the other hand, Jewel's attitude toward Cassia always puzzled her. Perhaps her mistrust of Cassia stemmed from the fact that Mitch and Cassia continued to have a special bond, even after the divorce. Cassia tried hard not to interfere in Mitch's relationship with Jewel. Mitch never cared if Jewel approved or disapproved of their friendship. Once he even stopped by Cassia's apartment to drop off chicken soup when he heard from a friend that she was sick. Jewel waited in the car. Many of their friends thought that it was a bit odd for them to remain friends after the divorce because so many inflated stories about what caused their breakup went flying throughout their social circle—stories that included Cassia stepping out on Mitch and Mitch picking up prostitutes on The Block. Cassia just brushed off the exaggerated stories. However, one story in particular really hurt Cassia. About a month after signing their divorce papers, Cassia was having lunch with another wedding planner. She told Cassia that

Jewel was telling everyone that she and Mitch had been lovers for a couple months before that "dumb bitch" caught them kissing. While Mitch and Cassia were mostly amicable throughout the divorce process, it still left Cassia mentally exhausted. She thought about Jewel's claim and wanted to talk to Mitch about it but, after more thought, decided against it after concluding that Jewel hated that she and Mitch were still friends, and this fictitious story was her way of killing their friendship and getting Cassia entirely out of the picture. Cassia refused to feed into Jewel's drama. Besides, she and Mitch were friends before they were lovers. She was determined to do whatever was necessary to preserve that friendship. Cassia's schedule was already off. She was leaving fifteen minutes later than her decided 5:30 a.m. departure, but she went back into her apartment to get her computer. The thought of not being able to communicate with Mitch, especially since her nightmare, made going back into her apartment for her computer necessary.

Inside the room, Cassia took her to-do list from her purse and readjusted her leaving time again. She picked up the bag that housed her computer. Turning the key into the deadbolt, Cassia shivered. She could not shake the creepy skin-crawling feeling since her nightmare. In her first e-mail to Mitch, she would, for the first time, tell him about her nightmare. When they were together and she woke up shaking and crying after having the same nightmare over and over, she would lie telling Mitch that she did not remember her bad dream. She knew that it would be like opening a can of worms if she told Mitch about her dream. If she let one worm escape, then all of them would come slithering out. However, now that Mitch knew about Uncle Charles and Ashby House, she felt ready to share the content of her nightmare and the new twist in last night's version. She would also demand answers about his undeniably strange reaction when she mentioned Uncle Charles's name at breakfast yesterday.

Cassia drove onto the I-95 south ramp. She glanced in the direction of the upscale retirement village where Grandma B called home for the last five years. The usual pang of guilt for not visiting her grandmother more often attacked Cassia. However, Cassia quickly squashed those feelings of guilt because she knew why her visits had become less and less frequent—Catherine Brittle was not an easy person to be around these days. Actually, she had never been an easy person to be near, but lately she was becoming more intolerable with every visit. Cassia wondered how Grandma B was able to keep the few church friends that she had. Even their numbers had dwindled over the years. Some were lost because of Catherine's inability to control her opinions and sharp tongue, but most were gone due to the fact that many were up in age and had died.

Cassia recalled how strikingly beautiful Grandma B was in seeing old pictures of her as a young woman. Many people compared her looks to Grace Kelly in her younger days—tall and thin, light velvety flawless skin, high cheekbones, and perfectly groomed blond hair that she wore off her face in a relaxed bun most of the time. Cassia glanced at herself in the rearview mirror. She wondered why she did not look like anyone in her family. It was not the first time that she questioned her genetics since her father was over six feet tall and blond too. Her mother looked like a clone of Grandma B. Cassia's hair was dark black, and she was barely five feet tall. Her catlike green eyes did not match anybody in the family. Once Cassia overheard Grandma B's friends whispering that Cassia must be the milkman's baby because she did not resemble her mother, Marianne, or her father, Michael, at all. At the time, Cassia did not understand the meaning of that saying and asked her grandmother what the milkman looked like. Grandma B was confused and said that they got their milk from the store.

Grandma Brittle lived for attention. At her famous tea parties that she held twice a year, she predictably bragged to all her friends about the number of suitors who regularly knocked at her door. It was not until her husband was dead five years that she finally accepted an invitation for brunch from a gentleman from her church. Her daughter, Marianne, had been dead six years by then. Cassia never really knew why Grandma B did not remarry because even in her fifties and sixties, she could still turn heads. Cassia thought maybe her grandfather, whom she never met, must have been the love of her grandmother's life. One thing she was certain about was that the other love of Grandma B's life was Cassia's mother, Marianne—Catherine's only child.

For just a moment, Cassia's heart softened for her grandmother when she thought about losing her own child, Elizabeth. She thought about the bedroom that Grandma B kept as a tribute to her daughter. She remembered how it was set up like a shrine with pictures, memorabilia, and one candle burning most of the time. Cassia's tender thoughts for her grandmother did not last long though. Her anger came bubbling up thinking about how her grandmother locked away into a storage unit all her mother's things when she moved from her house to the retirement village. Cassia believed that her mother's things should have been given to her. However, she was not surprised that she never got them considering what happened the day her grandmother caught her in her mother's room.

On the morning of Cassia's sixteenth birthday, Catherine left the house to pick up a cake for her party. When she returned, Catherine found Cassia sitting on her mother's bed looking through one of Marianne's journals. They were kept in a locked box in the closet. Cassia knew she was not allowed in that room, so she dropped the journal onto the floor when her grandmother entered the room. Catherine rushed over then picked up the journal. She shook it in front of Cassia's face shouting, "How did you get this? Did you go in my room and steal the key from my jewelry box?"

Cassia had never seen her grandmother's face so red. She leaned back supported only by her elbows on the bed trying to keep the book from brushing against her face. After a few seconds, she became uncomfortable in that position, and finally with her right hand, she pushed the journal away from her face. "Grandma, I didn't steal anything from your room. I found the key taped under the music box on the dresser."

Catherine put the journal on the dresser. She picked up the music box and turned it over.

A piece of tape dangled on the underside. Her anger did not lessen one bit as she ripped the tape off the box. "How much of your mother's journal did you read? You have no business going through your mother's things."

"I have every right to be in this room." Through angry tears, Cassia shouted, "You just don't get it. Yes, she was your daughter, but she was also my mother." Cassia ran out of the room.

Catherine took the journal to her bedroom. Marianne had written a large number six on the cover. She turned to the page in the middle written in red. It was a section of the journal that Catherine was familiar with—the pages that she never wanted Cassia to read. Catherine's fingers brushed over her daughter's written words. She then closed the book because she could not read those hurtful words today. Catherine buried the journal deep in the back of her closet.

Cassia could not control the tears welling up in her eyes as she tried to push the thought from her mind that her grandmother was hiding something from her about her mother. Cassia swerved onto the shoulder of the road but was able to correct her mistake without incident. She took the next exit for a coffee and donut. She got out of the car. The crisp air hitting her face felt refreshing. She decided right then that she was not going to let the thoughts that consumed her so many times upset her today.

Cassia returned to her car. Again, she tried to clear any negative thoughts from her head. However, her heart began throbbing and aching. She could not ignore the inevitable. Time was running out for her to find out any information about her mother. Grandma B refused to talk about Marianne. Now seventy-eight years old and more closed than ever, Cassia wondered if she would ever get the answers to the many questions that plagued her most of her life. She wished that she had enough time to stop at the retirement village and rub it into her grandmother's face that she had inherited Ashby House. Cassia started back onto the interstate. Her right foot pushed down hard on the gas pedal. Within a few seconds, her speedometer was at seventy miles per hour. The sudden rush of adrenaline made Cassia laugh. "Okay, Grandma Bitch, you said that I would never go back to that house. Well, I am not only going back, I now *own* Ashby House."

CHAPTER FIVE

Day 1—Ashby House
June 12, 2006

CASSIA'S CAR DROVE SLOWLY DOWN the driveway, passing under the steel Number Six Ashby House arch. Tightly gripping the steering wheel, she stretched her neck back as far as it would go and kept her eyes on the sign until it was behind her. The sun was in a fight with the early morning fog, and it was finally winning. Except for the stubborn cloud that veiled the uppermost section of the mansion, Cassia got her first look at the place she last visited when she was six years old. Ashby House was just as huge and magnificent as she remembered. Scanning the three-story mansion for the first time in many years, she was in awe of its snow-white façade and the six equally white pillars. She thought about Uncle Charles leaning against the pillar closest to the door with his favorite pipe clenched between his lips with collisions of sweet cherry tobacco and soft summer drizzle circling around him. Cassia once asked Uncle Charles why the house had six columns. He explained that six slaves died while building the original house, and each column represented the strength of each slave. Cassia loved Uncle Charles's stories and believed every word.

Cassia reached the large circular drive and got out of the car. She could not control the ladybugs fluttering in her stomach. She was glad to see that the house was not run-down at all. In fact, it looked better than she remembered. She thought about Mr. La Rue, the caretaker who was employed at Ashby House when she visited. He had to be retired by now—at least she hoped because he was not a very pleasant fellow, telling her so many times to stop writing with chalk on the driveway, stop swinging on the weeping willow tree branches, and to stay off of this and that section of the lawn. He even accused her of clogging up one of the downstairs toilets. She did, but would never admit it to him.

Cassia was falling in love with the house all over again. She scolded herself to stay focused and stick to the plan—settle the estate, put the house on the market, and get the hell out of there. Cassia checked her cell phone. It was already 10:16 a.m., and no sign of Mr. Oates. She hated when people were later than ten minutes. Cassia reached inside the car in an attempt to get the paper with Mr. Oates's number but got sidetracked when a large blackbird with a wingspan of at least five feet, larger than Cassia had ever seen on any bird, began screeching above the house. Cassia jumped. Her keys fell out of her hand and hit the blacktop. She bent down to retrieve them, and upon returning upright again, her eyes searched for the bird. Instead of locating the bird, her eyes stopped at the attic window. Cassia saw the curtain slightly move. She was sure someone was peeking out.

Cassia walked up to the front door and grabbed the large brass knocker. She banged hard enough for someone inside to hear. No one answered. She paced back and forth on the front porch. She looked up at the third-floor window, but the curtain no longer moved. The breeze was getting strong, and Cassia froze when she saw from the corner of her eye the long flowing branches of the weeping willow tree dancing back and forth. It was the tree in her nightmare, but today it seemed friendlier. It calmed her. Cassia's concentration on the tree was interrupted by the pinging of loose gravel beating against tires and rims. She watched a red pickup truck heading toward the house. The vehicle was shrouded in a cloud of white dust. Cassia's stomach sank remembering the day she saw a vehicle shrouded in a similar dusty cloud. It was the day that she was expecting her father Michael Westfield's vehicle. Instead, it was Grandma B's pink Cadillac that made the same sound coming down the same driveway many years earlier. The day that changed her life and Charles Winchester's.

CHAPTER SIX

MICHAEL WESTFIELD MET CHARLES WINCHESTER III in Paris when Charles was hired as a consultant for a special project for Michael's company. Working together they realized that they enjoyed many of the same things such as opera, the search for the perfect wine, and a good game of checkers. Michael's wife, Marianne, had accompanied him to Paris that year. She had been feeling down about their inability to conceive a child after a few years of trying. Michael suggested that perhaps a change of scenery might help them relax, and maybe that was all they needed. Just like Michael, Marianne felt a special bond with Charles almost immediately. Perhaps it was because he reminded her so much of Michael, not in looks but because of his quick wit and interesting storytelling. Soon, Charles, Michael, and Marianne were inseparable. While in Paris, they dined together almost every evening and attended operas and wine tasting on weekends. Marianne even challenged Charles to a few games of checkers when Michael had a bout of stomach distress one weekend. She was not as good as Michael, but she managed to come out the winner in a game or two.

Paris did not help produce a child, but Marianne never considered her trip a failure. Meeting Charles changed their lives forever. Grandma B did not share Marianne's enthusiasm for her newfound friend. Marianne never understood why Grandma B's attitude changed from bad to worse the first time that she mentioned the name *Charles Winchester III*. When Marianne questioned her about her apparent disdain for someone she had never met, all Grandma B said was that she knew the family and they were nothing but trouble.

Over the next year, Michael and Marianne visited Charles at his home Ashby House in Virginia whenever they could get away. Marianne paid no attention to Grandma B's intense objection to their growing friendship. She saw no reason to share with Michael or Charles her grandmother's negative feelings about the Winchester family. As far as Marianne was concerned, the Winchesters were just another family on her grandmother's list of people she hated. Marianne also saw no reason to share with Grandma B that she and Michael had asked Charles to be a sperm donor since the doctor had determined that Michael had low sperm motility and the probability that he could impregnate Marianne was very slim.

When Marianne became pregnant three months later, she, Michael, and Charles made a pact that the child's paternity would be their secret—a secret that they would never share with anyone. However, Marianne broke the agreement in her fifth month of her pregnancy. One day while meeting her grandmother for tea, they began arguing. Marianne had her fill of Grandma B's negative comments about Charles and the Winchester family. Before she left the table, Marianne blurted, "This baby has the blood of a Winchester, so I guess you will hate her too."

CHAPTER SEVEN

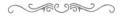

CATHERINE BRITTLE MET CHARLES WINCHESTER II at a charity event that he and his wife, Peaches, famously organized every year at Number Six Ashby House. Peaches Lawson Winchester was a tiny woman, an inch shorter than five feet, with long black hair and emerald-green eyes. She was ordinary in appearance, reserved, and sometimes her quiet nature was mistaken for unfriendliness. Peaches never confided in anyone about her feelings regarding her husband's habitual infidelity. Her friends all agreed that Peaches chose to ignore her husband's wandering eye. Some believed that she would eventually leave him. Others thought that she stayed with him because of their young child, Charles Winchester III.

Catherine and Douglas Brittle received an invitation to the Winchesters' charity event that year because Douglas's law firm now represented the interest of Winchester Enterprises—well, at least the charity portion of the company. Douglas saw the event as a business obligation. Catherine saw it as a chance to make a grand entrance into a room of potential admirers. When Catherine and Douglas arrived at the mansion twenty minutes late, Charles Winchester II was in the middle of toasting his guests and thanking them for their generosity. Catherine entered the room with Douglas on her arm, but it was as if Douglas was invisible. Every eye was on Catherine—tall and meticulously dressed in a flowing white chiffon gown with her hair in a stylish updo that included a sprig of strategically placed baby breaths. Charles looked up. Catherine smiled. Charles stumbled on every other word that followed in his speech. They became lovers a few weeks later. Six months into the affair, Catherine became pregnant. When Catherine told Charles about her pregnancy, he ended the affair. Hurt and bitter, Catherine contacted Peaches, who informed her that she was not her husband's first and probably not his last little whore. Peaches did not hear from Catherine again until twenty-three years later. It was the day that her daughter Marianne died giving birth to Cassia. Peaches could not understand why Catherine would blame the Winchester family for her daughter's death. Charles Winchester II had been dead for over five years by then. Peaches hung up on Catherine, never hearing from her again.

Douglas Brittle went to his grave believing that Marianne was his biological child. Catherine never confessed her affair to her husband. If Douglas did suspect that anything was amiss, he never questioned Marianne's paternity. He loved Marianne and was a good father to her. Catherine's secret was safe—at least for a while. Over the years, Charles Winchester II rarely crossed Catherine's mind. She was not even moved when she heard of his death. It was not until Charles Winchester III entered the lives of Michael and Marianne that Catherine's once buried secret began bubbling to the surface again.

CHAPTER EIGHT

CATHERINE WAS LESS THAN PLEASED when Michael asked her to drop Cassia off at Number Six Ashby House for the first time when Cassia was three years old. Michael and Charles had worked out a plan for Cassia to visit every July for the entire month while Michael attended his yearly meetings with his overseas clients. Michael always arrived at Ashby House on July 29, Cassia's birthday. He would stay on a few extra days to visit his friend Charles. However, before leaving for the airport right before Cassia's sixth birthday, Michael explained to Cassia that he would not be able to return from his trip on her birthday but would be delayed an extra day. With a big hug, Cassia told him that she would not turn six years old until he could be there.

In the early morning of July 28, Charles received a call from Michael letting him know that his last meeting was cancelled and he would be arriving at Ashby House in time for Cassia's birthday. When Cassia heard the news, she squealed and jumped up and down on the bed. Maddie was in midsentence telling Cassia that she needed to stop jumping when Cassia came too close to the edge. Maddie caught her before she hit the floor. Instead of scolding her, Maddie was so relieved that Cassia did not get hurt. She laughed right along with Cassia and hugged her tighter than she ever did before. That night, Cassia was still too excited to sleep, so Maddie promised that they would have a tea party in the morning while they waited for her father if she went right to sleep. Before the usual tucking in, Cassia told Maddie about the menu items she wanted to have for her tea party. Maddie was in awe by the enormous amount of thought that Cassia had put into the planning of the spur-of-the-moment tea party.

Cassia remembered the tea parties that Grandma B had at her house. She wanted to replicate the same etiquette—well, almost. Cassia insisted on a written menu like Grandma B always had. However, instead of tea, Cassia wanted chocolate milk. Little sandwiches with the crusts cut off were a must. Maddie agreed to make them, not with cucumbers and cream cheese or chicken salad, but with peanut butter and jelly. The dessert menu did not include scones, but pink cupcakes and rice crispy treats with colored sprinkles cut in the shape of ladybugs.

Cassia drifted off to sleep but not before asking Maddie to tuck her in really tight. Maddie happily complied and, as always, kissed each cheek and said, "Love you to pieces, child." Uncle Charles passed by the bedroom and announced that he was too excited to sleep too. He blew Cassia a kiss. She pretended to catch it and placed it on her cheek. Just like Cassia's, Uncle Charles's emerald-green eyes sparkled when he laughed.

Charles looked forward to his best friend's three-day visit every summer when he came to pick up Cassia. As with every summer visit, he had the board set up for their checkers game, ordered an assortment of Michael's favorite wines, and his favorite operas were ready to be played on the record player. Charles bought only vinyl records. He loved the popping sounds and white noise that came only with vinyl. He believed that his LPs produced a calming cordiality that called to the listener.

The next morning, Cassia ran down the stairs again jumping and squealing as she came into the kitchen. While holding six tiny fingers up, she announced to Uncle Charles and Maddie that it was her sixth birthday. Uncle Charles denied that he was aware of such a day. He smiled and winked at Maddie while hugging and wishing Cassia a happy birthday.

Maddie was already preparing their tea party treats. Cassia began her list of menu items on the page from the magnetic to-do list that Maddie kept attached to the refrigerator door. It had a picture of a finger with a string tied around it and underneath had many lines for writing. Maddie used the tablet for writing items that she needed from the store. It was her way of keeping an inventory of household necessities.

After all preparations were completed, Maddie carried the items in a large picnic basket in one hand and a blanket in the other. Cassia ran to the weeping willow tree. "This spot is perfect." Maddie set down the basket. The warm summer breeze interfered with Maddie's first attempt to spread the blanket just right onto the grass. Maddie and Cassia began unpacking their tea party items onto the blanket. They both stood up upon hearing tires kicking up gravel on the road. The branches of the weeping willow gently swept across their bodies. Cassia danced and jumped about uncontrollably for a few seconds. "Daddy's here, Daddy's here." She froze when the dust cleared and she saw Grandma B's car. She watched the pink Cadillac hurriedly pass by and come to a screeching stop at the long circular driveway. Grandma B got out of her car. She did not look over at Maddie or Cassia. She marched onto the porch where Uncle Charles was leaning against one of the columns on the front of the house. He was smoking his favorite pipe—the one he received as a gift from Cassia's father the previous summer.

Uncle Charles stood upright. He removed his pipe from his mouth as soon as Catherine exited her vehicle. They began an exchange of words even before she reached the front porch. Suddenly, Uncle Charles fell against the column as if he had been shot with a bullet. Cassia and Maddie watched from the blanket. The calm conversation quickly escalated into shouting. Cassia started toward the house, but Maddie outstretched her right arm in front of Cassia. "Stay here, child. I'll see what's going on." Before Maddie reached the house, Catherine shouted, "Cassia, get in the car." Pointing her finger at Maddie, who was almost to the house, she demanded, "Get her things from the house—all her things." Maddie looked at Uncle Charles. His eyes were red and teary. He nodded his head. Maddie went into the house.

Cassia was almost to the house when Grandma B turned around. She pointed to the car and shouted, "Cassia, get in the car *now*." Cassia did so without a word. Catherine walked from the porch to the car. She put her key in the trunk, and it popped open. Maddie came out of the house with her arms full of Cassia's belongings. When she reached the car, Catherine motioned for her to place them in the trunk. Without saying a word to Maddie or Uncle Charles, she got in her vehicle and started the engine. Cassia looked out of the window. She stared at Uncle Charles standing on the porch. She had never seen sadness in his green eyes before. He slightly smiled and waved at her. Maddie slammed the Cadillac's trunk. Cassia jumped. She clicked the seatbelt across her booster seat and said, "Grandma B, why can't I stay and wait for Daddy?" Catherine did not answer Cassia until the Cadillac passed under the Ashby House sign. "Your father was killed in a plane crash this morning." It was the last day she spent at Ashby House.

CHAPTER NINE

THE PINGING GRAVEL AGAINST TIRES was now replaced by a *whomp, whomp, whomp* of a diesel engine as it came to a stop at the circular driveway. Expecting Mr. Oates, Cassia was surprised to see a female exit the oversized red pickup truck. The older model beat-up pickup did not match the chicly dressed occupant with her designer dress and four-inch pumps. Her short blond hair blew slightly in the warm breeze as she briskly walked toward Cassia. Her wide smile was friendly and familiar, but Cassia was unable to place their connection until she removed her sunglasses and heard a memorable Southern twang, "Cassia, it's me, Annabelle Oates."

"Oh my god, Annabelle, it *is* you." The two women hugged and laughed.

Annabelle came to play with Cassia at Ashby House when her father, Raymond Oates, had business with Uncle Charles. That last summer at Ashby House, Annabelle visited almost every day, sometimes staying a couple of nights. They made a pact to be best friends forever.

Cassia had envied the fact that Annabelle's mother took great care in dressing her so girly every day. Cassia wore shorts and T-shirts most of the summer. Annabelle's mother thought it was necessary for her to wear dresses. However, that did not stop Annabelle from outrunning Cassia every time they raced to the tree house that Uncle Charles had built especially for her fifth birthday. The last time Cassia saw Annabelle was the day before she left Ashby House for good. Cassia could not forget that Annabelle wore a yellow sundress with a giant ladybug on the front. She fell in love with it the minute she saw it on Annabelle. She never knew that Annabelle's mother bought her the same dress for her sixth birthday.

Unlike Cassia's charcoal-black hair and Dorothy Hamill cut, Annabelle's blond hair flowed all the way down her back, almost reaching her butt. Every day her mother fixed her hair in two ponytails that set high on each side of her head. Constantly, Annabelle absentmindedly, throughout the day, separated and pulled at each pigtail to keep them tightened. Cassia only saw her hair down when she spent the night with her at Ashby House. Before going to bed, Maddie removed her ponytails and made one long braid before going to sleep. Sometimes Annabelle would go home with it braided but would always return the next time with the two ponytails again. Her sparkling blue eyes were trouble. Well, that's what Uncle Charles called them. Maddie agreed. She knew that when Cassia and Annabelle got together, her usual household duties would be interrupted so she could keep a close eye on those two. She often laughed when telling Uncle Charles, "Annabelle's energy and Cassia's inquisitiveness are a lethal combination."

Cassia released Annabelle from her grasp. "It's so good to see you. Your hair! Where did it go?"

"I cut it off a long time ago. My mother cried." Annabelle rolled her eyes. Her long locks were now shorter than Cassia's, but Annabelle still could have made the cover of any magazine. Her soft multi-highlighted shorter tresses only made her blue eyes seem more mischievous.

Cassia laughed. "Well, you look beautiful. What are you doing here? I was expecting your father."

"Well, Dad's a little under the weather today, so he asked me to drop the key off to you. Can you believe that you now own Ashby House?" Annabelle said with her wide smile and blue eyes sparkling like champagne that had just been poured.

"Don't own it yet. Your father said that there is a stipulation in the will that I must spend six days in the house before it's mine. What do you think about that?"

"Dad told me about that. Strange, but Charles Winchester was a little strange. Nice, generous, but strange. Or perhaps the politically correct term would be eccentric." Annabelle laughed. "And what a great storyteller he was. Remember how he told us all those crazy stories about Ashby House and ghosts that live here. Maddie would get so mad at him. I can hear her now." Annabelle placed her hand on her hip, and in a more pronounced than usual Southern accent, she began shaking her right index finger like Maddie often did, "Mr. Charles, Mr. Charles, stop those wild tales. You're scarin' those babies." They both laughed. Annabelle continued, "I know why she got so mad. It's because she had to deal with the fallout from the stories. Maddie was the one who had to sit with us—or sit with me until I fell asleep because I was so scared. But you—you were never scared," Annabelle said looking confused.

Annabelle was right. Cassia had no reason to fear the dead. The person whom she loved the most was dead. It was her mother. Cassia could never imagine being hurt by her. It was the living that did all the hurting. That theory was constantly being reaffirmed in her life. First, her father, who buried himself in his work because of the loss of his wife. Though he tried to hide it, Cassia felt the sting of his disconnect. Second, Grandma B's distantness, though Cassia wondered if it was just her personality, and her icy layer just got thicker when her daughter and husband died. Third, Mitch's affair. While she was deeply hurt by the loss of her own child, Cassia could not include her in the same category as those who hurt her. Instead, she put her on the same list as her mother, even imagining sometimes that her mother was taking care of Elizabeth somewhere in the afterlife.

Annabelle handed Cassia the key. The sun bounced off the two-carat princess cut diamond on Annabelle's left ring finger. It nearly blinded Cassia for a moment. "Wow, impressive. Who's the guy? Sunny La Rue Jr.?" They both laughed.

"No, I wouldn't mind it being Sunny, but my father would have a heart attack. Sunny La Rue Jr. is one beautiful man these days. Six five and a good f—" Annabelle stopped. Cassia did not notice the unfinished sentence.

"Remember how he would pull on your pigtails and take off as fast as he could? That boy could run. Whatever happened to him?"

"He took over as caretaker for Ashby House a few years ago after his father died. During the last year, when Uncle Charles's health started going downhill, he opened his own home improvement company while still keeping up his duties here. I think he was afraid that Ashby House would be sold and he would be out of a job. I believe that Charles even helped him finance some of his business. It's really taking off. I'm sure he'll be stopping by to check on the place."

"Is he here now? I thought I saw someone in the attic while I was waiting for the key."

"No, he's working on a roofing job on Lincoln Street."

"So…back to the fiancé. Who is he?"

"His name is Robert Marcus Brenneman Jr. He's a lawyer. His father is a lawyer, and his grandfather is a lawyer. I met him about six months ago when our fathers decided to merge their law firms, which should be finalized soon. I sometimes think that our getting together is part of that merger deal," Annabelle said sarcastically. "My father is ecstatic. He says, 'Lawyers breed lawyers.'"

Annabelle laughed. "Just what the world needs—more lawyers." She immediately regretted her negative comment. In an instant, the lawyer in Annabelle trying to persuade a jury surfaced, "Really, he is a great guy and gorgeous too."

"Hope I get a chance to meet him."

"Oh yeah, Dad said he'll be by tomorrow or the next day to go over the estate papers with you. He'll be in touch." Annabelle looked at her Gucci watch. "Damn, would love to stay longer, but I have to get to work. I just made partner, so I'm trying to be on my best behavior—at least for a little while," Annabelle said, flashing a Cheshire-cat-like grin. "Hey, maybe we can get together soon. Would love to hear what's going on in your life."

Cassia thought about her life—unhappy in her job and divorced. Every now and then, Cassia felt a pang of sadness regarding the demise of her marriage. This was one of those times. She hugged Annabelle. "Sure. And congratulations."

"Thank you." Annabelle turned around and headed toward the truck. She stopped and turned back around, throwing up her arms. "Damn, Cassia, this house is amazing, and it's yours."

"Yes, it's pretty awesome." Cassia nodded and whispered under her breath, "And I have no idea what the hell Uncle Charles was thinking, but it should get me out of debt." Cassia called out just before Annabelle started the truck and its loud engine would muffle her words, "Hey, Annabelle, want to come back later and have some dinner? I cook a decent lasagna. And we can celebrate your promotion and engagement. You can bring that gorgeous fiancé too."

"Okay, but let's make it a girls' night. And the lasagna, I'd prefer if it was *indecent*." They both laughed. "I'll bring lots of garlic bread and a vat of wine. Does six thirty work for you?"

Cassia nodded. Annabelle started her truck and waved. Cassia waved back and watched the truck exit the long driveway. She looked down at the key in her hand. "Okay, Uncle Charles, will you and your little friends be joining me?"

CHAPTER TEN

CASSIA TURNED THE KEY IN the deadbolt and pushed the door open. Looking down at the entryway floor with its shiny eggshell-white marble and tiny black flecks, Cassia smiled. She could not count the number of times that Maddie scolded her for running and sliding on that cold marble floor, "Child, you're gonna break your neck. Your daddy and Uncle Charles won't be happy. No. Not happy at all." Sometimes when Maddie was in another section of the house and Cassia walked by the den, Uncle Charles would emerge from his reading holding an old shawl that was usually thrown over his favorite chair. He would throw the shawl onto the shiny floor and whisper to Cassia, "Hurry, jump on," and away they would go with Uncle Charles pulling Cassia across the entire length of the twenty-foot-long foyer. Their laughter echoed throughout the house. Maddie knew exactly what was going on. When she finally made her way to the laughter, Uncle Charles would attempt to hide the shawl behind his back, but most of it would be dangling on the floor behind him. Both Uncle Charles and Cassia would shake their heads, denying doing anything wrong with Cheshire-cat-like grins on their faces. Cassia ran her hand across the carved oak curved banister. The twenty-tiered chandelier softly chimed as the crystals collided with the breeze that barged in through the open door. Cassia closed her eyes and breathed in deeply. The scent of cherry tobacco infused the air.

Cassia walked down the long hallway. Involuntary tears streamed down her face. Usually steering clear of melodrama, she was surprised by this sudden rush of emotions. Cassia was not sure if it was the scent of the cherry tobacco that caused the tsunami of memories to take over the part of her brain that she kept locked up so tight all these years, but her heart ached more and more with every memory that surfaced of her father, Uncle Charles, and Maddie. This house—Ashby House—was the place where she felt the closest to her father. This was the place where he put aside his work and hurt feelings caused by the death of his wife. This was the place where he laughed and played with Cassia. And this was the place where Cassia felt like she was part of a family. She pulled a tissue from her purse and wiped her eyes.

Cassia entered the den. Three life-size portraits overwhelmed the wall. Cassia stepped back outside the doorway so she could better examine them. She immediately noticed how handsome Charles Winchester II was in comparison to his son. Charles Winchester II was tall, thin, and *GQ*-like. His son, Charles Winchester III, was much shorter than his father, round-faced, and sported an overgrown mustache. He looked nothing like his father at all.

Cassia studied the portrait of Peaches Lawson Winchester. Dressed in a peach-colored flowered dress, she was a lovely petite lady but nowhere in the scope of a stunning beauty like Grandma B. The tints of gray mixed in with her short dark curls made her look like a nice grandma that Cassia only imagined in pictures. She exuded a wholesome kindness. Cassia felt it looking into Peaches's eyes. Charles III did have some of his mother's features like her dimpled chin and the same emerald-green eyes. Cassia took her compact makeup mirror from her purse and studied the color and shape of her own eyes. She was puzzled by the similarity but dismissed it as coincidence.

Cassia moved closer to inspect the little gold plaques attached at the bottom of each portrait:

Charles Winchester II
April 2, 1920–March 19, 1970

Peaches Lawson Winchester
May 21, 1922

Charles Winchester III
June 26, 1950–June 2, 2006

She was surprised by how quickly someone saw to the task of putting the date of Uncle Charles's death onto his picture frame since he had only been dead for more than a week. She wondered who was responsible for that detail. She also wondered what she would do with all the family heirlooms. Surely some relative would want them. Were there any relatives still alive? Could there be anyone who might contest the will since she was not related to Uncles Charles by blood? These were some of the many questions for Mr. Oates. Cassia scanned the portraits again. There was no date of death plaque attached to the portrait of Peaches Lawson Winchester. Cassia pulled out her to-do list from her purse. On the back, she began writing the questions she would ask Mr. Oates.

Cassia moved to the kitchen. She was happy to see that it had been updated. The practical part of her brain advised her that the updated kitchen would certainly increase the home's selling price. She was, however, a little sad because she missed the homey feeling of the old kitchen and the memories it held. Cassia ran her hand over the granite counters and stainless steel appliances. On the refrigerator was a magnetic notepad with a picture of a finger with a string tied around it. It was the same notepad that Maddie used when writing her shopping lists. Cassia removed the notepad, closed her eyes, and held it to her chest. She reflected on the day when she sat at the table with a pencil in her hand writing the tea party menu on the notepad, "Maddie, how do you spell *sprinkles*?"

Maddie stopped mixing the rice crispy treats and looked at Cassia. "Sound it out, child." Maddie never gave away the answers but would help Cassia with every sound until all words were spelled correctly.

Cassia opened her eyes and smiled. She placed the notepad back on the refrigerator and looked down at the black granite counter. There was a page torn from the notepad. In large cursive writing was written,

Cassia
    Stocked the refrigerator and cabinets with a few essentials. A variety of wines are in the wine rack. Welcome to Ashby House.
                            Raymond Oates

Cassia opened the refrigerator. It was packed with more than essentials. While she was grateful, she couldn't help but think that it was the least Mr. Oates could do since she *had* to stay six days. Cassia opened the cabinets, and there was enough food in them for her to probably stay a couple months. She laughed. "I'm staying six days, Mr. Oates—only six days." She began taking inventory searching for her lasagna ingredients. Cassia lined up the jars of spaghetti sauce and noodles on the counter. She opened the freezer. It too was well stocked with meats and other frozen items like lots of Rocky Road ice cream—her favorite. Cassia picked up one of the pints of ice cream and studied the label. It was the same brand she remembered eating when she stayed at Ashby House. Before placing the container back into the freezer, she said, "I will definitely see you later." Cassia located a pound of lean ground turkey and ground beef behind more Rocky Road ice cream. She settled on the turkey, which she immediately moved from the freezer to the refrigerator next to the mozzarella and container of fresh parmesan cheeses. Some of the items were not the brands that she normally used for her lasagna but decided that they would do just fine. She was happy that she did not have to drive into town to shop because she was tired from her drive from Baltimore to Richmond. She took her to-do list from her purse and penciled in "a short nap before starting dinner."

Cassia looked forward to her dinner with Annabelle and hearing more about her *perfect* life. She immediately scolded herself for her pettiness and made her mind up that this dinner would be a celebration, not a pity-party. Cassia looked around the kitchen, and an unexpected enthusiasm crept into her thinking. She would use the money that she would get from the sale of Ashby House and start a new and happy life. Perhaps it was time to get rid of some of her old ghosts. Cassia started for the stairs but changed her mind. Her nap would have to wait a couple minutes because she had to check out her favorite room.

CHAPTER ELEVEN

THE DINING ROOM OF ASHBY House was the size of a Victorian ballroom. While every piece of furniture was supersized, it did not shrink the room size one bit. The hardwood floors were buffed and shined so well that not even a tiny scratch showed through. The custom red drapery with wide valances and white sheers provided protection from any sun-damage to the room or its contents and allowed in just enough light to make the room cheerful and pleasing during a sunny day. Three twenty-tiered chandeliers strategically hung over the table—one at each end and one exactly in the middle. They provided additional lighting when needed. A dimmer switch offered a variety of illuminations ranging from a soft glow to a blinding brightness. Cassia was stunned when she saw the same huge table and oversized chairs that she sat in so many years ago.

During her first visit to Ashby House, Cassia was too small for the large chairs. Maddie placed two phone books on a chair so Cassia could reach the table properly. After Cassia slid to the floor when one of the phone books shifted during dinner one evening, Maddie purchased a booster seat the next day. After that occurrence, whenever she dined with Uncle Charles, he would ask if she was planning to eat dinner *at* the table or *under* the table. No matter how many times he said those words, they never failed to produce smiles on the faces of Cassia and Maddie. It was two more summers before Cassia was tall enough to reach the table without a booster.

Cassia ate breakfast and lunch in the kitchen with Maddie. Dinner was always eaten in the dining room with Uncle Charles. It was a formal affair. After playing all day in her shorts and T-shirt, Cassia looked forward to her bubble bath. She loved getting dressed up for dinner—stepping into a decorative dress and swanky shoes. Even Uncle Charles wore his fancier cowboy attire. He always sat at the head of the table on the only armed chair. To Cassia, he looked like a king sitting on his throne. Cassia ran her fingers over the huge round silver rivets holding the embroidered leather onto the chair's solid wood frame. The other eleven chairs were identical, except they were armless.

Maddie did all the cooking at Ashby House. She introduced many new Southern dishes to Uncle Charles—dishes that her momma cooked for her when she was a little girl. Cassia remembered how Maddie giggled when Uncle Charles complimented her cooking, sometimes using his limited French vocabulary. Even if Maddie had no idea what Uncle Charles was saying, his animated gestures and spirited smile broke through any language barrier that may have impeded his meaning.

During Cassia's last summer at Ashby House, she began helping Maddie set the table for dinner every evening. First, they would remove from the drawers in the china cabinet three of the ten napkins that Peaches Winchester made—the ones with the picture of Ashby House beautifully embroidered onto the cloth. Next, they would take three silverware servings and the snowflake trivets from the box at the bottom of the cabinet as well as the tall candelabra-like candlesticks and place them on the table. Lastly, Maddie usually placed the three plates from the cabinet onto the table. However, during Cassia's last visit to Ashby House, she was put in charge of the task because she was finally tall enough to reach the sophisticated Lennox gold inlay pattern "Westchester" china from the middle shelf. She liked being helpful and was proud that she never dropped a dish, though she did drop a piece of silverware or two. Maddie always took her seat across the table from Cassia after she placed all the food on the table. When Annabelle stayed, she sat next to Cassia. During her father's three-day visit every July, most meals were eaten in the screened gazebo in the back yard because Michael preferred a more relaxed dining experience after his hectic month of wining and dining clients.

Cassia enjoyed the informality of eating in the outside gazebo when her father visited, but her fondest memories of Uncle Charles took place in the dining room. Cassia was sure that this was her favorite room in the house. This was the room where Uncle Charles told the greatest stories about the history of Ashby House and about its former occupants—occupants who refused to leave. He never called them ghosts. He made them seem like old friends.

Most of the storytelling began while Maddie was cleaning up the table after dinner. Uncle Charles would fill his pipe with cherry tobacco. Then he would pull out the lighter that he always carried in his pocket. Cassia closed her eyes and heard the click, click of the lighter as Uncle Charles opened it to light his pipe. She saw the flame grow and retreat as he puffed and puffed on the end of the pipe. A veil of smoke dispersed into the room. With another click, the lighter was closed. Cassia watched Uncle Charles sitting at the head of the table with his glass of brandy in front of him. The chandeliers were never on because Uncle Charles preferred eating by candlelight. He made no secret of the fact that he knew he was not the best-looking gentleman. Once when Cassia asked Uncle Charles why they ate without the lights on, he replied, "I'm more handsome in candlelight."

Cassia watched herself as a child listening attentively as Uncle Charles began one of his many stories.

"My ancestors owned many slaves. That was the way life was in the South during that time. Most slaves who worked the fields were uneducated. However, a household slave named Frederick received an education from his previous owner. That was rare because white people did not believe that blacks should be educated because an intelligent black slave could be trouble, but occasionally a white slave owner did not agree with the times or the theory. When Frederick's owner died, he was bought at an auction to work as a butler, along with his wife to work as a cook. They had no children. When my ancestors found out that Frederick could read and write and do math, he immediately took over the task of tutoring their three young children—Elizabeth, Martha, and Douglas. Frederick's wife worked as the children's mammy. She stayed with the family until they were set free after the signing of Mr. Lincoln's emancipation document. They fled the house and never returned again." Uncle Charles leaned over to Cassia. He whispered, "Ahh, but after their deaths, they returned to this house."

Cassia eyes grew wider. "Why, Uncle Charles?"

Uncle Charles sat back in his chair to contemplate his answer because he had no idea why they returned to Ashby house. He also had no idea why they would not leave. He said, "They want to stay in a place where they were happy." Charles was making things up as he went along.

He knew that Frederick and his wife were not happy roaming the house because they were so solemn all the time. Charles also knew that Elizabeth, one of the daughters of the original owners of the house who walked the halls at night too, was unhappy. He would sometimes hear her sobbing, sitting at the bottom of the stairs. Charles's mother, Peaches, once hired a medium, a person who claimed she could speak to the dead. The medium surmised that the people in the house were unhappy because they wanted to join their families on the other side. The medium did tell the spirits to "go home" in an elaborate cleansing ritual of burning sage and chants. She told Peaches she would come back again for another smudging because she still felt their presence. Peaches walked the lady to her car. She opened her car door and suddenly stopped and stared at a group of trees in the distance that formed the property line. She said, "Mrs. Winchester, there is much unfinished emotional business here at Ashby House and one dark spirit wanting to disrupt the other benign entities. Up until now, he has remained outside of the house, but I feel that he is getting closer to coming inside." That was one piece of information that Peaches did not share with Charles. She moved out the next day.

Uncle Charles's eyebrows raised, and the wrinkles on his forehead deepened. "Ahh...the reason that I think they stay is because they like my music. I turn on Verdi's La traviata, and I invite Elizabeth to dance. She smiles." Uncle Charles got up from his chair and held his hand out to Cassia. He bowed. She learned to do the same in return. Then they danced with no music playing in the dining room. Like Elizabeth, Cassia smiled.

When Maddie came into the room to clear the last items from the table, Uncle Charles took hold of her hand. He began dancing with her. When Uncle Charles held Maddie, she giggled. With rosy cheeks and a schoolgirl shyness, she said, "Mr. Charles, you know I can't dance." He proved her wrong because Uncle Charles could lead anybody in a dance. He had Maddie matching him step for step, and every twirl was perfect. Uncle Charles made Maddie smile too.

CHAPTER TWELVE

CASSIA NEVER VISITED ASHBY HOUSE in the winter. She never got to see the roaring fire or feel the warmth of the six fireplaces. All the wood fireplaces in each of the five bedrooms were converted to gas many years ago, but the most impressive fireplace, and the only wood-burning one left, was located between the kitchen and living room. It was made from a natural stone extracted from the old quarry and was built large enough and tall enough that a short person or child could walk right through it—from the kitchen to the living room. Luckily, it was cleaned of soot after its winter use because in the summer, Cassia and Annabelle would sometimes run through it as a shortcut to get from the kitchen to the living room when playing tag in the house on a rainy day. The last summer that Cassia stayed at Ashby House, she had to duck her head slightly to clear the opening. Annabelle was bending down to avoid hitting her head the summer before.

Cassia ran her fingers over the cast-iron pot hanging on a hook in the middle of the fireplace. She studied the grooves and knots on the hand-carved wooden mantel. Uncle Charles long ago told Cassia that there was not another fireplace mantel like it in the whole world. It was made from the wood of the old barn that once stood on the grounds where the weeping willow tree now stands. He told her this story.

"Many slave owners came from the school of the same thoughts and traditions. My ancestors treated their house slaves fairly well. Unfortunately, slaves that worked the fields had a hard life. Just like managers are assigned by an owner to run a company, plantation owners assigned many overseers to manage the plantation. There was one very cruel overseer named Jonathan. People would say he became that way because at the age of six he was taken away from his dying mother." Uncle Charles thought that it was best to leave out how Jonathan's screams sounded like a wounded animal as he was dragged across the field and how he walked aimlessly for days with no food and drinking rainwater until he finally was discovered by a plantation owner who presented him as a gift to his wife. When she saw the sick child, she said, "What am I going to do with a sick nigger baby?" She kept him, but he was treated badly by her and her three very spoiled children. Uncle Charles continued his story, "Jonathan never saw his mother again. When he got older, he would search the face of every black woman that he came in contact with hoping to find his mother by the only thing he remembered about her—the three-inch scar on his mother's left cheek."

Cassia listened intensely while Uncle Charles continued his story, "When Jonathan was eight years old, he was sold to work the fields of another family member and then another family member. Over the years, the more he was abused, the meaner he got. When he was sold to work at Ashby House, he changed his last name from Roberts to Welts because he believed that he had the most scars from floggings than any slave in the entire South. Even though he knew the pain from being beaten, he overstepped his authority and abused many of the male slaves who worked the fields. Whippings were done in the barn but only when the owners were away. The beaten slaves knew not to complain to the owners because Jonathan threatened to kill their families if they told. One night, Christian and his wife, Angelina, returned to the plantation without notice and heard screams and cries coming from the barn. The owners rushed to the barn and saw what was going on. Christian, never a violent man, beat Jonathan with his own hands. He was beaten so badly that night that a doctor had to be called to the plantation. After his recovery from his injuries, he was sold. The stories of the horrors that occurred in the barn were passed down from generation to generation. When my parents moved in here, my mother ordered the barn be torn down immediately. She planted with her own hands that weeping willow tree that you love to have picnics under. That is the spot where the barn once stood." Maddie came into the room and caught the last part of the story. She scolded Charles for telling such a horrible tale to a young child.

Before Maddie left the room that day, she made Charles promise not to scare Cassia with his stories again. When Maddie returned to the kitchen, Uncle Charles uncrossed his fingers. Cassia laughed. She leaned in and begged Uncle Charles in a whisper, "Finish the story, Uncle Charles, please."

Leaning in closer to Cassia and whispering in her ear, Charles finished the sad tale, "If you stand long enough under that weeping willow tree, you will feel droplets of moisture. The droplets are the tears of all the beaten slaves."

Cassia was sad thinking about the little boy being taken from his mother. She felt a connection to him because she too had been taken away from her mother without any choice in the matter. Cassia's thoughts returned to Uncle Charles's storytelling. She smiled remembering what a flair he had for the dramatics. At the end of all his stories, he would lean in closer to Cassia and every time had her so engrossed in the story that she could not help but lean in and meet him halfway because she just *had* to hear the ending—every time.

Cassia looked out the window and stared at the weeping willow tree. Yes, there was a sad history connected to the house, but Cassia's own memories of her visits made her believe that Ashby House could once again bring her the joy that she experienced as a child. How great it would be to see Ashby House in all its winter beauty—the snow covering the house and the trees, running into the house after a snowball fight, and sitting by the fire with a glass of wine snuggling with Mi—no, not Mitch! That was the first time in a long while that she thought about being with Mitch in that way. Cassia was lonely. She finally admitted it. She walked to the refrigerator and pealed a page off the to-do list notepad. On the first line, she wrote, "Find a new man." She put the paper in her purse.

Cassia went to the car to retrieve her computer and suitcase. Taking another long look at the house, she realized something else—she wanted to keep Ashby House. Cassia rolled her suitcase up the long staircase to the bedroom. She left the computer in the foyer. Instinctively, she claimed her old bedroom. The room was the same as she remembered with the two twin canopy beds and ladybug bedspreads. Cassia always slept in the bed closest to the window, except when Annabelle visited. The other bed was close to a small closet that Annabelle was too scared to sleep near. The room had two closets—a big walk-in closet in the right corner of the bedroom. The other closet was only big enough for a small child to stand in. It was used for storage, and the girls began calling it the "munchkin closet" after watching *The Wizard of Oz* one rainy day. While Cassia never understood Annabelle's fears, she made sacrifices so that her friend would be comfortable during her stay. She liked it when Annabelle spent a night. In addition to changing beds, she allowed a night-light on even though Cassia preferred sleeping in a dark room.

Cassia sat on the bed, and her daydreams of keeping Ashby House faded when the practical side of her brain took over. She could never afford the costs associated with running a five-bedroom estate—taxes, maintenance, and utilities. Besides, her work was in Baltimore. She hoped Mr. Oates would be feeling better soon because she was anxious to go over the estate papers with him. Cassia pulled her to-do list from her purse and turned to the side with the questions. The more questions she wrote, the more she worried that offloading the house might not be so easy. There would probably be estate taxes to be paid, and she was basically broke. The real estate market was not the best, and she had no idea if any family members might crawl out of the woodwork and contest the will. This sale could drag on for years. On the side margin, Cassia wrote a note to herself to call Marcie to see if those five couples she met with before her Richmond trip came in to sign their contracts.

Cassia removed her shoes and stretched out across the bed. Her eyelids were heavy. She had gotten up too early, and driving always made her sleepy. She had not heard one sound since entering the house, so Cassia dismissed the thought that someone might be in the attic. She checked the time on her cell phone and set the alarm. One hour would refresh her. That would give her enough time to get a shower and then start dinner.

Cassia woke not to her alarm but to a loud thud. The noise came from downstairs. She wondered if Sunny La Rue had let himself in to take care of something in the house. She was certain that he must have a key, but she would give him a piece of her mind if he came in without knocking because he surely could see that her car was in the driveway. Barely able to open her eyes fully, Cassia squinted checking the time on her phone. She had only been asleep for about a half hour. Suddenly, like a puff of spray from an automatic infuser, the scent of cherry tobacco filled her nostrils. Cassia rolled over and buried her nose in the bedspread. She was sure that the tobacco scent was absorbed into the fabric since Uncle Charles walked throughout the house smoking his pipe regularly. Breathing in deeply, she detected no odor of cherries in the spread. Cassia sat up and sniffed the air. The odor was definitely hovering all about. She put on her shoes, ran her fingers through her hair, and started making her way down the steps. She called out, "Hello, anybody there?"

CHAPTER THIRTEEN

Cassia removed the pepper spray from her purse that she had hung on the banister at the bottom of the stairs. She cautiously crept down the hall checking out the dining room, living room, and then the kitchen. Nothing was out of place. She checked the front and back doors. They both were locked. Cassia exhaled a sigh of relief and placed the pepper spray on the kitchen counter. She convinced herself that old houses creak all the time but had a hard time believing that the thud she heard was just a normal house settling sound.

Cassia leaned against the counter. She scanned the kitchen and stopped at the coffeepot that was next to the toaster oven. Her half-awake eyes opened wide. "Ahh…coffeepot means there is probably coffee here somewhere. Don't fail me now, Mr. Oates." Cassia opened the pantry door. She frantically moved several cans of tomatoes and beans to the side, and there it was—a red Folgers coffee container. Cassia held the can and smiled at the little sunrise peeking over the mountain and the words "Mountain Grown" written across the can. Thoughts of her favorite Folgers commercial popped in her head. It was the little girl welcoming her big brother home at Christmas. Cassia wondered what it would be like to have a brother.

Cassia pulled the tab off the can of coffee and closed her eyes. She called out, "Thank you, thank you, Mr. Oates." Cassia breathed in deeply. She just smelled coffee. This was the first time since entering the house that she did not smell the remnants of Uncle Charles's pipe tobacco. With the coffee brewing, she sat at the kitchen table and adjusted her to-do list. Once again, Cassia drew a line through

6 p.m. Even before the loud beep sounded indicating that the coffee was done brewing, Cassia poured a cup. She was thankful for the "brew pause" feature on the coffeepot. She picked up her cell phone and headed for the den. Walking through the foyer, she grabbed the bag that housed her computer. Cassia was anxious to see if Mitch had e-mailed her, though she believed that he was probably still settling in or sleeping. The photo shoot of the royal family started tomorrow. She might not hear from him for several days because according to Mitch, the assignment had him on the move following them around London while they make several public appearances. The second week he would be doing still-shots of them at Buckingham Palace, capturing their everyday life. Even if she did not have a message from Mitch, she would e-mail anyway.

Cassia entered the den. Again, focused on the three portraits on the wall, she did not look down to see the large book on the floor in her path. Cassia tripped on the book, spilling nearly half of her coffee. A few drops fell on the book, but most of the coffee spilled on the hardwood floor. "Shit." Cassia put her computer and what was left of her coffee on the desk. She pulled a few tissues from the box on the desk and stooped down to clean the liquid off the book and floor.

She was sure that the book was not there when she was in the den earlier. Cassia knew instantly that it was the book hitting the floor that caused the loud thud that woke her from her sleep. Perhaps it was too close to the edge of the little round table with the lamp, but that did not explain how it got knocked to the floor. Cassia looked around the room for any plausible answers. She found none. After placing the wet tissues into the small trashcan next to the desk, Cassia bent down to pick up the book. She had to use both hands to pick it up and carry it back to the table. It was heavy—too heavy to have fallen by itself. She ran her fingers over the four-inch slightly raised gold lettering on the padded cover. It had just one printed word, "BIBLE."

Cassia picked up the Bible from the table and placed it on the desk next to what was left of her cup of coffee. She took another tissue and cleaned up the remaining moister under the cup so it would not cause any water stains on the flawless oak desk. Cassia sat on the overstuffed leather desk chair and opened the book. She never read the Bible. She was angry at God if he did in fact exist. Grandma B sent her to a Christian Sunday school and church after her father died, but Cassia refused to continue going to church when she was in high school. As she got older, she had a hard time with the church's teaching of a loving god who gave the world his son to die for man so the gates of heaven could open again. That same "loving" god took away so much from her.

Cassia studied the book. She was struck by the exquisiteness of it. The thick padded ivory front and back covers provided protection for the golden framework of the pages. Each page was outlined in a golden tint, which at first appeared unremarkable when looking at a single page. However, it was when the book was closed that the full effect of the golden outline could then be appreciated. The first few pages listed a family tree. It was not the Winchester Family Bible but Uncle Charles's mother's—the Lawson family. Cassia studied the names and dates of those family members that once lived and died. The name *Elizabeth* jumped off the page. Cassia tried to keep her sadness from overwhelming her at the sight of the name, but ever since she lost her baby, it felt like a punch to the heart whenever she saw or heard the name *Elizabeth*. She turned the page quickly. On the next page was Uncle Charles's name with his date of birth and date of death in large fancy cursive writing. In fact, the entire family Bible was written in the same lovely calligraphy. Again, Cassia was surprised that Uncle Charles's date of death was already filled in. Above Uncle Charles's name was listed his father, Charles Winchester II, with date of birth and date of death. Next to him was listed his wife, Peaches Lawson Winchester, with her date of birth but no date of death. Cassia knew that the absence of a date of death for Peaches Winchester again was more than a coincidence. Cassia picked up her phone and called Mr. Oates's cell phone. No answer. She left a message.

Cassia flipped further into the pages of the Bible. Tucked in the middle was a folded letter. The ink was faded and pages yellowed. Cassia carefully opened the brittle document and read it aloud.

July, 1867

My dearest sister Martha,

Today, standing side-by-side with former plantation owners and poor white farmers, I realize the south will never be the same. With the devastation of war and the freeing of our black slaves, southerners are expressing feelings of bitterness, anger, fear, and cries of injustice. Momma says that poppa is not well since returning home and finding the house in ruins. We are waiting on word about cousins Virgil and James but fear the worst. How goes it with you?

Today in town I overheard a conversation that seemed to sum up how people are feeling since the freeing of our black slaves. I know that it is a sin to eavesdrop and I pray that God will forgive me. The conversation was between two southerners. They were plantation owners who lost everything, just like poppa. They were angry and worried about how the south will recover without free labor, now that the blacks are freedmen. Our economy will never recover and they feared for the safety of their wives and young daughters. I sensed so much hatred and desperation in their voices that I had to fight back tears.

I, too, my dearest sister am upset about the freeing of our black slaves, especially the loss of our Mammy. I cannot believe she is gone. My heart is broken because she never even said good-bye. Remember the beautiful shawls she knitted for us? Every time I look at mine I cry because I miss her so.

Your loving sister, Elizabeth

Cassia carefully folded the fragile letter and placed it back into the pages of the Bible. She closed the book. Cassia sat back in the chair and closed her eyes trying to comprehend the author's words and feelings. She did not understand the woman's attachment to her slave. When Cassia opened her eyes a few seconds later, a figure was standing in the doorway. At first, the form was not clear, looking like a bad satellite television image with its pixels fading in and out. Within a few seconds, the lady's image became sharper. Cassia got a good look at her—it was the beautiful lady that she had seen in the attic with Uncle Charles that last summer she stayed at Ashby House.

Cassia sat frozen. She was not afraid but mesmerized by the image. She scrutinized every inch of the lady. First thing that Cassia surmised was that she was not of our time. She was perhaps of the Civil War era and in her early thirties. The lady was dressed in a lovely pale-pink crinoline-line skirt and a high-collared white puffy-sleeved blouse. A beautifully knitted snow-white shawl was draped over her shoulders. The lady held the ends tightly in her delicate hands. Her charcoal-black hair with long flowing locks of curls was partially tied back with soft pink flowing ribbons that matched her dress and hung just a little longer than her hair. She was indeed beautiful, but her tear-filled emerald-green eyes conveyed an obvious sadness. Cassia finally said hello. The lady turned away, and Cassia raced to the doorway. For a few seconds, she just stood in the doorway watching the lady walk down the hall. Her dress swooshed from side to side in an elegant rhythm, but neither the crinoline nor the lady made any sound. Cassia started toward the lady. Her image completely faded in the same manner that it appeared by the time Cassia caught up to her.

Cassia's attention shifted when she heard a loud knock at the door. She went to the door and tried to make out the image of the person standing outside but was unable to clearly see through the stained-glass window in the door that distorted the tall image. Cassia opened the door. A dazzling smiling face stood before her. "Hi, I'm not sure if you remember me. My father worked for Mr. Winchester many years ago, and I sometimes would come to work with him. I took over as caretaker of Ashby House a couple years ago. I'm Sunny, and you must be Cassia."

Annabelle did not lie. Sunny was as gorgeous as she said. Most of the men in Cassia's social circle were of the *GQ* or *GQ*-ish type.

Sunny La Rue did not fit into that sphere, but she was willing to start a new loop just for him. Sunny was over six feet tall. His collar-length blond sun-highlighted hair was the look many women paid big bucks for and spent many hours in the salon to achieve. While his slightly wavy hair was parted in the middle, he intermittently ran his fingers through it to keep it off his face as he talked to Cassia. She was not sure if it was something he did when nervous or just out of habit. His light-blue eyes look lighter than they really were against his sun-tanned face. It was apparent that he spent many hours working in the sun, but his skin was not a leathery bronze-like color. Instead, just a soft golden hue. He wore Levi's jeans and work boots. His upper bicep muscles spilled out of the arms of his plain black T-shirt. Cassia settled on this stylish description for Sunny—blue-collar chic. Cassia extended her hand to Sunny and said, "Of course, I remember you."

Cassia recalled an annoying scrawny-like kid and was in awe of this beautiful man standing in front of her. She wished that she had not taken a nap. Her sleepy eyes and messed-up hair certainly were not the look she was going for when trying to make a good first impression. Although, Mitch always told her that it was her sexiest look. But then again, Mitch was in love with her and preferred morning sex, and he knew they were the words to get it started.

"I'm on my way to finish a roofing job on Lincoln Street, but I thought that I should stop to check if that repair that I made to a pipe under the kitchen sink is still holding." Sunny stood motionless on the front porch holding a huge plumbing wrench in his hands. He was waiting for an invitation from Cassia to enter Ashby House.

Cassia finally got the message and said, "I'm sorry. Where are my manners? Please come in."

CHAPTER FOURTEEN

THE KITCHEN SINK CHECKED OUT with no leaks. Cassia wrote her cell phone number on a piece of paper. She handed it to Sunny hoping that he got the message that he should not show up without calling first again. Before Sunny left, he gave Cassia his business card saying, "Just in case you need me." Cassia smiled and said goodbye. She tried not to allow herself to read too much into his comment, but it swirled around and around in her imagination. She started hoping that something would break down in the house and laughed at the thought that maybe she would break something herself and have to call him—perhaps in the middle of the night.

Before going into the kitchen to start dinner, Cassia stared down the long hallway. The beautiful lady was nowhere to be found. Cassia thought of lots of questions as she sat on a swivel stool at the kitchen counter with her hand resting on her chin. Who is she? What does she want? What triggered her appearance? And would she come again?

Cassia wondered if the answers were in the attic since that is where she saw her with Uncle Charles. Cassia glanced at the time on the microwave. It was five thirty. No time for the attic right now. She got up from the stool. Cassia opened the pantry that housed the pots and pans. She pulled out the big spaghetti pot. She filled it with water and added a pinch of salt and a little olive oil. Cassia placed the pot on the stove and waited for the water to boil. She then put in the lasagna noodles and lowered the temperature to medium. While the meat slowly cooked, she removed a bottle of wine from the corner wine rack without checking the label. Unlike her father and Uncle Charles, she had no knack for distinguishing a so-so wine from a more expensive one. Cassia placed the card with Sunny's number on the counter and stared at it. While taking her first sip of wine, Cassia thought about the first guy she slept with after her breakup with Mitch. He was not in the same category as Sunny, but he was *GQ* fine.

For the first few weeks after catching Mitch in that passionate kiss with Jewel, Mitch slept on the couch, not because he wanted to but because he knew that if he did not, Cassia would have. The couch was uncomfortable, and Mitch knew it was the right thing to do. Even though Mitch swore that this was the first kiss that he and Jewel ever shared, Cassia did not care because since she lost the baby, she began pushing Mitch away at every opportunity. While it upset Cassia to see Mitch kissing Jewel, it provided her with another excuse to create more layers to the invisible wedge that she had been building between them for months. Since she lost the baby eight months ago, Cassia criticized everything Mitch did. According to Cassia, Mitch did not grieve properly. She even accused him of being relieved that she lost the baby. She also felt that he did not comfort her in a way she thought he should and blamed him for her lack of interest in sex.

The morning of their sixth wedding anniversary, Mitch got up before Cassia and went to the grocery store to buy her giant sunflowers, Cassia's favorite. He got six—one for each year of their marriage. He had them on the table in a tall glass vase with clear rocks on the bottom to steady them. He arranged her favorite bagels and variety of cream cheeses on a plate. He had coffee ready too. Mitch did not get the reaction that he hoped for when Cassia walked into the room. Instead of throwing her arms around him and smothering his with kisses like she once did, she pointed her right index finger at each flower and counted—one, two, three, four, five, *six*. She said, "How could you?" Mitch picked up his photography equipment and slammed the door behind him without saying a word. Afterward, Cassia sat at the table and began to cry. She felt guilty about the way she had been treating Mitch. She knew that she needed professional help dealing with her grief and probably with a few of her other quirks. Mitch had given her months ago a name of a psychologist who primarily dealt with grief. Cassia picked up the card from the table where it sat for weeks—Nora Michaels, PhD. She dialed the number and made her first appointment for the following week. Cassia felt relieved and excited for the first time in a long while. She took out her to-do list from her purse and saw penciled in at noon "picnic lunch with Mitch." Cassia had arranged lunch with Mitch last week and now saw it as an opportunity to make up for her shitty behavior that morning and tell him about her appointment with Dr. Michaels. She wrote on the back of her list the menu items that she would get from the store, which included Mitch's favorite fried chicken from Royal Farms.

Cassia arrived at Mitch's office at eleven fifty. The door was open. Cassia walked in. The picnic basket slipped from her hands onto the floor. The crashing sound of bottles clinking against each other as the basket hit the tile floor caused Mitch and Jewel to break free from their embrace. They both looked at Cassia. Tears flooded Cassia's emerald-green eyes. She turned around and briskly walked down the hallway. She did not say a word. Mitch followed close behind apologizing. For days he apologized profusely, but Cassia made excuses to be away from the apartment more and more. She spent nights with girlfriends and one night with Mitch's friend Ollie.

Ollie was a photographer like Mitch and worked for the same wedding planning company. During that time, Cassia struggled dealing with bubbly brides and planning their happily ever after. She was miserable but continued working because she had no choice. She needed the money. After one particularly long wedding with lots of excessive sugariness, Cassia made it to her car, and the floodgates opened. She was thankful that all the guests were gone. Cassia had her head against her crossed arms leaning on the steering wheel. Ollie was on his way to put his last piece of equipment in his truck when he saw Cassia. Ollie knew about the breakup between Cassia and Mitch. Their entire social circle was buzzing about the news. Ollie and Cassia talked in her car, and she told him that she did not want to go home. He invited her to stay at his place for the night. He got in his truck, and Cassia followed in her car. After a few drinks and many more tears, Ollie and Cassia began kissing. Cassia was surprised at how easy it was for her to make love to Ollie without a shred of love. Later, Dr. Michaels explained that what she had with Ollie was just plain sex. She was able to turn off any emotion connected to love. With Mitch, she could not turn off her love and just have sex with him. Mitch and Cassia were connected by love to other emotions like anger and resentment. Cassia left in the morning while Ollie was still asleep. He texted her later in the day stating that he was there for her if she wanted to "talk" again. She never told Mitch about her night with Ollie. As far as she knew, he never said anything either.

After Cassia's night with Ollie, she felt guilty. She could not cope with the nice things that Mitch continued doing for her. After a few more days in hellish limbo, Cassia told Mitch to leave the apartment. He moved out the next day. They had no children and only a few assets, so the divorce was swift. Except for Mitch's clothes, cameras, and personal items, he left everything else in the apartment with Cassia. He even continued paying half the rent for the five months remaining on the lease while he moved in with a cousin. Cassia swore that she would never again sleep with someone so quickly. She stuck to her three-date rule most of the time. Cassia picked up the card with Sunny's number and walked to the fireplace. She leaned the card against the clock on the mantel. She gulped down the last of her glass of wine and chuckled. "Well, Sunny, I am willing to consider your earlier visit our *first* date."

CHAPTER FIFTEEN

CASSIA TOOK THE LASAGNA OUT of the oven. She heard a knock at the door. Annabelle stood in the doorway holding in one hand a loaf of Italian bread hanging out of the bag by several inches and in the other hand a bottle of wine. While it was not the large vat of wine that she promised, it was enough to eventually make them giggly and sentimental. Cassia did not feel dressed up enough to eat in the dining room, so she started setting up the kitchen table for dinner. Cassia retrieved candles, candlesticks, and three snowflake trivets from the china cabinet. They were the items that Maddie used when setting the table. While Cassia was in the dining room, Annabelle walked around the kitchen. She pulled out a few bottles of wine from the rack and said, "Hmm, good taste, Dad." She saw Sunny's business card on the fireplace mantel. She picked it up and flung it back onto the mantel.

Annabelle quickly turned away from the mantel when Cassia entered the kitchen. She made no comment about the card as she helped Cassia arrange the trivets on the table and light the candles. Cassia placed the lasagna and garlic bread on the table while Annabelle opened the bottle of wine. She filled both glasses. Before taking their first bite of food, they lifted their glasses and toasted to old friends. They began exchanging life stories. Cassia talked about how unhappy she was in her job and confessed her divorce. Annabelle was not willing to divulge any dirt in her life, if there was any. She continued painting a perfect picture of her life. When they were done eating, Annabelle and Cassia refilled their glasses and moved to the living room. Annabelle removed her shoes and sat "Indian style." Cassia did the same. They sat facing each other and raised their glasses and toasted once more—to a great dinner.

Cassia looked around the room. She said, "This place has brought back so many memories. Before I got here, my plan was to sell Ashby House and go back to Baltimore. But, Belle, I have been secretly fantasizing about keeping it." Cassia did not realize that she called Annabelle by the nickname she used when they were younger. Annabelle smiled because only one other person ever calls her Belle. Cassia continued, "I'm not even sure that will be financially possible. Do you think your father will be up to bringing the papers by tomorrow?"

"Ummm…Cass, I think my father is depressed right now about Charles's passing. He is acting very strange. I know you are anxious to get together with him, but I have a feeling that it might be another day or two before he can come to this house."

"Sure. I understand. They were friends for a long time."

Annabelle smiled and leaned in closely. "They were more than friends. For the last five years, they were lovers. My father came out of the closet about that time. He and my mother divorced. It was bad at first, but now everything is fine. She is remarried and very happy."

"Wow," Cassia said with her emerald eyes nearly bulging out of their sockets. "Did they live here together?"

Annabelle laughed. "No. No. My father always maintained his own place, but he did spend a lot of time here."

Many questions raced through Cassia's mind, but she chose the one that might answer why Uncle Charles left her Ashby House. "Belle, why didn't he leave Ashby House to your father?"

Annabelle said, "Charles told my father that he wanted to keep Ashby House in the family. I assume that his mother did not want it back, so I guess he decided to leave it to someone he considered family—you."

Cassia uncrossed her legs and placed her feet on the floor. "So, Uncle Charles's mother *is* still alive. Well, that explains why there is no date of death listed for her on her portrait or in the family Bible." Cassia began processing the second part of Annabelle's revelation. She did not understand why Uncle Charles considered her family since they had not seen or spoken to each other since Grandma B removed her from Ashby House the summer that her father died.

Annabelle rose from the couch and took her last sip of wine. "Peaches Winchester is very much alive. I saw her at Charles's funeral. Why do you think she is dead?" Cassia stood up. Without pausing to catch her breath, her mouth was moving as quickly as her feet were pacing back and forth. Cassia said, "I need to talk to her immediately. Does she live close by?"

Annabelle was taken aback by Cassia's change in demeanor. "Yes…Mrs. Winchester lives about ten miles from here. I believe after the funeral she went out of town for a few days. I think she is visiting her friend somewhere in Florida. My father probably knows when she'll be back. Let me call him."

Annabelle went to the kitchen to get her cell phone from her purse. In a few seconds, she returned to the living room and called her father. Cassia stayed in the living room just long enough to hear Annabelle say, "Dad, do you know when Mrs. Winchester will be back from her visit with her friend in Florida?"

Cassia returned from the kitchen with another bottle of wine. She refilled her glass. Annabelle was now off the phone. She said, "My father believes that Mrs. Winchester will be back on Thursday or Friday. He promised to call you tomorrow to set up a meeting to go over the papers with you." Annabelle wrote down the phone number and address that she got from her father for Peaches Winchester. She handed it to Cassia. Cassia thanked her and poured more wine into Annabelle's glass. Cassia wanted more answers to the many questions she had itemized on the mental list in her head, but tonight she was overwhelmed from too much wine and the confusing information swirling in her head.

Annabelle insisted on helping Cassia clean up before leaving. She took one more sip from her full glass of wine and followed Cassia into the kitchen. Annabelle rinsed the plates and put them in the dishwasher without saying a word. She glanced over at the fireplace where Sunny's business card was lying facedown. Cassia paid no attention to Annabelle's silence. She was deep in her own thoughts. Cassia wrapped up the leftover lasagna and bread and placed them in the refrigerator. She took the apple crisp from the oven and cut up a piece and placed it in a container for Annabelle to take with her.

Annabelle finally broke the silence. "Hey, Cass, do you remember that time capsule we buried in the yard that last summer you were here? Wasn't it near the tree house?"

Cassia thought for a moment. "Damn, I forgot all about it until now. I think you're right."

"We counted about five feet to the right of the tree house and then placed that large rock over the hole that we covered with dirt." Cassia laughed. "Remember how you, Sunny, and I struggled to move that humongous rock over the dirt to cover the time capsule? I wonder if it's still there. Do you remember what we put in it?"

"Let me think. I know we put a lock of mine, yours, and Sunny's hair in there and a cassette tape of my favorite Journey song." Annabelle began singing into a spatula that she picked up off the counter. "Just a small-town girl. Livin' in a lonely world."

Cassia joined in, "She took the midnight train. Goin' anywhere." They both laughed.

"I don't remember what else we put in there," Annabelle said while drying her hands with the dishtowel one last time before making her way to the front door.

Before Annabelle made her way out the door, Cassia said, "Oh yeah, I forgot to tell you Sunny La Rue stopped by earlier to check on a pipe in the kitchen. Belle, you are so right about Sunny. Wow! He left his card with his number." Cassia giggled like a schoolgirl. "I sure hope nothing breaks down and I have to call him in the middle of the night."

Annabelle turned around. She looked at Cassia without changing her expression or acknowledging her comment. She said, "Listen, I have an idea. I don't have court until noon, so how about I come back in the morning, and we can try to find our time capsule. I'll bring Robert along for some muscle. Does that work for you?"

Cassia did not understand why Annabelle completely ignored her comment about Sunny, but she was excited at the prospect of meeting Robert and locating their childhood treasure. Annabelle and

Cassia exchanged cell phone numbers. They hugged and said good-bye. Cassia watched Annabelle's truck disappear into the darkness.

Cassia locked the door. She wanted to check her e-mails, but the wine and information overload left her brain tired. She went straight upstairs to the bedroom. She pulled out her pajamas from her unpacked suitcase and made several notes on her to-do list for the next day—unpack, e-mail Mitch, call Marcie, and call to check in on Grandma B. While brushing her teeth, Cassia looked in the mirror like she had done a thousand times before. However, this time her own eyes haunted her for the first time. She looked away and blocked out the thought of any similarity between her eyes and Uncle Charles's. She turned off the bathroom light and got into bed. Before drifting off to sleep, Cassia realized that Annabelle never mentioned Maddie being at Uncle Charles's funeral. She was angry at herself for allowing her brain to obsess about Peaches Winchester. Tomorrow she would definitely ask Annabelle about Maddie. Cassia wanted to get out of bed and add Maddie to her to-do list, but the room was now spinning. She stayed put and drifted off to sleep.

Cassia began dreaming. She and Annabelle were playing tag and laughing and running through the fireplace between the kitchen and living room just like they did when they were kids. However, now they were adults. They began running without ducking because the opening to the fireplace was now very tall. Maddie began scolding them, but seconds later, she had ice cream on the table for them and began laughing with them. Then Maddie said to Cassia, "Love you to pieces, child." Cassia was once again a child. She hugged Maddie's neck.

CHAPTER SIXTEEN

Day 2—June 13, 2006

CASSIA WAS AWOKEN BY THE ringing of her cell phone. In her sleep stupor she reached for the snooze button on the bedside alarm clock, but after several attempts at trying to make it stop, Cassia realized that it was her phone ringing. Cassia picked up her phone next to the clock, and with her half-asleep squinted eyes, she tried to make out the number. It was a Richmond area code and assumed that it was Mr. Oates calling arranging a time for them to get together. By the time Cassia collected her thoughts, the call went into voice mail. She immediately listened to the message. It was not Mr. Oates, but instead it was Annabelle letting her know that Robert had court that morning, and because she had court in the afternoon, they would not be able to come over until about five o'clock. Cassia decided to call her back after she got at least her first cup of coffee. She hoped that the caffeine would bring her back to life.

Cassia sat up in bed. Her head was pounding. It was another "never again" morning. She was not much of a drinker and vowed to stay within her two-glass limit the next time she drank. Cassia thought it was best to move slowly, so she allowed her feet to dangle over the side of the bed for a few minutes before making her way to the bathroom. Once in the bathroom, she leaned against the vanity and looked into the mirror. Unlike last night, she could not ignore the familiar eyes staring back at her. Cassia made a plan to study the two portraits on the wall more closely when she got downstairs. Cassia brushed her teeth. She washed her face and quietly whimpered while the cold water absorbed into her dehydrated pores.

While hanging the towel back on the rack, there was a knock on the front door. "Shit." Cassia frantically ran a brush through her morning hair believing it must be Sunny again. She grabbed her cell phone from the bedside table and started down the stairs. "Damn, doesn't he know how to use a cell phone?" Cassia gave her hair one last fluffing and opened the door. It was not Sunny but a middle-aged black woman clutching a wicker basket in her hands. She said, "Child, I would recognize those beautiful green eyes anywhere."

Cassia knew that familiar dimple on the woman's right cheek and that small faded scar on her left cheek when she smiled. She knew the sound of her voice. And she knew that nobody else in the world called her "child." Cassia threw her arms around Maddie. She hugged her in return. They both laughed because the basket that Maddie was holding was nearly smashed between them.

Cassia released Maddie from her grasp. "I am so sorry. I hope that I did not ruin your basket. It is so good to see you. Please come in."

Maddie entered the foyer. She looked up at the chandelier that began gently chiming. She said, "I've always loved that heavenly sound." Tears filled her eyes as she sniffed the air. "I can still smell his tobacco."

Maddie followed Cassia to the kitchen. She placed the basket on the table. Her eyes scanned the renovated kitchen. She sat down and shook her head in approval. "Wow, it looks great in here. Cassia, I'm sorry to just show up, but when I heard that you were at Ashby House, I tried to get your number from Raymond (Oates), but he did not call me back. So, I got up early this morning, went to the bakery in town, and bought some muffins. I hope you don't mind."

Cassia studied Maddie's face. She was surprised that Maddie still looked so young. Her youthful skin and bright smile hid the reality of her fifty-four years on this earth. Cassia realized that Maddie was probably only in her early thirties the last time she visited Ashby House. Then she thought that to a six-year-old child, anybody over thirty is old.

"I am thrilled that you are here," said Cassia while reaching into the cabinet to get the can of coffee that she opened yesterday. She poured water into the carafe and placed three scoops of coffee into the filter. The smell of coffee brewing immediately permeated throughout the kitchen. Cassia placed plates, cups, napkins, and a spoon on the table. She asked Maddie if she used cream and sugar. At that moment, Cassia realized that she knew nothing about this person who had always been so warm and caring to her. Cassia did not know that Maddie started working for Uncle Charles when she was twenty-five years old after her divorce from an abusive husband. She moved from Atlanta, Georgia, to Richmond, Virginia, after several violations of a restraining order, one of which landed her in the hospital for a week. When she recovered, Maddie traveled as far north as she could afford to go. With her money dwindling down to almost nothing, she stopped in Richmond and stayed at a cheap motel. During the day, she answered ads for a live-in housekeeper. Maddie told her story to Charles. He hired her that day. For the first couple months, if they needed anything in town, Charles made sure that she never went alone. He helped her secretly communicate with her family, who kept her informed of when her ex was in or out of jail. Charles even paid to fly family members to visit Maddie at Ashby House on several occasions when she became homesick.

Charles never treated Maddie like hired help, but she could never break the habit of calling him "Mr. Charles." They became friends—they dined together, took walks together, and on occasion traveled together. Unable to have children of her own, Maddie was excited when Cassia started her yearly visits. Over the years, she became quite attached to Charles and credited him with saving her life. She terminated her employment with Charles Winchester one year after Cassia's last summer visit at Ashby House. She moved back to Georgia with her family after the death of her ex-husband from a heroin overdose but kept in close contact with Charles. She even visited Ashby House with her new husband several times over the years.

With their coffees now poured and muffins on their plates, Maddie began wiping the tears that started down her cheeks. "I am so sorry that I could not be at Mr. Charles's funeral. I was in Atlanta burying my momma the same day."

Cassia gently patted Maddie's hand. "I am so sorry for your loss. How old was she?"

"Seventy-five years old and in good health until about a year ago when she was diagnosed with lung cancer. My daddy died five years earlier from colon cancer. Despicable diseases."

Cassia said, "I didn't know that Uncle Charles died until I got a call last week from Mr. Oates telling me that I was named in his will to inherit Ashby House. I was told that he wanted to keep Ashby House in the family. I still don't know what to make of it."

Maddie took Cassia's hands from across the table and looked into her eyes. "Child, your Uncle Charles loved you. You *are* his family. He was heartbroken when your grandmother took you away that day—wicked woman." Maddie usually spoke her mind without regrets but apologized immediately fearing that she may have hurt Cassia's feelings with her comment about Grandma B.

Cassia laughed. "Don't apologize. She was and still is just as wicked."

"I remember the day when she came and got you. Didn't even give you a chance to say goodbye. She hauled you off in her car and sped away." Shaking her head, she said, "With the news of your father's death and your leaving, Mr. Charles was never the same."

"I'm so sorry that I didn't say goodbye," Cassia said, lowering her head.

Maddie leaned in close to Cassia and picked up her chin with her right index finger. "Not your fault, child. You were only doing what she told you to do."

Cassia cleared the plates and cups from the table. She closed the dishwasher and turned to Maddie. "Do you remember anything about my parents when they visited Ashby House?"

Maddie's eyes widened. "Child, your mother and father were so much in love and so happy when she got pregnant. I remember when your mother was just starting to show—when you were in her belly—and your father and Mr. Charles were getting ready to leave for the store. Your father kissed your mother so tenderly and then stooped down and kissed her belly. Mr. Charles laughed at me because I couldn't control the tears that came pouring down my face watching that lovely moment."

Cassia smiled. She thought about the scrapbook and pictures of her mother and father that she put together after her father died. She had no trouble imagining that scene.

"The three of them—your mother, father, and Mr. Charles sat at this very table many nights playing cards and other games. Mostly, they told stories late into the night."

Cassia thought that it was a great opportunity to bring up the subject of the ghosts. "Maddie, were they the same stories that Uncle Charles told me—the ones about the ghosts?"

Maddie laughed. "Do you remember those crazy stories?" The serious expression on Cassia's face gave Maddie her answer.

"Maddie, have you ever seen any apparitions here at Ashby House?"

Maddie's appearance grew serious too. "No, I never saw any ghosts, but there were a few nights when I heard crying—a woman crying. A couple times I got up to check but found no one. I asked Mr. Charles about it, and he told me that it was Elizabeth, a daughter of the original owners of this house. He said that she was sad. He didn't know how to help her."

Cassia thought about the letter that she found in the pages of the Bible, the one written by Elizabeth to her sister Martha. Cassia got up from the table and took Maddie's hand. "Come with me to the den. I want to show you something."

Maddie and Cassia walked down the hall. Maddie looked at the portraits on the wall as she entered the den. She stared at Charles's face for a few seconds before following Cassia to the desk where the Bible sat. Cassia opened the Bible. She flipped open the pages to the middle and pulled out the old letter. Cassia handed the letter to Maddie. She read it to herself, put her hand over her mouth, and gasped when she got to the end and saw that the author of the letter was Elizabeth.

"I think I saw Elizabeth yesterday," Cassia said. She began pacing back and forth in front of the desk. "A lady was standing in the doorway after I finished reading the letter. It *had* to be her. It *had* to be the Elizabeth from the letter. I followed her down the hall, but she vanished before I could reach her." Cassia mischievously smiled. She looked at Maddie without blinking. Her pupils were dilated like she had just ingested a large dose of stimulants. With her head slightly cocked to one side, she said, "Are you feeling adventurous today?"

Maddie smiled, and with a nervous resonance and a bit of apprehension in her voice, she said, "Why? What do you have in mind?"

"I keep thinking that the answers have to be in the attic. That is where I saw Uncle Charles and Elizabeth that last summer at Ashby House. Will you go up in the attic with me?"

Maddie thought about Cassia's question for a few seconds. She had never been in the attic the entire time that she lived at Ashby House. Charles told her that it was just for storage. He would take care of that area of the house himself. Maddie had to admit that she was curious about what was in the attic. There were so many days when she watched Mr. Charles go up the stairs with a few vinyl records tucked under his arm. He would be gone for hours. She sometimes would hear the music from his favorite operas blaring down the stairs when she walked by. Maddie respected his request and stayed out of the attic figuring it was just his man cave and gave him his privacy.

Maddie's eyes widened. A nervous quivering laugh involuntarily came out of her mouth. The sound surprised Cassia, and even Maddie wondered where it came from. She said, "Okay, let's do it."

CHAPTER SEVENTEEN

CASSIA AND MADDIE WALKED UP the steps to the second floor. They headed down the hall toward the stairs to the third floor. Maddie's nervousness turned to sentimentality when she came upon her bedroom—the bedroom she stayed in during her years at Ashby House. Maddie had to go inside and look around. She said, "Cassia, please give me a minute."

Cassia stayed in the doorway and watched Maddie move slowly about the room. She watched as Maddie's fingers traveled along the carved cherrywood of the four-poster queen-size bed. And she watched her turn toward the window wiping the tears that she tried to hide. Only Maddie knew the comfort and safety that the room symbolized. It was a place where all her fears had disappeared. No longer did she wake up with a feeling of disgust and self-loathing because of the despicable sexual acts that she was forced to perform the night before. No longer did she wake up to the hurtful words that eventually eroded her self-esteem. The tears that Maddie could not hold back today were for Charles Winchester, the man who supplied her those years of protection and peace.

When Maddie moved into Ashby House and for the first time heard the lady crying in the night, she was afraid. After talking to Mr. Charles, she realized that the lady meant her no harm. Later, when Maddie heard the lady softly sobbing in the distance before falling asleep, it made Maddie sad—sad to think that Ashby House did not bring Elizabeth the same comfort that it provided her.

Unlike Cassia, Maddie was content to never see the apparition or learn anything more about the spirit or spirits that roamed Ashby House. She was thankful that Elizabeth never came into her bedroom at night. She thought perhaps Elizabeth somehow knew the turmoil that she had been through and therefore left Maddie undisturbed in her serenity. Now, Maddie wanted to change her mind believing that she might somehow be breaking their unstated pact. However, her curiosity about what might be in the attic won over her apprehension about breaching their agreement. She followed Cassia down the hallway and up the stairs to the third floor. When they reached the door, Maddie froze. She stared at Cassia and timidly said, "I hear Elizabeth crying. I think the sound is coming from downstairs. Cassia, she is not in the attic."

Cassia turned and faced Maddie. "I hear her too, but we've come this far, and now I need to see what is in here."

Cassia placed her hand on the doorknob. She held onto it for a few seconds without turning the handle or saying one word. In the stillness, Cassia absorbed the sounds and smells that were moving abruptly in and out of her acutely heightened senses. Elizabeth's crying was now amplified in Cassia's ears. Uncle Charles's cherry tobacco invaded her olfactory system and burned her nostrils. Cassia let go of the doorknob. She placed her hands over her ears to try and quiet the crying. She shivered as an icy cold breeze passed through her like a minus-eighty-degree windchill on a Chicago winter morning. Cassia felt sick. She remembered the story that Uncle Charles told about Jonathan Welts, the cruel overseer. For the first time, she was afraid. No longer was she certain that the spirit or spirits that roamed Ashby House were all benign. She closed her eyes and silently asked her mother for protection. Immediately, the crying stopped. The doorknob turned without assistance. Cassia cautiously pushed the door open and peeked inside. Cassia could not turn around to leave even if she wanted because Maddie was standing so close behind her that she had no choice but to step inside the room.

Maddie and Cassia stood side by side. They looked around the room. Maddie finally broke the silence, "Child, I'm glad that Mr. Charles never made me clean up *this* mess." They laughed. Cassia put her hand over her mouth and coughed and laughed harder as dust invaded her lungs.

Cassia finally gained her composure. "Wow, so this is Uncle Charles's man cave."

"Look, Cassia, there is Mr. Charles's record player. And look, his favorite record is still set up waiting to be played. Now I know why he liked coming up here. What a great recliner," Maddie said pointing to the chair in the corner. The overstuffed broken-in leather chair stood adjacent to a table covered with a large cloth checkerboard. The red-and-black checkers matched the board in size. It was set up waiting for someone to play. The room was certainly very different than the pristine condition of the downstairs. Maddie found an old piece of cloth. She shook it until the dust stopped flying. She then dusted off the leather chair and sank into it like a memory foam mattress. She said, "You know, Cassia, I can imagine him sitting with a silly grin on his face holding a snifter of brandy with a light fog of smoke circling around his head and waving his hands like a conductor to the music. That man loved music."

Cassia thought about the many times that he danced with her and Maddie. She wanted to bring up the dancing but was afraid she would let the news of Uncle Charles's sexuality slip out in the conversation. She did not know how Maddie would feel about the information, so her only reply was, "He sure did."

Maddie said, "I always thought that it was so strange how he loved dancing with women even though he preferred the company of men."

Cassia smiled. "So you know about him and Mr. Oates."

"I lived in this house for a long time, child. Mr. Charles was very discreet, but he brought home a few lovers over the years. But when he and Raymond got together, that was true love. I heard that Raymond was by his side until the very end."

Cassia walked to the other side of the room. She strained to see through the undisturbed dust and cobwebs that covered the dimly lit area of the room where grimy windows let in only the faintest light. Entangled in the dust and cobwebs were various size boxes stacked almost to the ceiling, mountains of books piled high and unsteady, and broken pieces of discarded furniture. Dust filled her lungs, eyes, and hair. Cassia coughed again while pushing her way through the thick webs. She called to Maddie, "Come and take a look at this!"

Maddie struggled to get out of the chair that seemed to refuse to release her from its grip. After several attempts of wiggling and using all of her upper-body strength, she managed to free herself from the chair. Maddie went to the far-left corner of the room where Cassia was standing next to the makeshift box filled with brittle straw and tattered rags enclosed by a shabby wooden frame.

"Wow, it's an eagle's nest," Cassia said laughing.

A somber look came over Maddie's face. She stared at the structure on the floor. "Cassia, this is a slave's bed."

Cassia's eyes grew wide. "Really? Why do you think it is here?"

"Well, Mr. Charles's stories about his ancestors owning slaves were true, I guess. I don't know why this heartbreaking piece of the past would have been saved. It is an appalling reminder of a horrendous time in America." Maddie reached down into the straw for a faded cloth bag that she noticed was wedged between the straw and the top of the bed frame. She picked up the bag, opened it, and inside were two small wooden caps about one and a half inches long. Maddie never knitted a thing in her life, but she knew that these caps were needle guards. She watched her mother place similar ones over her own knitting needles after she was done using them.

Maddie's heart ached thinking about her mother. She missed her so much already. She had told her husband before she left for Richmond that she has had holes in her heart before, but this is the biggest one now. Maddie thought about the time and love her mother put into all her knitting. She called her finished products "masterpieces." And they were works of art that Maddie vowed to forever treasure while packing up her mother's belongings. Maddie still could not believe that such beautiful things could be made from just a few skeins of yarn. She was in awe every time her mother completed a scarf for her and proudly showed it off to her friends at school. Her eyes bulged with tears that she fought to contain remembering the countless blankets that her mother made in order to match the latest color change that Maddie had to make in her bedroom.

Holding the guards in her hand, Maddie thought about the day when her mother attempted to teach her how to knit. Her mother said as she removed the protective cap from her favorite needle, "Maddie, these guards protect the needles when not in use. Always protect the tips of your needles. Now watch as I loop this end through another loop, and then I tighten a little, and then I draw another loop, and after that, more loops and more tightening. Look, I've made a nice chain." Maddie's head was spinning trying to comprehend all that tightening and looping. Now she wondered, perhaps if she had taken more of an interest in staying home and knitting, she might not have gotten involved with her first husband, who turned out to be such an evil man.

Maddie put the needle guards back into the bag. She handed it to Cassia while explaining what was in the bag and their purpose. Cassia peeked inside the bag. She wondered if the contents of the bag held any clues to solving the mysteries of Number Six Ashby House.

Cassia and Maddie moved to the other side of the room where huge framed old portraits were heaped against each other. The first portrait leaning against the stack was of the beautiful lady. The plaque attached to the portrait read, "Elizabeth Lawson Morris, 1855–1875." Cassia was about to tell Maddie that this was the lady she saw yesterday, but the constant ringing of her cell phone downstairs interrupted her thoughts. The dust and heavy attic air troubled her breathing. Holding tightly onto the knitting bag, she said to Maddie, "Let's go downstairs," and staggered as fast as she could down the steps with Maddie following closely behind.

CHAPTER EIGHTEEN

CASSIA PLACED THE KNITTING BAG on the kitchen table next to her cell phone. She was surprised that she not only had three missed calls but one text too. Maddie interrupted her before Cassia could check her messages, "Cassia, I am only going to be in town until tomorrow afternoon. I would like to pay my respects to Mr. Charles this afternoon by visiting his grave site. Would you please go with me?"

"Yes, but I need to get a shower first," she said, laughing and removing pieces of cobwebs from the sleeve of her pajama top. Cassia reached over and removed a cobweb from Maddie's hair.

"I probably should get a shower too. I need to check into my hotel room. I can pick you up in about an hour or an hour and a half," Maddie said while looking at the 12:30 time on the microwave. "Does that work for you?"

"Hotel room? You are not staying in a hotel when I have four bedrooms not in use. Please cancel your reservation and stay with me. Besides, Mr. Oates's daughter, Annabelle, will be here later. I know she would love to see you. She's bringing her fiancé too."

Maddie was a little reluctant to stay, but after some more coaxing from Cassia, she agreed. She hoped that the sleeping pills she brought with her would give her a restful night. Maddie was surprised to hear that Annabelle was engaged. She thought that girl would never settle down. The few times that she visited Ashby House after terminating her employment with Charles Winchester, she would hear lots of negative gossip about Annabelle.

"Cassia, may I please borrow your phone to call the hotel and my husband? My phone is dead, and my charger is in the car. Also,

I need to call Raymond because we have an appointment tomorrow morning at my hotel. Is it okay if we meet here at Ashby House?"

"That's fine with me, but Annabelle told me that her father is having a difficult time right now dealing with Uncle Charles's death. I'm not sure if he is ready to visit Ashby House just yet."

Maddie looked down and shook her head. "I feel bad because I never really gave that any consideration. Unfortunately, I cannot put off meeting with Raymond because I have a flight scheduled for home later in the afternoon. I had to use time off without pay to come here because company policy only allows bereavement time for next of kin." Maddie's face reddened. "That rule makes my blood boil."

Cassia agreed. She felt lucky that she had the freedom to make her own schedule with her job, but that perk came with many disadvantages too. Cassia got paid on straight commission and no benefits. She had no paid time off for vacations, bereavement, or personal days. She also had to supply her own health insurance.

Maddie continued, "I did get three paid days off for my momma's funeral." Her eyes once again filled to the brim with tears.

Cassia felt so helpless seeing Maddie so distraught. She had never witnessed that display of pain at the loss of another human being except on the news or in movies. Cassia always knew that Grandma B and her father were affected by the loss of her mother, but she never saw firsthand any heart-wrenching scene like this one. She did however remember how reserved Mitch and Grandma B were when she lost Elizabeth. Tears burned her hot face. The doctor's words once again resonated in her head, "This type of thing happens sometimes." She hugged Maddie as tight as Maddie had held her in her dream. "I'm so sorry for all your losses." After a few seconds, Cassia released Maddie from her grip. She handed Maddie a tissue and kept one for herself. She smiled at Maddie with remnants of tears still on her own face. "We are a sappy pair, aren't we?"

Those words gave Maddie the best laugh that she had in a long time. While Maddie was happily married to a kind man and had three wonderful stepchildren who adored her, her mother's and father's illnesses and ultimate deaths had Maddie sinking into a dark place. She was having trouble finding her way out. Now adding Charles Winchester's death into the mix sent her sinking into sadness even further. Her husband was growing more concerned because ever since her father died and then leading up to her mother's death, Maddie's nightmares were increasing. When they first married, she had a nightmare about every other month or so. They increased to about once a week after her father's death. Since her mother's death a week ago, Maddie woke up screaming almost every night.

Maddie's nightmares stemmed from her painful past experiences during her first marriage—some real and some so bizarre that it sometimes took Maddie's husband, George, hours to calm her down. There were two nightmares that she had most often. The first was her ex-husband chasing her down a dark street with a knife while she is naked. Every person she asks for help ignores her pleas. The second and more disturbing dream was her ex-husband ripping her child from her womb with a coat hanger. There is blood all over her. Her husband is standing over her. She continues hearing his sinister laughter as she wakes up screaming.

"Maddie, maybe you can suggest meeting Mr. Oates at his office, but if he does want to meet here, I can provide you all the privacy that you need." Cassia handed Maddie her phone. Maddie thanked Cassia. She began making her first call as Cassia headed upstairs. She heard Maddie say, "George, how are you? I miss you so much, my love." Cassia smiled.

CHAPTER NINETEEN

CASSIA RINSED THE SHAMPOO FROM her hair. She turned the water to the hottest that she could stand but still felt the remnants of an unfriendly icy coldness that she had experienced before entering the attic. She once again asked her mother to protect her from any aggressive spirits that may be attached to Ashby House. Cassia could not get the story out of her head—the one Uncle Charles told about Jonathan Welts, the violent overseer who flogged and tortured many of the slaves who worked the fields of Ashby House. She felt that getting together with Peaches Lawson Winchester was more important than ever. Perhaps she could shed some light on the history of the house and the people who once lived here.

Cassia stepped out of the shower. With just a towel wrapped around her, she sat on the edge of the bed. She reached inside the side pocket of her suitcase. She pulled out the ladybug brooch that she always kept with her. It was the one trinket that Grandma B gave her from her mother's belongings. Grandma B told Cassia that it was her mother's favorite piece of jewelry.

Grandma B never knew that it was a gift from Peaches Winchester. During one of Michael and Marianne's visits to Ashby House, Peaches stopped by to see Charles about the investments in her portfolio. Marianne commented about the lovely ladybug brooch that Peaches was wearing on her dress. Charles's father had the brooch specially made for his wife during an overseas trip to Paris. It was an "I'm sorry" gift for yet another one of his affairs that she found out about. Before Peaches left the house that day, she removed the brooch and gave it to Marianne. It was the kind of thing that Peaches was known to do. It was the one and only time that they ever saw each other. Marianne's married name was *Westfield*. Peaches never knew that her maiden name was *Brittle*—a name that was *very* familiar to Peaches. She had no idea that Marianne was her late husband's lovechild. Cassia cupped the ladybug inside her hand, closed her eyes, and this time she asked her mother to look after Maddie too. She opened her eyes and placed the brooch back inside the suitcase and zipped it up.

Cassia got dressed and waited downstairs for Maddie to finish getting ready. She picked up her phone and read her text. It was a short message from Mitch, "Sent you an email." She checked the time and decided that reading Mitch's text would have to wait until later. Cassia listened to her voice mails. One was from Marcie, who was happy to let Cassia know that all five contracts were signed, and she wanted to renegotiate *her* contract with Cassia when she returned from Richmond. Cassia rolled her eyes and deleted the message. The second message was from Mr. Oates saying he wanted to arrange a time for their meeting. The third message was from Annabelle calling to again confirm the time change for their "treasure hunt." Cassia smiled because Annabelle giggled like she did when they were kids when she said the words "treasure hunt."

Cassia dialed Annabelle's number to confirm that the time change worked for her. Annabelle was excited that Maddie would be joining them too. Cassia asked if leftover lasagna would be okay with her. Annabelle had no problem with that. Cassia took her to-do list from her purse. She penciled in all the changes. Once again, she crossed out the 6:00 p.m. slot. Just as she was penciling in her new items, Maddie came into the kitchen. Her eyes were no longer puffy. With her hair now pulled back, Cassia saw the kindest brown eyes and youthful light-brown face looking back at her.

Cassia said, "I waited to call Mr. Oates because I wanted to find out if you had confirmed your plans with him yet."

Maddie said, "Oh, I spoke to Raymond and set up a time. He's meeting me here at Ashby House tomorrow morning at ten. He said he had no problem meeting with me here instead of his office. He also said that it would work for him to meet with you right afterward. He said to call him if that plan did not work for you."

Cassia placed her cell phone and keys into her purse. "Okay, that works for me. Let's go. Oh yeah, Annabelle and her fiancé, Robert, will be staying for dinner. Will you be able to join us?"

"I would love to, but I've already made plans for dinner with an old friend in town. My dinner plans are not until 7:00 p.m., so I can stay until about six thirty. I would love to see Annabelle again. It's been four or five years since I've seen her. I would love to meet her fiancé. What time will they be here?"

Cassia said, "About five thirty. That is perfect."

The graveyard was about forty minutes from Ashby House. On the way, Cassia shared her story about losing baby Elizabeth, her divorce from Mitch, and how they were still friends. Maddie told Cassia how sorry she was for the loss of her child and that she had lost several babies too. They were early in her pregnancy. She never told Cassia the details of her miscarriages and why she was eventually unable to have children of her own. Maddie told Cassia that her husband, George, wanted to accompany her to Richmond, but their youngest granddaughter, who just turned six last month, had a dance recital. She talked him into staying because she wanted at least one of them to be there. At a red light, Maddie pulled out pictures of George, the children, and grandchildren and showed them to Cassia. Maddie glanced over from time to time identifying each person in the picture by name, including their five-year-old golden retriever, Samantha. Her eyes lit up every time she talked about her family in Georgia. Though Maddie was unable to have children of her own, it was evident to Cassia that George's children and grandchildren were no less Maddie's. By the time Maddie and Cassia reached the graveyard, Cassia was in love with Maddie's family too.

CHAPTER TWENTY

Maddie's car proceeded through the gates of Oakwood Cemetery. She had been there once before accompanying Charles when his cousin Albert died many years ago. Maddie pulled up to the caretaker's office. She had forgotten how large the cemetery was and knew that finding Charles Winchester's grave without any assistance would be like finding a needle in a haystack. Maddie shook her head while looking at the rows and rows of tombstones. "I should have asked Raymond for the location of Mr. Charles's grave when I spoke to him earlier." Maddie stepped out of the car. She said, "I hope someone inside can help us."

Cassia stood by the car while Maddie rang the bell at the caretaker's office. They waited a few minutes, but the only answer they got was a "go away I mean business" bark from a dog inside. Maddie backed away from the office door. She looked at Cassia and shrugged her shoulders.

"Maybe we should call Mr. Oates," Cassia said.

"He won't be picking up his phone now. When I talked to him earlier, he said that he would be in court for the rest of the day."

After standing in front of the office for a few minutes, Maddie said, "Let's drive around and look for freshly dug graves. Perhaps we'll get lucky."

Cassia and Maddie got into the car. They drove slowly up and down the curvy narrow roads searching for areas of the ground that possibly still had heaps of flowers stacked or cleaned areas of ground with no grass yet grown over. Coming up over a hill, Cassia saw a woman kneeling at a grave. Maddie jumped when she shouted out, "Stop the car. I see a woman over there near that large angel statue. I doubt that she knows where Uncle Charles's grave is, but she might know the whereabouts of the caretaker. Hell, she might be the caretaker."

"Child, I don't see anybody." Maddie's eyes scanned statues of various saints with their hands folded in prayer, a statue of the Blessed Mother holding baby Jesus, and more statues of angels than she could count. Then Maddie pointed to the tallest angel. "Did you mean that one?"

"Yes." The statue was about twenty feet off the road imbedded in a row of smaller statues and grave markers.

Cassia said, "Wait here. I'll be right back."

Cassia walked toward the woman. She did not know if there was such a thing as graveyard etiquette when walking through since she had only been to a cemetery a few times. She visited her daughter's grave but stopped after two times. The idea of Elizabeth being so far down in the cold ground made Cassia only sadder. She never visited her parents' graves for the same reason. Cassia was only at the graveyard now to support Maddie.

Cassia walked the short distance to the woman. She was wearing a shabby white cotton dress and a red-and-white Aunt Jemima–like head scarf. Cassia was surprised that the woman was shoeless and her feet were heavily calloused. She was sitting with her legs to the side with one hand on the ground as if to keep her balance. Her other hand was pulling out the grass and weeds that had overgrown onto a grave marker. Cassia could not clearly see the woman's facial features at first because she was thoroughly engaged in her work and seemed oblivious to everything around her. Cassia softly said hello, careful not to startle the woman.

Cassia had a feeling that the woman somehow sensed that she was there. Her body didn't flinch or jerk at all. She did not move off the ground but did look up at Cassia while shielding her eyes from the sun with her right hand. Cassia looked back at her. She could not take her eyes off the deep scar on the woman's left cheek. After a few seconds, Cassia was able to refocus her attention. Cassia surmised that the woman was probably in her late thirties or early forties.

Cassia now thought how ridiculous it was to ask if the woman knew the whereabouts of Uncle Charles's grave even though she could have passed for the caretaker from the way she was dressed and how focused she was at cleaning that grave marker. In order not to offend the woman, Cassia only asked if she knew where the caretaker might be.

The woman shook her head from side to side. She was not interested in any conversation with Cassia. She put her head back down and proceeded with her work. Cassia thanked the lady but got no response. On the way back to Maddie's car, Cassia wondered if perhaps the lady was cleaning the grass and weeds from her child's grave. An overwhelming sadness came over Cassia thinking that her own daughter's grave might be in disarray and she did not even know.

Cassia reached the car and wanted to share the details of her encounter with the lady, but before she could begin her story, Maddie said, "Look, I think the caretaker's there now."

Maddie drove to the caretaker's office. The door was open. The dog that was barking when they first stopped by stood straight up when Maddie and Cassia entered the office. Next to the dog stood a tall balding man. He was about as thin as the toothpick that was hanging out of his mouth. Cassia guessed from his wrinkled appearance that he was probably in his seventies—maybe even eighties. He wore a stained white T-shirt hidden mostly behind his faded blue denim suspenders. His boots were muddy. He turned from the file cabinet to see who had entered. He said with a wide grin, "Hello, ladies. My name is Gus, caretaker extraordinaire." Pointing to the erect eighty-pound Doberman by his side, he continued, "And this is my sidekick Zeus. What can we do for you?"

Maddie said, "We are looking for Charles Winchester's grave. He was buried about a week ago."

Gus shook his head. "Mmm…Charles Winchester. Poor bastard. I went to school with him."

Since he was a classmate of Uncle Charles, Cassia believed that Gus must be about the same age as Uncle Charles, but he looked a lot older—maybe as much as twenty years older based on his wrinkled appearance. Cassia then realized that she was comparing the old man to the Uncle Charles that she remembered. That was not fair.

Gus smirked. "Everyone in high school knew that Charlie Winchester was a fruit except Charlie Winchester. Poor bastard."

Cassia and Maddie looked at each other. Neither one could speak for a few seconds. Cassia shook off the remark and thought it was best to ignore it. She began her story about seeing the barefoot woman. Before she could get too far into her story, Gus interrupted. His eyes grew large. "What lady? Ma'am, you two are the only visitors here today so far. There is a sensor on the front gate that counts the cars coming through. It registers right here," he said while pointing to a box behind his desk. "The owner of the cemetery put in the counter about a month ago because he wants to adjust the hours of this place based on the number of visitors. Less hours means I'm fucked—can't get my work done and can't survive on less pay," Gus said while throwing up his hands in the air without an apology. He opened his eyes wider. With his bushy eyebrows nearly reaching his receding hairline, he winked. "I found a way around that. Most days I drive my car in and out of the gate at least twenty or thirty times because the one thing that the counter can't tell is *what* cars came through." Gus smiled, exposing his yellow stained teeth but still holding onto that toothpick that appeared to be glued to his bottom lip. "Today, haven't done my little trick, so it's just been me—one car and you ladies equal two cars through the gate."

Maddie looked over at the counter. Gus was right. Only two cars registered passing through the gate. Gus said again, "See, one for my car and two for your car."

Maddie thought for a moment. "Maybe she walked in."

Gus threw his hands in the air. "That's crazy, lady. We're in no-man's-land. There are no houses for at least ten miles. And remember, your gal had no shoes on."

Cassia spoke, "Maybe she got dropped off. Maybe she took her shoes off and put them behind one of the statues and I just didn't see them."

Gus scratched his head. "I guess that's possible, but who in their right mind gets dropped off to spend the day at a graveyard?" Cassia hated to admit it, but what Gus said made sense. Gus continued, "Come outside and show me where you saw her." Zeus attempted to follow Gus to the door. Gus put his hand out, and without a word, Zeus stopped. When Gus and the women got outside, Cassia pointed to the angel statue up the hill where she saw the woman.

Gus strained his neck looking in the direction where Cassia pointed. He said, "I don't see anybody. Maybe I'll let Zeus find her." Gus chuckled, causing the toothpick dangling from the corner of his mouth to finally fall to the ground. Seeing the appalling expression on the women's faces, a look he certainly was trying to achieve, he just grinned and said, "Just kiddin', ladies."

Gus's playful expression turned serious. He pointed up the hill where Cassia claimed to have seen the lady. "That section up there where you say you saw a woman—nobody visits that area anymore. Those people buried up there died in the 1800s. My boss is always on my ass to get up there and clean it up better, but why bother. All their relatives are dead too. Nobody visits up there anymore."

Gus got into his motorized cart that he used to make his way around the cemetery. He said, "Show me where you saw the woman. Then I'll show you Winchester's grave."

Maddie and Cassia got into Maddie's car. Gus followed closely behind. Cassia spoke, "I don't like him. He is rude, and I don't find him funny at all. He better not scare that woman."

Maddie nodded her head in agreement with Cassia. They drove up the hill. Maddie told Cassia to let her know when to stop.

Seeing the tall angel from the road, Cassia said, "Maddie, stop."

Maddie and Gus followed Cassia to the place where she saw the woman. She looked behind several of the large statues that surrounded the area. The woman was nowhere to be found. Cassia pointed to the grave marker. It was the one she saw the woman weeding around.

Gus looked at the marker and the other surrounding markers. He scratched his head. "Something's not right. This is the only marker in this section that has been trimmed around. All the others are nearly covered over with grass and weeds." He thought for another second and then shouted out, "Goddamn it, somebody was here."

Maddie looked down at the grave marker and read the name out loud, "Jonathan Welts. Who is Jonathan Welts?"

Cassia crossed her arms in front of her body to stop her trembling. All color was gone from her face.

CHAPTER TWENTY-ONE

Maddie and Cassia followed Gus to Uncle Charles's grave. He stretched his right arm out and pointed to a grassless area where flowers were still stacked high. He then drove off without any form of farewell. Maddie and Cassia sat in the car. They watched Gus's cart disappear over the hill in the direction of the office. Neither one of them said a word about the mysterious woman. Maddie looked at Cassia before opening the car door. This was the first time that she noticed the anemic look of Cassia's face and the beads of perspiration covering her forehead. Cassia adjusted the car's air vent closest to her. It was now aimed directly at her face. Maddie turned the air conditioner up a little higher.

Maddie said, "Are you okay?"

"No, I'm not feeling well. Do you mind if I stay in the car?"

"Not at all. I will only be a few minutes."

Cassia sat in the car. She closed her eyes thinking about Gus and now knew that if he sent Zeus looking for the woman, the dog would not find her. She opened her eyes. The air hitting her face made her feel better. She looked out the window at Maddie standing over Uncle Charles's grave. She thought about the day she watched Maddie and Uncle Charles through the closed window of her grandmother's car. She would demand answers from Grandma B when she returns to Baltimore. She needed to know why she was kept from Ashby House all these years. Her heart was no longer racing. It was aching.

Maddie's back faced Cassia. Her head was down, so Cassia could not tell if she was praying, talking, or crying. Cassia wanted to get out of the car to comfort Maddie. However, once again a feeling of sadness overwhelmed her—it was the sadness of knowing that another person whom she loved was *six* feet in the ground. While she did not feel the same connection to Uncle Charles that she felt to her child, Elizabeth, the sadness that she was experiencing gave her the same crushing feeling nonetheless.

Maddie returned to the car wiping tears from her eyes. "I wish that I had picked up some flowers for Mr. Charles." Maddie felt guilty. She always felt that she did not do enough to repay Charles for all the things he had done for her over the years even though Charles never asked for anything in return. She did bring him a bottle of wine every time she and her husband, George, visited. Since neither she nor George were drinkers and knew nothing about wine, they would stop and scour the aisles of Golden Liquors, the closest liquor store to Ashby House, to find a nice wine—well, one that would fit their budget, usually around $25. Sometimes they would solicit the opinions of customers in the aisles or from the owner of the store who knew Charles very well. They never knew if their choice was a good one because Charles always had the same reaction when they handed him the bag with the wine inside. He would remove the bottle from the gift bag and hold it away at arm's length, straining to read the label without his reading glasses. Maddie's tears stopped as she thought about Charles's emerald-green eyes and that silly grin peeking out from his overgrown mustache saying, "Ahhh, perfect."

Cassia smiled and pointed to the large heap of flowers still on Uncle Charles's grave that Gus would soon collect and discard with the front loader that was parked next to the office. She said, "I think he has enough flowers." She and Maddie laughed. Maddie was glad to see the color return to Cassia's face. She said, "You look better."

Cassia smiled. "I feel better. Let's get out of here." Cassia was almost certain that Maddie did not remember Uncle Charles's story about the cruel overseer Jonathan Welts because of her lack of reaction when she read his name on the grave marker. She decided not to share with Maddie the information that she knew about Jonathan Welts and her feeling that he was probably one of the many spirits still roaming in or near Ashby House. She certainly did not want to frighten her since she was staying the night. Maddie's car was almost to the front gate of the cemetery. Cassia said, "I should check my cell phone." Cassia turned around and reached in the back seat for her purse. Her eyes glanced upward. In the middle of the road was the woman who Cassia saw cleaning the grave marker. She stood with her arms crossed in front of her watching them leave the cemetery.

CHAPTER TWENTY-TWO

CASSIA DID NOT SAY A word to Maddie about seeing the woman again. And they did not converse in the same easy manner like they did on the way to the graveyard. Instead, they engaged in snippets of small talk during the forty-minute drive back to Ashby House. Maddie was thinking about her husband, George, and missing her family. Cassia could not get the woman in the graveyard out of her head. When they reached Ashby House, Maddie told Cassia that she would like to rest for about one hour before Annabelle and her fiancé were due to arrive. Cassia was thankful for the time alone. She wanted to check the Internet for any information about the history of Ashby House. Cassia was reasonably sure that Googling *Jonathan Welts* would render no results, but perhaps Googling *Ashby House* might let her in on its secrets.

Cassia returned to the kitchen and poured herself a glass of wine from the open bottle left over from the night before. She reached inside the refrigerator taking out the covered dish of lasagna and placing it in the oven to reheat. Her computer was in the den, so she grabbed her cell phone and glass of wine and headed to the den to begin her search. The mental list of questions in her head was growing longer. Cassia hoped to find out something about Ashby House and why its afterlife occupants were so hell-bent on not leaving. She thought about the woman at the graveyard and felt that she must be somehow connected to Ashby House. And the idea of someone as wicked as Jonathan Welts possibly roaming the house sent chills through her again. Cassia wanted answers now and became more anxious thinking about her meeting with Peaches Winchester. What if Peaches did not want to meet with her? All she could do at this point was call her when she returned from visiting her friend. Hopefully, she would be open to providing some of the missing puzzle pieces.

Cassia shook her head as she entered the den. She looked up at the portraits of the Winchester family and wanted to scream. She wondered why Uncle Charles stuck her with unraveling this ghostly mess. Cassia then reminded herself about her mission—settle the estate, sell the house, and then return to Baltimore—to her *boring* life of lists and unfulfilling work and to her loveless existence. Now Cassia wanted to scream for an entirely different reason.

Cassia logged into her computer. Instead of checking into the Internet for information about Ashby House, she remembered the text she received from Mitch yesterday, "sent you an email." Cassia opened her mail, and about forty new messages appeared. Most of them were junk mail, but two were from Marcie and three were from Mitch. She opened the latest one from Mitch first. "Why haven't you acknowledged my messages. I'm sorry. Maybe I am asking too much from you. Maybe you forgot your computer. Mitch." The second message read, "I really need your shoulder Cassie. It's important. Mitch." The earlier message was longer.

> *Dear Cassie,*
>
> *On Saturday Jewel will be joining me in England. She emailed me a long letter today outlining her unhappiness 'with our stagnant relationship' (her words). I'm sure it's her family putting pressure on her. While she believes that moving in together was a big step for me, she wants more. She wants to get married. Here, in England! If I am agreeable to this, I am to meet her at the airport with a ring and flowers. If not, she will consider her trip to England a vacation and call it quits when we return home.*
>
> *You know me. I do not like ultimatums but I guess she has a right to want more than I've given her in this relationship. We have been together a long time. I hope this is not too weird running this by you but you are my best friend and you know me*

better than anybody else. I wish that I was a list-maker like you. That way I could argue the pros and cons of this decision. Thanks for listening.

Hope all is going well at the {haunted}mansion. Please be careful because I really do love you and care about what happens to you.

Love,
Mitch

Cassia slumped back onto the desk chair. She never really had thought about how she would feel about Mitch remarrying until now. It took her by surprise when her breathing intensified. Maddie came into the den and saw the distress on Cassia's face and heard her exaggerated breaths. She knew exactly what to do because she had panic attacks too. Maddie rushed into the kitchen rifling through drawers and cabinets until she found a paper bag. She ran into the den and told Cassia to breathe into the bag. Cassia complied. Within a few seconds, Cassia's breathing was once again normal.

Maddie said while still rubbing Cassia's back, "Did you see another ghost?"

Cassia chuckled through labored breathing, "I wish it was that. No, Mitch sent me an e-mail. He's getting married in England. Well, when his girlfriend arrives, she wants to get married. I'm not making any sense, am I?"

"I think I understand. Are you still in love with Mitch?"

Cassia paused and thought before answering Maddie's question, "No, I don't think so."

Maddie hugged Cassia. It was a mother's comforting hug—one that Cassia had longed for. Cassia did not want to let go. She closed her eyes and pretended that she was hugging her mother, and the tears flowed.

Maddie wanted so much to help Cassia through this difficult time, but she did not know what to say, so she held on to Cassia a little longer. She remembered Cassia's eyes lighting up describing her relationship with Mitch on their ride to the graveyard and thinking how sweet it was that they were still friends after everything they had been through. Maddie did not know any more than Cassia if Cassia was still in love with Mitch or just taken aback by the thought that Mitch getting married might change the close relationship that they had painstakingly created since the divorce. Maddie released Cassia from her grip. She smiled at her while wiping her hair from her face. "Child, go wash your face. You'll feel better. Annabelle and Robert will be here in about ten minutes."

Cassia shut down her computer. She headed for the stairs to her bedroom. Maddie wanted to tell Cassia about her dream—no, nightmare about Jonathan Welts, but in light of the condition that she found Cassia when she entered the den, Maddie thought that it was best to wait until later.

CHAPTER TWENTY-THREE

CASSIA STARED INTO THE BATHROOM mirror. She was used to her emerald eyes becoming a darker green when she cried or got angry, but this time the green pigment looked a little peculiar, like a storm brewing. While brushing her hair and refreshing her makeup, Cassia made another mental list of the things that she would say and the things that she would keep to herself when e-mailing Mitch later. Cassia came down the stairs a few minutes before five thirty. Maddie was at the bottom of the steps and smiled at Cassia. There was no trace of panic left on her face.

Cassia opened the front door when she heard Robert's truck pull into the driveway. Annabelle exited the driver's side of the truck holding a large bowl of salad. Robert carried a bottle of salad dressing in each hand. Watching them coming up the walkway gave Cassia an opportunity to assess Annabelle's "Mr. Wonderful." At first look, Robert Marcus Brenneman Jr. was not exactly the picture that Cassia had drawn in her head, even though Cassia could not remember Annabelle ever giving any specific details about Robert's physical appearance except to say that he was gorgeous. The picture Cassia drew was based on her own imagination of Annabelle's seemingly perfect life, so Robert was perfect in her mind.

The first thing that stood out about Robert was his height—well, lack of it. He was almost two inches shorter than Annabelle—and she was wearing flats. His dark-brown hair was styled in a short preppy-type cut. As he got closer to the house, Cassia saw that his face sported a permanent five o'clock shadow. Cassia guessed that he probably shaved right before coming to Ashby House. He wore plaid shorts and boat shoes with no socks. He sported a look that Cassia despised—he wore a cable-knit sweater wrapped over the shoulders of his polo shirt. Cassia wanted to ask him where his tennis racket was but held her tongue.

Annabelle introduced Robert to Cassia when they entered the house. He shook Cassia's hand, said a quick hello, and said, "Do you have any mosquito spray?" He then shot Annabelle a nasty look. "I can't believe you forgot the friggin' bug spray. I'll probably wind up with bites and diseases trying to find your little time capsule."

Cassia told Robert that she saw some Cutter in the medicine cabinet upstairs. She asked him if he was allergic to Deet. Robert ignored her question. Cassia pointed the way to the kitchen. Robert took large fast steps and was a good two feet ahead of Annabelle and Cassia. Annabelle grabbed Cassia's arm and pulled her farther away from Robert. She whispered, "He just lost a big case today, and he gets like this when that happens. He'll shake it off eventually. I am so sorry."

Cassia was pretty sure that this was Robert's general disposition. She wondered what the hell Annabelle was doing with someone so unpleasant. Maddie was putting the lasagna back into the oven after checking on it at Cassia's request when they reached the kitchen. Annabelle and Robert deposited the bowl of salad and dressing onto the counter. Cassia put them in the refrigerator. Maddie hugged Annabelle. She shook Robert's hand after a brief introduction. Annabelle was right. Robert was a tad friendlier now, but Cassia made her mind up. She did not like him. She concluded that Robert must save all his "charm" for the jury because he certainly was not winning her over with the sparingly amount of charisma he was using on this group. He did smile once or twice, showing off his unnaturally white perfectly straightened teeth.

Cassia thought about the TV episode of *Friends*, the one where Ross gets his teeth whitened for a date, and it goes all wrong. They glow when he turns off the lights. Instead of the darkness leading to an intimate moment, the girl thinks he is a freak. Cassia stared at Robert's teeth, imagining them lighting the way on a dark night. Cassia had a hard time keeping the smirk off her face every time he opened his mouth and his teeth showed. Cassia stood back watching

Maddie, Annabelle, and Robert in deep conversation. Still focused on Robert's mouth, her thoughts drifted back to the day when she and Mitch watched the *Friends* episode together. The next night, Mitch came to bed and surprised Cassia by wearing cheap plastic glow-in-the dark vampire teeth that he purchased at a Halloween shop. Cassia turned over to face Mitch to say goodnight, and Mitch smiled. Illuminated teeth stared at her in the darkness. They tried to make love that night, but one or both of them would start laughing. The next night, it was Cassia who did the surprising—she emerged from the bathroom wearing a sexy female vampire outfit complete with black fishnet stockings and matching stilettos. She decided against the fake wig after observing herself in the bathroom mirror. Her dark hair and emerald-green eyes completed the outfit perfectly. Without glowing teeth and any laughter that night, Cassia and Mitch had no trouble accomplishing what they set out to do the night before.

After Halloween, Cassia was drawn back into the costume shop by the "50 percent off" advertisement painted across the front window. She purchased two more outfits—sexy cat woman and naughty policewoman. Mitch's favorite was the lady vampire. In an instant, Cassia began obsessing. Could Mitch be making Jewel laugh with the vampire teeth? She had not seen the teeth since Mitch left the apartment. That was *their* joke! How could he? Cassia never allowed herself to think about Mitch's intimate relationship with Jewel—at least not until this moment. She was sure that this sudden fixation had something to do with Mitch's e-mail. Cassia wanted those thoughts out of her head, but images of Mitch and Jewel laughing, hugging, and making love kept running through her mind like a fast-forward slideshow that would not stop. Cassia was relieved when Annabelle's voice interrupted her fast-moving thoughts, "Cass, the bug spray… can you please check if you have any?"

Cassia retrieved the insect repellent from the upstairs cabinet. She gave it to Annabelle. Cassia then asked if anyone would like a drink, but before anyone could answer, Robert interrupted, "Listen, ladies, I am hungry. I have not eaten since breakfast. And on the way here, I saw dark clouds heading toward Ashby House. I am *not* standing out in a storm looking for your little time capsule. So, let's vamoose!"

Cassia, Annabelle, and Maddie followed Robert out the back door without saying a word. He stopped at his brand-new black Hummer and opened the back hatch. He said, "I need to get my gloves, safety goggles, and shovel out of the back. Oh, I need to change into my steel-toe boots too. You can start heading down to the tree house. I'll be right behind you."

Robert began spraying himself with the bug spray. Cassia watched for a minute mumbling under her breath while lagging just a little behind Annabelle and Maddie, "He has a natural repellent in him, so he's just wasting that can of spray. Idiot."

Robert yelled to Annabelle, "And, sweetie, do you think those white $300 tennis shoes were a good choice for the dig?" Annabelle ignored his comment. Cassia caught up with Annabelle and Maddie. The three women walked arm in arm until they reached the tree house. There were indeed dark clouds in the distant sky, and they were moving fast.

Robert caught up to the women by the time they reached the tree house. Annabelle pointed to the large rock that she believed covered the time capsule. Cassia and Annabelle helped Robert push the rock to the side. After moving the rock, Cassia and Annabelle began reminiscing about their times in the tree house. Robert hit the ground with the pointed shovel. "This ground is so friggin' hard. I'm probably going to get a hernia trying to move this dirt."

Annabelle rolled her eyes. "It can't be very far down. We were kids when we buried it. Just try, okay?"

Maddie looked at her watch. "I really like to stay longer, but I need to leave now. My friend and I have dinner reservations at Stella's." She hugged Annabelle. "Maybe you and Robert will still be here when I get back. If not, it was nice seeing you." She could not bring herself to congratulating Annabelle on her engagement to such an asshole. She said, "Bye, Robert, it was nice meeting you." Under her breath, she mumbled, "Not really."

Robert continued digging out small chunks of hard dirt. He huffed and puffed without looking up at Maddie. "Yeah, yeah, you too."

Robert's progress was slow. Cassia saw the dark clouds rolling in faster and faster. While Annabelle watched Maddie's car leaving Ashby House, Robert called out, "Hey, can somebody grab that hoe leaning against the tree and help me?" Annabelle's attention was now focused on a green truck, one that she was familiar with, pulling into the driveway. It parked close to the front of the house and was now out of sight from where Cassia, Annabelle, and Robert stood. Annabelle was oblivious to Robert's request for help, so Cassia reluctantly picked up the hoe. Annabelle announced that she would like a cold drink and it looked like Robert could use one too. Cassia offered to go back to the house and make them some ice tea, but Annabelle insisted on getting the drinks. About halfway to the house, Annabelle turned around. "You stay and guide Robert because you probably remember better than I do where the time capsule might be."

Robert removed his goggles and gloves. He shouted out to Annabelle, "Hey, babe, I like two lemon slices in my tea. And don't forget I'm allergic to that artificial sweetener shit. I need real sugar." Annabelle did not turn around again. She just waved her right hand in the air.

Cassia was not sure at first whether she or Robert was to blame for her feeling of awkwardness at that moment. After some thought, she was certain that it was Robert because she had always been able to easily converse with just about anybody. Cassia hit the ground with the hoe. The next hit was to the shovel that Robert had in his hand. Robert threw down the shovel and yanked the hoe from Cassia's hand. He began frantically chopping at the hard ground. Cassia thought her head was going to explode. She had to get away from Robert. She said, "I'm going to the house to help Annabelle with the drinks." On the way to the house, Cassia thought about Sunny. She was sure that he would have had that time capsule out by now. Cassia thought about calling him.

Instead of going in the back door, Cassia cut across the lawn. She wanted to get some notes out of her car. When she reached the front of the house, in addition to Robert's Hummer, there was a pickup truck in the driveway. When she entered the house, she heard giggling and whispering coming from the kitchen. It was Annabelle's and a man's voice. Cassia stopped before reaching the kitchen when she heard Annabelle say, "Not now, Sunny, Robert is right outside."

Sunny began singing an old Tee Set song from 1970, "Ma Belle Amie, I'm in love with you…" Cassia could hear kissing and more giggling.

Cassia returned to the front door. She quietly opened it and slammed it hard enough for Annabelle and Sunny to hear. She walked into the kitchen. Annabelle was standing with a tray of drinks in her hands. Sunny was leaning against the sink, holding a drink in his hand.

Annabelle smiled at Cassia. Her face was flushed and glowing. Talking quickly, she said, "Look who I found. Sunny came to check on—" Annabelle stopped. She could not even pretend that she knew why Sunny stopped by. She looked inquisitively at Sunny and said, "Why did you stop by again?"

Sunny ran his fingers through his hair like he did the first time that Cassia met him. She still could not conclude whether he did this out of nervousness or habit. He certainly had reason to be nervous, but Sunny looked calmer and more relaxed than Annabelle. Cassia thought that it was strange that Sunny was cooler under pressure considering Annabelle's profession.

Sunny said, "Just came by to change the filter in the HVAC system."

"Isn't that in the basement?" Cassia sarcastically quipped.

Sunny then began stumbling on his words, "Umm…yes…it is, and that's where I am going…downstairs right now." Cassia concluded that all cheaters, male and female, are terrible liars.

Annabelle might not have been a good liar, but she was good at reading people's faces. She was certain that Cassia knew what was going on. She began to explain, "Listen, Cass…"

Annabelle stopped. She heard Robert come in through the back door. He was now standing in the kitchen holding a rusty four-by-six-inch tin box in his right gloved hand. He said, "Found it, and thanks for the drinks, ladies."

CHAPTER TWENTY-FOUR

ROBERT PLACED THE BOX ONTO the paper towels that Cassia situated on the counter. Cassia removed the scissors that were housed in the Cuisinart knife set. She cut through the copious amount of duct tape that secured the box shut. Annabelle moved closer to see its contents. Both Annabelle and Cassia had forgotten that they had put a smaller box inside of the first box. It too was overly duct-taped but not rusty at all because underneath the duct tape there were several layers of Saran Wrap. Cassia pulled the smaller box out and removed the next round of tape with scissors. At that moment, Sunny returned from the basement. Cassia put down the scissors and looked at Robert. Annabelle quickly said in a run-on sentence, "Robert, this is Sunny, a childhood friend of mine and Cassia's, he helped put together and bury the time capsule and is now the caretaker here at Ashby house, and he just stopped by to take care of a few things." Annabelle was out of breath.

Robert extended his hand to Sunny, and the first round of thunder began, "Hey, buddy, if I had known you were here, I would have had you do the manual labor in finding the box since that's sort of your job here at Ashby House, right?"

Sunny gave Robert a smile that was as phony as a twenty-dollar bill with a picture of Santa Claus on it. He shook his hand and quipped back, "Robby, I'm going to let you have this one because I sense that you don't get too much attention from the ladies."

Robert stared so intensely at Sunny that it probably would have bore a hole through him if Annabelle had not stepped in between the two men. The thunder clapped louder, and flashes of light were successive. Cassia wanted to end the standoff before it escalated any further. She was going to ask both men to leave, but before Cassia could make that request, Robert said, "Let's go, Annabelle."

Sunny craned his neck around Annabelle. He said directly to Robert, "No. Stay, I'm leaving anyway." He then looked at Annabelle and smiled. "I have some important *manual labor* to take care of later tonight." Sunny turned around and began whistling the last few notes of the Hinder song "Lips of an Angel" until he was out the front door.

Robert's face was almost as red as the merlot in the half-empty wineglass on the counter. For a few seconds, no one said a word. The only sounds that could be heard were the crunching and pinging of gravel against Sunny's truck tires as he drove down the driveway and a crash of thunder every couple of seconds. Cassia knew that this evening might be unpleasant the moment that she met Robert, but now she sensed that it would be even more awkward than she originally concluded. Annabelle broke the silence, "Cass, we should probably go. Come on, Robert."

Robert sniffed the air. "Cassia, that lasagna smells delicious, and I'm hungry." Robert reached for the opened bottle of wine on the counter and poured himself a glass. He took a seat at the counter and leaned back so far on the stool that Cassia thought he might fall off. She secretly wished that he would but caught himself just in time. Robert said, "Well, ladies, shall we finish unveiling so we can eat?"

Robert got up from the stool. The storm was directly over Ashby House. With one more deafening thunder and a sky full of streaking lightning, Ashby House went dark. Cassia and Annabelle jumped at the sheer sequence of events. The storm seemed to finally succeed at what it planned to do all along. Only faint flashes of light and far-away sounds of rolling thunder in the distance could now be heard. It was dusk, and a hint of the setting sun quickly peeked through the dark clouds rapidly rolling away after nature's grand finale. The small trace of sun provided enough light for Annabelle to gather several candles and place them on the kitchen table where the plates were set for dinner. Cassia called the power company. Robert said, "At least dinner got done before the power went out."

Robert went to Annabelle and kissed her on the cheek. He never said a word, but Cassia was sure that it was an "I'm sorry" kiss. Cassia was baffled. She had never met someone who could run so hot and then so cold in a nanosecond. Annabelle patted Robert's hand twice. The atmosphere outside and in the room was calm now. Annabelle poured two glasses of wine. She kept the glass that was filled almost to the top and handed Cassia the half-filled one. Cassia thought about proposing a toast at that moment but could only come up with tasteless humor like, "Here's to the *perfect* couple—Robert the asshole and Annabelle the slut." Instead of saying anything, Cassia gulped down her half glass of wine like it was a shot of whiskey. Cassia never considered herself ugly, but she knew that she did not possess the kind of beauty like Annabelle, her mother, or even her grandmother—the kind of beauty that men fight over. She also felt like a fool remembering the comment that she made the night before to Annabelle about Sunny.

Robert began doing a rhythmic drumroll with his hands slapping his thighs. "The first item of mystery is…" Cassia got the message. She unraveled the cellophane from the first item. It was the cassette tape of Journey. It was in perfect condition. Cassia was glad that Maddie helped secure the items because they would have never thought of waterproofing them so well.

Annabelle took the cassette from Cassia's hand. She read the label and laughed, "This was my cassette. I loved their music. After you were gone, Cassia, I made my mother buy me another copy. I told her that I lost the first one." Cassia and Annabelle laughed when Annabelle held the cassette to her chest and admitted that Journey's lead singer Steve Perry could still cause her heart to skip a beat.

Robert looked on without any interest in the time capsule items. He was hungry, and his only thought now was that he wanted to eat. He walked over to the kitchen wine rack and began checking out the bottles. He took another bottle from the rack, opened it, and poured himself one more glass. He then took one of the candles from the table and proceeded down the hallway with his glass of wine toward the den without saying a word.

Annabelle watched Robert walking down the hallway until he was out of sight. She began explaining to Cassia in a low voice, "Cass, my father was so upset with me when I started dating Sunny a couple of years ago because he said that Sunny was a loser, meaning he is not a lawyer. I love my father, and it took us a long time to build a good relationship again after he left my mother. I broke it off with Sunny, and then when the merger between the law firms began, Robert and I were practically forced together by our fathers. My father was so happy, and so to please him, I just went along with everything. Then, out of nowhere, Robert proposed to me and presented me with a huge diamond at a board meeting. What could I say with our fathers and all our colleagues staring at me and waiting for my response to Robert's question? I said yes. Then, about two months ago, I ran into Sunny after a particularly bad day at the office. I spilled my guts to him. I told him that I was still in love with him, because I really am. I have to find a way to break this to my father."

Robert was coming back down the hallway toward the kitchen before Cassia could respond to Annabelle's confession. Robert's glass was now empty. He reached for the open bottle and poured just a little into his glass. Slightly slurring his words, he said, "Well, girls, what secrets have you uncovered?"

Cassia spoke first, "Well, you saw the cassette tape of the group Journey." Cassia then began pulling out and describing the remaining items, "A lock of Annabelle's hair in a baggie, a lock of my hair in a baggie, and—" Cassia put the lock of Sunny's hair onto the counter but did not announce who it belonged to. She remembered how hard Annabelle chased Sunny to get a piece of his hair for the time capsule and how Sunny pretended that Annabelle was strong enough to hold him down while Cassia cut a small amount of hair from his head. Cassia decided that it was not a good time to share that story, so she continued with the inventory of the box, "A few of Annabelle's hair ribbons, and what is this?" Cassia removed the cellophane. It was a gingerbread man that Maddie had made. Cassia thought about how Maddie would make them every time she visited because that was her favorite cookie. She and Annabelle sometimes pretended that the gingerbread cookies were dancing, and when they got tired of making them dance, they would dip their heads in milk and break them off and eat them. Maddie would hear them giggling from another room. She knew exactly what they had done. "Girls, I hear the gingerbread men screaming in there. Are you biting their heads off again?" Annabelle and Cassia giggled louder.

Annabelle picked up the gingerbread man and pretended to eat its head off. "Yumm, a twenty-something-year-old cookie."

Robert said, "I don't care how old it is. I'm going to take it from you and start eating it if you don't get this dinner on the table soon."

Annabelle shot Robert a nasty look. "Almost done."

Cassia pulled out another baggie and placed her hand inside. She felt something hairy. She quickly pulled her hand out of the baggie and threw it down. It hit the floor. A head of a Barbie doll with long blond hair fell out of the baggie. Annabelle picked it and laughed. "What the hell were we thinking? Oh yeah, I remember now. We couldn't get the whole Barbie doll in the box, so we popped the head off and put it in. Cass, I think that was your idea."

"I do remember that now." Cassia laughed. She felt around the box one more time. She found a small journal that was folded in half to make it fit inside the box. Cassia unfolded the black soft-covered book. She said, "Belle, this is the old journal that I found in that room—the one that was being renovated that last summer that I spent here. I wanted to ask Uncle Charles about it, but since I was told not to go into that room, I could not very well ask him about something that I found in a place where I was not supposed to be."

Cassia opened the journal. The pages were yellowed and brittle. Cassia flipped to the last entry in the book and began reading it to herself. For a moment, she was oblivious to everyone around her. *Summer, 1867, They are calling us freedmen—*

Robert interrupted, "Umm, ladies, dinner, now." Annabelle shot him another nasty look. Robert smiled at Annabelle. "But I'm hungry. Okay…please…"

Cassia closed the journal. She placed it in the cabinet next to the open can of coffee.

CHAPTER TWENTY-FIVE

CASSIA TOOK THE HEATED LASAGNA from the oven then placed it on the snowflake trivets that she retrieved from the dining room earlier. Annabelle removed the salad and dressings from the unlit refrigerator and placed them on the table. She searched the drawers of the cabinets until she found the salad tongs. They sat down to eat. Cassia was surprised by how easy the conversation flowed during dinner. Of course, Robert was tipsy by then but seemed to recover a little when his dinner began absorbing some of the alcohol in his stomach. Annabelle was uncharacteristically quiet. Most of the conversation occurred between Robert and Cassia. He seemed very interested in the wedding planning business.

"Cassia, I can see Ashby House as a wedding venue. I've been to a couple of weddings that took place in mansions—mansions that were not half as nice as this one. Don't you think this would be a great place to have our wedding, Annabelle?" Annabelle did not respond. She was distracted by the constant vibrating of the phone in her purse across the room. She was thankful that no one else seemed to notice the noise. Robert said louder, "Annabelle, did you hear what I said?"

Annabelle halfway snapped out of her stupor. "What?"

"I said, don't you think Ashby House would be a great place to have a wedding—our wedding?"

Annabelle said unenthusiastically, "Sure."

Robert ignored her half-hearted response. He continued to zealously converse with Cassia. He even suggested that he might be willing to become a partner if she needed some financial backing.

The more Robert talked, the more passionate he became about the prospect of Ashby House becoming, as he put it, "a top-notch wedding venue." He even took off the pen that he routinely kept attached to his shirt for such an occasion. He went to the refrigerator and took a page off the magnetic notepad. Based on the information he got from Cassia, he started working on some numbers for her to consider. Up until now, Cassia never thought about turning Ashby House into any kind of moneymaking business. Even though Robert was the last person she would consider going into business with, she liked some of his ideas. She started disliking him just a little less now. Well, at least until the next nasty comment came out of his mouth.

Cassia looked over at Annabelle's plate. She saw that she barely touched her dinner. Cassia said, "Maybe it wasn't such a good idea having lasagna two days in a row."

Annabelle said, "No, this is great. My stomach was upset earlier too." Cassia tried to muster some sympathy, but she knew that Annabelle's stomach trouble was probably caused by her trying to juggle two men at the same time. Cassia tried to look at the situation from Annabelle's perspective. At first, she could not gather one iota of compassion for her friend's predicament. Sure, Robert was an ass, and Cassia tried to understand Annabelle wanting to keep a relationship going with her father. Why deceive so many people? She then wondered what kind of relationship she would have had with her own father as an adult if he had not died. Would she ever have gone to such great lengths to please him? She started feeling a little less indifferent toward Annabelle's circumstances because she could not put herself in Annabelle's shoes.

Annabelle got up from the table. She remembered seeing another flashlight in one of the kitchen cabinet drawers. She grabbed her purse and got the flashlight from the drawer. She excused herself from the table, "I'll be back." Annabelle headed up the stairs to the bathroom. She returned about five minutes later. Despite her sick stomach, Annabelle's flush face took on a beautiful blushing glow in the candlelight. She put the flashlight back in the drawer. "Robert, we really need to go. I do not feel well."

Robert rose from his seat. "Okay."

Cassia wrapped up some of the apple crisp for Robert to take home. Annabelle did offer to help clean up, but Cassia insisted that she didn't mind doing it herself. She was glad the evening was ending. In the back of her mind, she continued editing her response to Mitch's e-mail. She wanted to get it out to him while her thoughts were fresh. Cassia walked her guests to the door holding the flashlight that Annabelle had used to see her way to the bathroom. As soon as she opened the front door, Cassia saw headlights and the sound of tires stirring up the gravel. The car came to a stop in the circular drive. Luckily, the headlights to Maddie's car stayed on for a few seconds even after she exited the vehicle. They provided enough light for Robert and Annabelle to find their way to Robert's Hummer in the darkness and for Maddie to make her way safely to the porch. Maddie waved to Robert and Annabelle. Maddie said to Cassia, "What a storm. How long has the power been out?"

"A couple of hours," Cassia answered.

"How was dinner with Mr. Personality?" Maddie leaned in and whispered with a laugh.

"Surprisingly, dinner was not bad." Cassia put her arm around Maddie's shoulder. "Come inside, my friend, and I'll tell you *all* about the drama that came *before* dinner."

Cassia told Maddie about what transpired between the love triangle of Annabelle, Robert, and Sunny. Maddie did not seem surprised because she always believed that wherever Annabelle went, drama was never too far behind.

Maddie followed Cassia and the flashlight beam to the kitchen. She was beginning to worry that the power would not come on before the batteries went dead in the only flashlight they could find. Cassia was relieved when Maddie checked through the kitchen cabinets and found two more flashlights and a pack of fresh batteries. Cassia dialed the power company to get an update on the estimated time for the power to return to the area. The recording stated that power would be out at least another two hours. Cassia was hoping they were wrong. Maddie suggested using candles in the kitchen and saving the flashlight batteries to find their way upstairs to the bedrooms should the power not be restored before they went to bed. Cassia agreed.

Cassia began rinsing the dirty dishes. She placed them in the dishwasher. She then wrapped all leftovers and placed them in the trashcan. Maddie picked up the two snowflake trivets from the table. She offered to return them to the china cabinet in the dining room.

Maddie chuckled. "Cassia, I think it's best if I use my flashlight to see my way to the dining room. Sometimes I have a tendency to be clumsy, and it's probably safer for me and Ashby House if I walk with a flashlight instead of a lit candle." Maddie was truthful about her clumsiness. She was afraid of burning herself or burning down Ashby House, but she was more afraid of the candle going out and leaving her in complete darkness. In all the years that she had spent at Ashby House, Maddie never feared Elizabeth because of the implied pact that they had entered into years ago. However, ever since the nightmare that she had when she napped earlier, Maddie no longer felt comfortable at Ashby House. In fact, she considered staying at a hotel for the night but decided against it because she did not want to alarm Cassia.

Cassia understood and agreed with Maddie's reasoning behind taking the flashlight to the den. Cassia took her own flashlight when disposing of the plastic bag of leftovers from the kitchen trashcan to the larger can in the back yard. She and Maddie returned to the kitchen at the same time. They sat at the table and turned off their flashlights, keeping them within reaching distance on the table. The only light visible now was the dancing glow from the two candles in the middle of the table. Maddie knew it was time to tell Cassia about her frightening dream. However, she was not aware that Cassia had an even more chilling tale to tell.

CHAPTER TWENTY-SIX

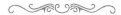

CASSIA POURED HERSELF AND MADDIE a glass of tea. The smells of the evening's dinner were now replaced with a strong scent of cherry tobacco. Maddie moved in closer and sniffed the burning candles on the table. Cassia looked on. "It's not the candles. I smell it again too."

Maddie smiled. "Do you think Mr. Charles is still in this house?"

Cassia shook her head. "I don't know about Uncle Charles, but I think Jonathan Welts might be here." Against her better judgment, Cassia relayed the story that Uncle Charles told her about the cruel overseer who once was in charge of all the slaves who worked the fields of Ashby House. Maddie now shivered every time Cassia said his name. Cassia and Maddie watched the candle flames sputter to the point of almost extinguishing and then relighting again like two unseen entities in a war—one trying to snuff out the flames, the other trying to keep them going. Maddie and Cassia turned on their flashlights just in case.

Maddie said, "I know who Jonathan Welts is. I don't remember the story that Mr. Charles told about him, but when I was napping earlier, I had a horrible dream. I think it was Jonathan and his mother in my nightmare."

Cassia leaned in closer like she did when Uncles Charles told one of his stories. "Please, tell me about it."

Maddie hesitated for a moment. Taking in a deep breath, she began, "The beginning of the dream was not horrible. It started with a tender scene between a little black boy. He was about six years old. He and his mother were walking across a beautiful field of the greenest grass. It was the kind of luscious green fields you see in the Deep South. The woman stopped and stood face-to-face with the boy. She gently held the child's small face in her hands. She began lovingly lecturing her son, 'Jonathan Roberts, you can be anything you want to be in this world. God will light the way for you.' At that moment, a group of men laughing and drinking hard liquor from bottles came across the field. One of them called her by name, 'Lily Roberts, you have been charged with stealing food for your little bastard child. You must pay for your crime.'" Maddie took another deep breath. She continued her story, "The woman screamed to her boy that he should run, but the little boy stood there like his feet were stuck to the grass. He just stood there with big crocodile tears streaming down his face screaming for his mama the whole time that she was being beaten and raped by these men."

Cassia said, "What did the woman look like?"

"She had a red do-rag on her head and a deep scar on her left cheek—"

Before Maddie could say another word, Cassia put her hand over her mouth and said, "Oh my god, the woman at the grave-yard—she is his mother."

Cassia decided against telling Maddie that she believed that she saw Jonathan Welts standing next to the weeping willow tree when she shined her flashlight around the yard when she took out the trash. She believed that Maddie was within inches of bolting out the door even without hearing that information.

Cassia checked the time on her cell phone. It had been almost two hours since she checked in with the power company. It was almost midnight. Cassia and Maddie were taking turns yawning. With the absence of any sound from the refrigerator compressor and no clinking together of the chains on the ceiling fan above the kitchen table, Cassia and Maddie continued talking just to keep the silence from happening. Finally, Cassia announced that she was ready for bed. She assured Maddie that the power would be coming back on any minute. The women took their flashlights with them up the stairs to their respective bedrooms.

Within a few minutes, Cassia heard a knock on her door. She opened it and found Maddie standing with her flashlight in her hand. "Do you mind if I stay in your room tonight?"

Cassia did not mind at all. She was thankful for the company. Cassia pulled the bedspread down from the adjacent twin bed. She motioned for Maddie to sit down. She said, "I want to show you something. It was my mother's. I hold it in my hands whenever I am afraid and ask my mother to protect me. I believe she hears me. Earlier, I asked her to look after you too." Cassia removed the ladybug brooch from the side pocket of her suitcase and held it out for Maddie to see. Maddie shined her flashlight on it to get a better look.

Maddie gasped. "Where did your mother get this?"

"I'm not sure." Cassia quickly pulled the brooch away from Maddie as if she feared that she might take it away from her. Cassia held it tight in her right hand and then cradled it near her heart. Cassia continued, "My grandmother gave it to me. She told me it was my mother's but never said where my mother got it." Instantly, the silence of the house was broken. The ceiling fan above the bed was now buzzing and the lights were on. Both Cassia and Maddie jumped from the unexpected return of power.

"Cassia, that brooch in your hand—it is the same brooch that Peaches Winchester is wearing in her portrait downstairs in the den. One day I commented on how beautiful it was, and she told me that her husband had just given it to her. He had it specially made for her by a top jeweler in France. Mr. Charles later told me that she gave the brooch away when she found out that it was just another one of her husband's I'm-sorry-for-cheating gifts. I didn't know that she gave the brooch to your mother."

Cassia held onto the brooch and bolted from the room. She made her way down the stairs to the den. She could not believe that she never noticed the ladybug brooch on Peaches's dress. Cassia prided herself on her attention to detail, but once in a while, something slipped by her, like the time that Mitch planted a small tree outside of her office window as a birthday present. She did not notice it for about a week. It was her favorite tree—a weeping willow.

Cassia stood in front and stared at the portrait of Peaches Winchester. The ladybug brooch stood self-assuredly on the pastel dress covered in unobtrusive flowers. Cassia opened her hand slowly to uncover the hidden brooch. Maddie caught up with Cassia and was now standing next to her. No great study of the brooch was necessary to determine that the brooch on Peaches Winchester's dress and the brooch cradled in Cassia's hand were the same. Cassia added another question to the running list in her head. The question about the brooch was filed away in her "ask Peaches Winchester" list. She had another list for Raymond Oates and one more for Grandma B.

Maddie and Cassia returned to the upstairs bedroom. When they settled in for the night, it did not take long for Cassia to hear the soft breathing of Maddie's peaceful slumber. Cassia was not afforded the same luxury of falling asleep and forgetting her troubles. She was not sure if it was the light from the night-light that she left on for Maddie, just like she did when Annabelle spent the night years ago, or the words in the e-mail that she planned to send to Mitch that continued swirling in her head. Maybe it was the discovery of the brooch she relied on for comfort was a gift from Peaches Winchester to her mother. She watched the time changing on the clock on the table by her bed until the last reading that she remembered was 2:45 a.m. At 3:45 a.m., Cassia was woken by a terrifying scream.

Cassia was thankful for the night-light, even though she believed that it was partly to blame for keeping her awake, because it enabled her to see that no one else was in the room—just her and Maddie. Cassia went over to Maddie. She was now sitting up on the bed sobbing. Her face and hair were drenched in sweat, like someone waking up after a fever had broken.

Cassia held Maddie tightly and rocked with her back and forth on the bed like she comforted herself after her own nightmares. "Shhh…it's going to be okay."

Within a few seconds, Maddie assured Cassia that she was fine. She went into the bathroom to wash her face. When she returned to the bedroom, Cassia was still sitting in the same spot on Maddie's bed. She had taken the brooch out of her bag and was once again holding it in her hand.

"Child, I am so sorry. I should have stayed at the hotel. You see, I have these nightmares. I see a psychiatrist, and he prescribed medication. It was helping at first because I started having them less frequently. However, since my momma died, I have been having them every night again. My psychiatrist said that the stress of my mother's death is intensifying the rate of occurrence and that they will once again subside in time."

Cassia brushed back the hair from Maddie's face. "Do you want to talk about the nightmare that you just had?"

Maddie nodded her head, confirming that she would. She knew that telling her nightmare to Cassia would make her feel better because it always helped when she told George about her bad dreams. She secretly wished that it was George in the room with her instead of Cassia.

Maddie began her story, "Cassia, I usually have the same few nightmares over and over. They are always about my ex-husband abusing me in the most shocking manner. However, the nightmare that I had tonight was a new one. Jonathan Welts and his mother, Lily, were in it. Lily Roberts was chasing down my ex-husband and stabbing him to death while her son and I looked on. During this entire attack, Jonathan had this deep crazed laughter going. My ex-husband was screaming and begging me to make her stop. Instead of asking her stop, I cheered her on. With every stab, his blood spattered on me, and my body jolted back like it was convulsing. By the time that she was finished, his blood covered every inch of my body."

Maddie did feel better after sharing her nightmare with Cassia. She quickly fell back to sleep. The sheer amount of violence that occurred in Maddie's dream and the fact that Jonathan Welts and his mother were now a part of Maddie's dream sequence left Cassia with an uneasy feeling. Cassia did not realize how tight she was still clutching the brooch in her hand. She released it from her grasp. She saw an imprint that the ladybug left on the palm of her hand. She followed the grooves of the outline left by the brooch with her finger. The indentations left in the palm of Cassia's hand did not extract a picture of a ladybug. They spelled out the word M-O-M. Cassia closed her eyes and once again asked her mother to protect her and Maddie before placing the brooch underneath her pillow. Both Maddie and Cassia slept the rest of the night without dreaming.

CHAPTER TWENTY-SEVEN

Day 3—June 14, 2006

CASSIA WAS ALREADY DOWNSTAIRS IN the kitchen making coffee when Maddie woke. Maddie could not remember when she slept in until nine thirty but felt rejuvenated from doing so. After having one of her nightmares, she usually woke with a feeling of dread. However, this morning she felt a calmness that she welcomed but did not understand. She decided to attribute her feeling of tranquility to the fact that she was going home that day and would be reunited with her family again. Maddie put on her robe and made her way downstairs to the kitchen. The smell of coffee brewing amplified Maddie's good mood.

"Good morning," Maddie said smiling with such a sincere grin—a grin that Cassia had only seen on her when talking about George and her family.

Cassia was sitting at the table with her laptop in front of her. She smiled back at Maddie.

"Good morning to you too. Well, you look wonderful this morning." Cassia saw a change in Maddie. She could not put her finger on exactly what was going on but was glad to see no negative residual effects from last night's nightmare.

"I feel wonderful. How long have you been up?"

Cassia said, "I came down a few minutes ago. I thought I should respond to Mitch's e-mail about his girlfriend's ultimatum. I have been writing this letter in my head ever since I got his e-mail, but I can't seem to transfer my thoughts from my head to the computer. I know Mitch expects me to come up with something profound to help him in his decision, but the only thing that I can think of to tell him is that it is his decision to make."

The coffeepot began beeping, signaling that it was done brewing. Maddie poured herself and Cassia a cup of coffee. Handing Cassia her cup, Maddie said, "Well, maybe that's what you need to tell him."

Cassia did not want to influence Mitch's decision in any way. She remembered how sure he was when he asked her to marry him. It was such a well-thought-out decision. He was so happy. She was so happy too. His uncertainty and dragging of his feet made her believe that his heart just wasn't completely in it this time.

Maddie pointed to the black soft-covered journal next to Cassia's computer. "Where did you get that journal? It looks really old."

"It was one of the items in our time capsule. Remember when the west wing of the house was being renovated? I found it in the torn-up floorboards. It is a journal that was kept by one of the house slaves here at Ashby House. I wanted to ask Uncle Charles about it, but I was afraid that I would get in trouble because he specifically forbade me from going into that part of the house during its reconstruction. I forgot I put the journal in the time capsule until we pulled it from the ground yesterday."

Maddie laughed. "I remember that I told you to stay away from that part of the house too. I guess you did not listen."

"Sometimes I gave you a hard time, huh?" Cassia smiled at Maddie.

Maddie bent down and kissed Cassia's forehead. "I loved you anyway, child." With her coffee still in her hand, Maddie said, "I'm going upstairs to get ready for my appointment with Raymond."

Cassia sat at the table. She took another sip of her coffee. She ran her fingers over the word *journal* that was written in bold white letters that contrasted the blackness of the book. Cassia would have rather read the journal than answer Mitch's e-mail. She was still not sure what she was going to write. Cassia opened her laptop. She heard the pinging of gravel against tires coming toward Ashby House. Cassia checked the time on the microwave. She grabbed her stomach to calm down those familiar ladybugs fluttering in her insides. Mr.

Oates was early. He was not due to arrive until ten o'clock. It was nine forty-five.

Cassia closed her laptop. She got up from the chair and met Mr. Oates at the door. Watching him walking toward the house, Cassia tried to find something familiar about him that she remembered, but he was a total stranger to her. It was probably because his visits to Ashby House were brief, usually dropping off or picking up Annabelle. Sometimes Cassia never saw him at all because he would be in his car waiting for Annabelle impatiently, honking his car horn sometimes more than once for her to come out.

Extending his right hand to Cassia as he walked up to the front door looking very lawyer-ish with his neatly pressed suit and black briefcase tightly gripped in his left hand, he smiled and said, "Hello, I'm Raymond."

Cassia saw the resemblance between Raymond Oates and Annabelle. She inherited his tall, slim physique, and his smile was unmistakably Annabelle's.

Cassia said, "It's nice to see you. Please, come inside. And thank you for your thoughtfulness—the food, the wine, everything was perfect."

"I'm glad that everything was satisfactory," Raymond said in a businesslike manner.

"I'll let Maddie know that you are here."

Raymond waited in the foyer while Cassia went up the stairs to let Maddie know that Raymond was downstairs waiting for her. A few seconds later, Cassia returned to the foyer. The aroma of cherry tobacco overpowered any residual smells of brewed coffee. Raymond did not say a word, but Cassia saw him remove his handkerchief from the inside pocket of his blue pin-striped suit. Cassia believed he was wiping his eyes even though he was turned away from her. Raymond turned around when Cassia gently touched the sleeve on his custom-made Italian suit jacket. "Maddie will be down in just a minute. Where would you like to meet with her?"

Raymond discreetly returned his handkerchief to the inside pocket of his suit. He said, "I think the den will be fine."

Maddie came down the stairs. Smiling and extending her right hand, she said, "Raymond, it is so good to see you." Maddie continued holding his hand for just an extra second. "I am so sorry for your loss. Mr. Charles was a good man—good to everybody."

Raymond thanked Maddie for her sincere condolences, "I know you loved him too."

Cassia quietly interrupted, "Would anyone like coffee, and I can warm up some apple crisp?"

Raymond and Maddie declined Cassia's offer. They were anxious to get business settled. Maddie had told Cassia that she had to leave right after her meeting with Raymond to allow enough time to return her rental car and make it through security in time to catch her flight back to Georgia. Her bags were already packed. Cassia stood in the foyer. She watched them walk down the hallway and enter the den. She heard the click of the door as it closed behind them.

Cassia returned to the kitchen. She poured herself another cup of coffee. She was not sure how long Maddie and Raymond would be in their meeting but hoped long enough so she could answer Mitch's e-mail. When Cassia opened her laptop and logged in, she once again had numerous junk e-mails, but was surprised to see another e-mail from Mitch.

> *Dear Cassie,*
>
> *I hope the reason that I have not heard from you is that you forgot your computer. I thought about calling you but I was afraid that I would screw up what I need to say to you because so much miscommunication can occur when talking cell to cell, especially during an out of the country call. Cassia, in order to accept Jewel's marriage proposal (ultimatum), I need to clean my emotional slate. Ideally, I would rather tell you what I need to say in person, but Jewel's marriage proposal (ultimatum) does not allow me the chance to do that face-to-face. I could kick myself when I think about all the opportunities that I just blew—times that I could have talked to*

you like during our lunches and dinners but you were always in such a good mood that I could not bring up all the hurtful stuff that we so conveniently swept under the rug all these years.

Cassie, ever since we got divorced, I feel that emotionally I have been in a limbo status. I need to get out of this middle state in order to move forward. I take full responsibility for our marriage breakup. Of course, I was a jerk about that kiss with Jewel. I am so sorry that I hurt you like that. I swear to you that was the first time that I kissed her. I was an even bigger jerk about the way I acted when you lost the baby. If I had done some research and not listened to your grandmother, maybe things would have turned out differently. Let me explain.

When you were four months pregnant, your grandmother called me to meet her for lunch at her house. She told me to come alone. She asked me not tell you. I was somewhat apprehensive about her request but I did what she asked. Before we even began lunch (which never happened), Catherine revealed a secret to me that she had been carrying for a long time. She told me that many years ago she had an affair with a man named Charles Winchester II, your Uncle Charles' father. Your mother was the product of that affair.

She then told me that your mother and father coincidentally met Charles Winchester's son during a business trip to Paris. They became fast friends. When your grandmother heard about this relationship, she discouraged it but never told your mother the real reason. Charles II had been dead several years by then.

Apparently, your mother and father struggled with conceiving a child. Having tried for a couple of years, they asked Charles III if he would be willing to donate his sperm. He agreed. When your mother became pregnant, all three of them, Charles, your mother, and your father made a pact to never tell anyone about Charles being your biological father.

When your mother was five months pregnant with you, she and your grandmother had an argument about your parent's relationship with Charles. Well, during that argument, your mother broke the pact and told your grandmother about Charles being your biological father.

Catherine never told your mother or father about her affair with Charles II.

When you mother died during childbirth, Catherine swore that she was being punished for her sin (affair) and that all generations that followed would be punished because, as she put it, 'the merging of Winchester genes.' She convinced me that you would die giving birth just like your mother. Cassie, so many nights when you thought that I was asleep, I saw you sitting in the chair in our bedroom holding the picture of your mother, stroking her face, and crying. I never wanted that kind of heartache for our child. I feel so foolish now because I should have told you. We could have gone to a doctor to have genetic testing done of the baby. I should not have let your grandmother convince me that you would die giving birth. I was so scared that I might lose you and I lost you anyway.

Cassie, I don't know why your grandmother or Uncle Charles never told you. I just know that I wish that I had told you when I found out from Catherine. We could have dealt with things together. Instead, I withdrew from the baby and inadvertently pushed you away, too. I really wanted you to know because if you ever decide to have another

*baby, you have this information. I am so sorry that
I did not tell you sooner.*

*You might not get this email until after Jewel
and I are married and for that I am sorry. I am
still feeling somewhat bitter about how she strong-
armed me into this decision but maybe that is what
I needed.*

Love, Mitch

Cassia felt sick. She wanted to close the lid to the computer and pretend that she never read the e-mail from Mitch. She could not move. As soon as the door opened to the den, Cassia heard amplified chattering from Raymond and Maddie. They were talking, but their words sounded like gibberish. She watched Raymond and Maddie shaking hands. Their meeting was over.

Maddie was smiling walking down the hall. When Raymond called her last week about needing to be present at the reading of the will, Maddie believed that Mr. Charles left her some sort of trinket, perhaps his collection of San Francisco music boxes and carousels. She routinely admired their exquisiteness whenever she dusted them in the curio cabinet. Never did she imagine that Charles would leave her fifty thousand dollars. Walking down the hall, Maddie saw Cassia sitting at the kitchen table. However, she was too excited to notice the horrified look on Cassia's face. Maddie excused herself when she came to the stairs, telling Cassia she was going to retrieve her luggage from the bedroom. Cassia heard sounds coming from Maddie, but once again comprehended nothing.

Raymond returned to the den and began preparing for his meeting with Cassia. He stopped what he was doing when he heard a loud crash and then a thump. Raymond hurried out of the den and down the hallway toward the kitchen. He nearly collided with Maddie, who was quickly coming down the stairs to check out the noise too. Maddie and Raymond reached Cassia at the same time. She was passed out on the kitchen floor. A broken coffee cup with its contents spilled was next to her. Maddie went into "mother mode." She cradled Cassia while Raymond reached for his cell phone in his jacket. Before he could dial 911, Cassia came to. She told Maddie and Raymond that she was fine and did not need any medical help. Raymond put his phone away.

Cassia was not ready to share the information that Mitch had sent to her with Maddie or Raymond. Cassia blamed her light-headedness on not eating anything that morning. She reassured Maddie and Raymond that she was fine. Maddie made Cassia drink a glass of orange juice and made her toast before leaving for the airport. Maddie hugged Cassia and promised to call later when she got home to check on her. Cassia thanked Maddie and wished her a safe flight home. She then apologized to Raymond and asked if they could reschedule their meeting for the next day. He agreed to call her later to work out an agreeable time. Raymond returned to the den to gather up his papers. Cassia walked them to the front door and said her goodbyes. She then returned to the kitchen.

Cassia sat at the table. She welcomed the silence. She opened her computer and reread Mitch's e-mail. Her brain started sorting information. She added many more questions to her mental lists. Some things started making sense to her—her lack of resemblance to anyone in her family, why Uncle Charles left her Ashby House, and her emerald-green "Winchester eyes." Cassia took out the makeup mirror from her purse. She studied her eyes in the mirror. Cassia threw down the mirror onto the table, and it shattered into tiny pieces. She jumped up from the chair and ran down the hallway to the den. Cassia looked into the eyes of the portrait of Charles Winchester II. She then looked into the eyes of Peaches Winchester. Lastly, she looked into the eyes of Charles Winchester III. Her tears flowed—uncontrollable ones like when she first arrived at Ashby House and walked down the hall for the first time after so many years. She closed her eyes and shook her head. She realized that they were not "Winchester eyes" at all.

CHAPTER TWENTY-EIGHT

CASSIA RETURNED TO THE KITCHEN. Her face was red and tearstained. She was angry at everyone in her life who kept the truth from her—Mitch, her father, Uncle Charles, and most of all Grandma B. She ripped four sheets of paper from the to-do list pad attached to the refrigerator. She removed a pen from her purse. With only those items in her hand, Cassia went out the back door and followed the walkway stones to the screened-in gazebo in the backyard. Cassia sat at the glass-top table on a plush patio chair similar to the one she would climb up on to sit on her father's lap during his visits to Ashby House. The gazebo was her father's favorite part of Ashby House. Despite her anger, Cassia wanted to be close to him at that moment. She wondered if her father would have told her the truth when she was old enough to understand. She imagined him sitting across the table from her spilling out the details of why Uncle Charles was chosen as her biological father and how much she was wanted and loved. Cassia's anger toward her father lessened. However, her anger toward Grandma B intensified.

Cassia placed the four pages from the to-do pad side by side on the table in front of her. On top of the first paper, she wrote *Mitch.* On the second, *Grandma B.* On the third, *Raymond Oates.* And on the last one, *Peaches Winchester.* Cassia wrote a number one on Mitch's page. She leaned back into the comfortable chair and closed her eyes. Once again, those familiar ladybugs in her stomach took flight. She opened her eyes, and they were pulled to a figure standing against the weeping willow tree. It was Jonathan Welts. He stood there with his arms folded in front of him. He was the only spirit that frightened her. She wanted him gone.

Cassia rose from her chair. Opening the door to the gazebo, she quickly walked the same path back to the house that she followed earlier. Once in the house, she grabbed her purse and keys from the counter. She went out the front door. As Cassia sat in her car entering an address into the GPS, she felt Jonathan's eyes on her but did not look in his direction. However, driving away from Ashby House, Cassia glanced toward the weeping willow tree. Jonathan Welts's eyes made her shiver.

Cassia turned right out of the driveway. She drove about forty minutes until she reached the same cemetery that she visited with Maddie the day before. Instead of looking for Uncle Charles's grave or stopping to see caretaker Gus, she drove her car up the hill searching for the statue of the angel. Cassia stopped her car a few feet from the statue and exited her vehicle. She walked to the same location where she had previously seen the woman cleaning the grave marker. Cassia found the barefoot woman wearing the same dress and red head scarf that she had on yesterday. This time the woman was not sitting down. Instead, she was leaning against the angel statue. The woman showed no surprise at seeing Cassia again. She said, "You're here about my boy, right?"

Cassia said, "I'm afraid of him."

The woman smiled, exposing a mouth full of yellow-stained but evenly aligned teeth. "Awww, he ain't gonna hurt nobody."

Cassia answered, "Miss Roberts, I think your son needs you."

Lily Roberts got into the passenger side of Cassia's car. As Cassia drove her car in the direction of Ashby House, Lily began telling a story about a little boy—her little boy. She said, "Jonathan was a perfect child with a lovin' heart. That boy pick wildflowers from the fields from morn to night. He then hide dem behind his back and smile. He make me guess what he had for me. I pretend I be surprised every time. He live like he got no care in the world. That boy love his mamma so. Then one day dem men took his innocence." Tears filled Lily's eyes to the brim, but she was determined not to let one fall. She then shook her head. Her tear-filled eyes grew larger. "What dem men did to me no child should ever see. I never seen my boy again." The tears that Lily tried so hard to contain finally flowed down her brown cheeks.

Cassia gently patted Lily's hand. "Miss Roberts, I am going to take you to your son."

Cassia's car came to a stop at the driveway of Ashby House. Jonathan Welts was still standing against the weeping willow tree. Cassia got out of the car. Lily did the same. She stood by the vehicle for a few seconds, shielding her eyes from the sun with her right hand. She saw her son. Lily began walking toward him. At first at a slow pace and then nearly running as she got closer. Cassia watched Jonathan touch the scar on his mother's left cheek with his right hand. His left hand was hidden behind his back. When he swung it around to the front, he presented her with a large bouquet of wildflowers. They hugged for a few seconds and then walked arm in arm away from Ashby House.

The crash of thunder woke Cassia. She looked around the gazebo. The four pieces of paper that were on the table in front of her were now scattered on the floor. The wind was violently blowing. The rain was starting to fall. Cassia rubbed the sleep from her eyes. She got up from the chair and stooped down and gathered the papers and pen from the floor of the gazebo. When Cassia stood upright, she looked in the direction of the weeping willow tree. Jonathan Roberts Welts was gone.

Cassia exited the gazebo. She ran down the stony path entering the house through the kitchen door. She took a clean kitchen towel from the cabinet drawer and wiped the rain from her face and arms. The lightning and thunder were on the same mission as last night and did not let up until it once again accomplished its goal. Cassia took another sheet of paper off the refrigerator notepad. On the top line, she wrote, "Get a generator.' Though it was only late afternoon, the dark skies concealed most signs of daylight. Cassia lit a few candles on the table and kept a flashlight nearby. She stared at her laptop, and that queasy feeling in her stomach returned. The silence that once again took over Ashby House made Cassia jump when her phone rang. The caller was Raymond Oates rescheduling their meeting to discuss Uncle Charles's last wishes for 10:00 a.m.

the next day. Cassia wanted to drill Raymond right then and there on the phone about how much he knew about the circumstances surrounding her paternity but thought it was best to talk face-to-face. Considering how close he and Uncle Charles were, surely he knew something. He might have even provided legal counsel to Uncle Charles in this matter.

Cassia dialed the power company. She decided they use the same message every time the power goes out. It said that the power would likely be restored within two hours. Same message as yesterday. When she finished her call, instead of opening her laptop and reading Mitch's letter for the third time like she had planned to do, she took the old slave journal and flashlight off the table and started down the hallway toward the den. She was on a quest to find something among Uncle Charles's books and papers that might give her the answers as to why he waited until his death to finally reach out to her. While Grandma B stopped her visits to Ashby House as a child, she could not understand why he did not get in touch with her when she became an adult. Shining her flashlight in front of her as she walked, Cassia entered the den without acknowledging the three portraits hanging on the wall this time. She walked over to the desk. For a minute she sat motionless at the desk with her arms folded in front of her contemplating where to begin looking for something that might give her some answers. Cassia sank back into the chair. She wondered if what she was looking for even existed. Cassia then took her flashlight and began feverishly rifling through the drawers of the desk. Paper clips, rubber bands, and other office supplies were sent flying into disarray from their neat order. Some hitting the floor. The desk must have been cleaned out because there was not one piece of paper inside. Cassia reached down to clean up the scattered mess that she had made. The old slave journal, which she had forgotten was on her lap, fell to the floor too. When she returned to an upright position, an old black man stood in the doorway of the den. He was a distinguished-looking, light-skin-colored black man with salt-and-pepper hair. The stocky-built gentleman sported a thin-lined mustache and had a spirited glint in his piercing hazel eyes. He wore slightly baggy white dress pants, a brown unbuttoned suit jacket, tan button-down vest, a crisp white collared shirt, and a slightly crooked brown bowtie. He was holding a book in his left hand. Cassia could not make out the title on the plain brown wrapper. Like Elizabeth, who stood in that same doorway two days ago, the man's image faded in and out at first, but within a few seconds became clearer and more defined. Unlike Elizabeth, who hurried down the hallway as soon as Cassia came closer to her, this apparition walked into the den toward Cassia. She banged her fists on the desk and shouted at him, "What do you want from me, ghost? I have enough problems of my own to try and sort out. Please go away." Within a few seconds, the man's image became more and more transparent until it was completely gone, as if a magician had waved a magic wand and chanted "abracadabra" or some other nonsensical word.

Cassia sat back into the chair again. She felt a small pang of guilt for yelling at the gentleman. She then felt silly thinking that she could have hurt his feelings—ghosts have no feelings. Then she thought about her mother. Cassia would surely never yell at her like that, but perhaps that was all she had to do to get the ghosts to go away. She did not know how many were in the house, but that was going to be her new plan—to rid the house of all apparitions. The silence in the room was broken by the growling of Cassia's hungry stomach. It was late afternoon, and she had not eaten since the piece of toast that Maddie had fixed her for breakfast.

Cassia got up from the desk chair and immediately heard the soft chiming of the chandelier in the foyer. She left the den, and walking down the hall to the foyer, she saw a cloud of smoke slowly swirling around the light fixture, causing the glass pieces to collide into one another. The cloud of smoke went from moving slowly to a more rapid pace. The soft chiming turned to loud clanging. The smell of cherry tobacco filled the foyer so completely that Cassia began coughing. Cassia looked up and watched the rapid movement of the chandelier pieces. She shouted through a wheezing cough. However, this time she was not asking any apparitions to go away. She yelled, "Uncle Charles, *you*, I want to talk to." Slowly the smoke dispersed until it dissolved completely. The aroma of cherry tobacco lingered. Ashby House was silent once again.

Cassia stomped into the kitchen like a child having a temper tantrum. She threw her cell phone into her purse and grabbed her keys off the counter. By the time she reached the front door, the click-click of the ceiling fan and the humming of the refrigerator motor were the only sounds that could be heard. The power was back on. Cassia placed her hand on the front doorknob and turned around. With no concrete person to address, she turned her eyes up toward the chandelier. In a trembling voice, she said, "Uncle Charles, explain something to me. Why is it that random ghosts appear to me but you won't, my father won't, and my mother won't? All I want to do is touch my mother's face one time—just one time. Is that too much to ask for?" Cassia waited a few seconds for a response, but all she got was silence. She could no longer control the angry tears that vertically lined her face. Before slamming the door behind her, she yelled out, "You all can go to hell for all I care."

CHAPTER TWENTY-NINE

CASSIA GOT INTO HER CAR. She took a deep breath but was able to control it enough to avoid hyperventilating like she did before. She wanted to stay in a hotel that night, but with only fifty dollars in her wallet and a credit card maxed out, she felt that she had no other choice but to return to Ashby House that evening. Cassia thought about driving home to Baltimore and forgetting the whole deal, but she really wanted some answers from Mr. Oates. She had so many questions that she needed answers to about her mother and father and why Uncle Charles was chosen to be her biological father. Raymond Oates was probably the person closest to Uncle Charles and hopefully knew all his secrets and hopefully would share them with her. Peaches Winchester was another reason not to leave. Cassia wondered if Peaches Winchester was even aware that she was her granddaughter.

Cassia sat in her car for a few minutes. She made up her mind that she would not go back to Ashby House that night. She chuckled to herself thinking who would tell that she did not stay there—the ghosts? She figured out how to get the money too. Cassia reached inside her purse for her cell phone. She called Annabelle, who answered on the first ring. Annabelle's "hello" sounded distorted. Cassia could not tell if she had woken her, if she had been crying, or if she had someone with her. Annabelle offered no explanation. Cassia invited Annabelle to meet her for a drink. Annabelle confessed that she was glad that Cassia called because she really needed to talk to someone. They agreed on meeting up at the TGIF on West Broad Street. She could be there in twenty minutes. Cassia hung up the phone. Immediately, she regretted calling Annabelle. She said aloud, "Do I have *psychiatrist* written across my forehead? The ghosts want me to listen to them—even though they don't actually talk to me, Mitch wants me to listen to his problems, and now Annabelle wants to talk." Cassia stopped herself from ranting, and in a singsong manner, she said, "You are talking to yourself again, Cassia…You are losing it, Cassia…" She thought about Mitch even though she was still angry at him. Cassia could hear him laughing at her ranting. She missed his sense of humor.

Cassia arrived at the restaurant before Annabelle. She asked for a booth closest to the door so she could get Annabelle's attention when she walked in. She was pretty sure that Annabelle would want a glass of merlot but decided not to order for her just in case she was in the mood for something else. Besides, her waitress was less than friendly and probably would not like having to send a drink back. Instead, she just ordered a Long Island ice tea for herself. She knew better than to drink on an empty stomach because the amount of liquor in a Long Island ice tea was sure to interfere with her thought process, so she ordered a sample appetizer platter. She was hungry.

Before arriving at the restaurant, Cassia had it worked out in her head how she would ask Annabelle for the one hundred dollars. She would tell her that she must have lost her bank card yesterday while at the cemetery with Maddie. Cassia did not like lying but did not trust Annabelle enough to tell her the truth. Cassia thought about the last time that she asked someone for money. It was Grandma B—a few weeks before getting married. She saw a marked-down designer dress at Macy's that she fell in love with. She did not have the $350 to buy it herself. She got the money and a lecture from Grandma B about finances and made her sign a paper that she would pay the money back no more than six months after the wedding. Cassia paid Grandma B back the next day after the wedding with the money they got from friends in their wedding cards. Cassia thought back to her wedding day.

Being in the wedding planning business gave Cassia a unique perspective on what to do when planning a wedding as well as what not to do. Her conclusion was to keep it simple, so that is what she and Mitch decided when planning their wedding. They went to the justice of the peace at the courthouse. Cassia saved her designer dress for the reception. Two days later, they had a small reception of about fifty people at Grandma B's. Cassia and Mitch were surprised when Grandma B offered to host the affair but realized her ulterior motive the day of the party. Grandma B had just purchased an expensive painting by the French artist Pierre-Auguste Renoir and wanted to show it off. Cassia still remembers her grandmother referring to the painting as "her baby." Grandma B's plan backfired because Cassia's and Mitch's circle of friends did not know much about or did not care about art. Most of those in attendance were their friends in the wedding planning business. Grandma B was able to impress a few friends that she had invited.

Mitch's mother and father, Laura and Bob Burns, flew in from South Dakota. Cassia liked them just fine. She did not see them enough to form any sort of relationship with them. Mitch was an only child. He loved his parents but did not seem especially close to them. He called them once a week and visited them once a year. Since the divorce, she lost all contact with them. Sometimes she would ask Mitch how they were doing when they met for lunch or dinner. Mitch's reply was always the same, "They are fine." He never mentioned if they ever asked about her.

Laura and Bob Burns were originally from Maryland but moved to the Black Hills in South Dakota about a year before she and Mitch married. Mitch's father worked for a small jewelry company in Baltimore. His took his boss up on an offer to open a new store in the Black Hills near Mount Rushmore. Cassia benefited from their move because she and Mitch visited once a year. Mount Rushmore became her favorite tourist attraction. She also loved the unique pieces of jewelry that she was able to purchase using her father-in-law's discount. Their wedding set was from the Black Hills too. Cassia chose a one-carat round center diamond surrounded by twelve-carat leaves with three (2 pt.) diamonds directly under the leaves. Mitch's wedding band matched Cassia's ring but minus the large diamond. Mitch would never have been able to afford such an expensive wedding ring had it not been for his father's discount. Cassia thought about selling her wedding ring a few times since the divorce, especially when money got tight, but could not part with such a beautiful piece of jewelry. She kept it locked away with a few other memory-filled trinkets in an old pink jewelry box with a ballerina that dances when you open the lid. Grandma B gave her the jewelry box with an expensive angel necklace inside for her sixteenth birthday. The angel necklace sits next to the ring, perhaps guarding it because the cheap lock on the jewelry box can be broken with just a slight twist. Cassia wondered what Mitch did with his wedding band. She never would ask him because she would be heartbroken all over again if he told her that he got rid of it in any manner. She knew that her thinking was ridiculous, but Cassia could not control her heart sometimes, even today, when it came to Mitch.

The only sign of tradition at the wedding that both Mitch and Cassia would not forgo was the wedding cake. Since Grandma B offered to pay for their small reception, Cassia and Mitch took advantage of her generosity by being somewhat extravagant in one area of the celebration by ordering their wedding cake from Herman's Bakery, one of the best bakeries in the Baltimore area. Mitch and Cassia compromised when ordering the cake. Cassia chose the design for the outside of the cake, and Mitch chose the inside cake flavors. The final product was a three-tier white cake with black-and-red ladybugs climbing around the outside of the cake to the top. One layer was red velvet cake, the second layer was Boston cream, and the third layer was chocolate with chocolate chips. The cake topper was made by their photographer friend Carl, who owns a side business making personalized cake toppers. The groom was holding a camera, and he was photographing the bride, who was holding a to-do list in her hand. The cake was a hit with all their party guests, especially those who knew them well.

Cassia's drink and appetizers arrived. She took her first sip of the cold drink. The icy chill meandering down her throat at first startled her senses but then left her immediately refreshed. The alcohol instantly went to her brain and numbed her thoughts. The calmness enabled her to shift her thinking from the stressful events at Ashby House that day to more mellow thoughts. She dipped a hot mozzarella stick into the red marinara sauce. She marveled at how long the cheese stretched before it reached its breaking point. Her thoughts then drifted back to Ashby House, and she wondered if she had reached her breaking point with the ghosts. Perhaps she pissed them off, and they are all gone now. After some thought, Cassia did not really believe that was true, so she decided that she would return to Ashby House after her drinks with Annabelle. She would confront the ghosts even if that meant going back into the attic.

Cassia looked around the restaurant at happy people laughing and talking. Usually, those kinds of scenes made her feel lonely, but this evening, she was okay with being by herself. Cassia was beginning to worry if perhaps she had crossed that line of being content. That was how Cassia described it—the point when she realized that it is so much easier not getting involved with someone and all their drama. No one had caught her eye in a long time, except maybe her brief fantasy she allowed herself when she met Sunny. Cassia had not been out on a date in months, and no one has shown any interest in her. She did get a text every now and then from Mitch's friend Ollie asking her if she wanted to come over and "talk" again, even though he now has a girlfriend. What an asshole! Cassia then thought about Sunny again. She believed that he would have been a lot of fun but probably not long-term commitment material. It was a moot point anyway to even think about Sunny because he had his mind made up that he wanted Annabelle. Cassia's thoughts were interrupted when she saw Annabelle coming through the front door of the restaurant. She was not alone.

Sunny slid into the booth opposite Cassia. Annabelle hugged Cassia and whispered in her ear, "Hope you don't mind," before sliding in next to Sunny. Cassia felt that she had no choice but to say that she did not mind. Before Cassia could reply to Annabelle, the waitress was standing next to their table asking Annabelle and Sunny for their drink orders. Surprisingly, Annabelle ordered a glass of ice water with a lemon wedge. Sunny said that he would take a glass of anything on tap. The once unfriendly waitress became flirty and begged Sunny not to give her the heavy burden of picking a beer for someone so nice. Cassia shook her head watching the smiling woman as she named all the beers that were available on tap. Annabelle sat silent, not saying a word about the woman's obvious flirting. Cassia was not sure if Annabelle was oblivious to the woman's flirtatious manner or was it because she was so sure about her relationship with Sunny that she allowed this woman to believe that she had a chance. Sunny put his arm around Annabelle. He smiled back at the waitress and said, "I'll have a Sam Adams." The waitress's smile disappeared. Before the waitress reached the bar to put in Sunny's draft beer order, Annabelle said, "Cassia, I'm pregnant."

Cassia put on her usual "I'm happy for you" face. However, the hemorrhaging of the gaping hole in her heart that refused to close since she lost her child started again. Cassia's therapist assured her that it was normal to experience feelings of ambiguity when hearing about someone's pregnancy. This time, Cassia's heart hurt. She crossed her arms in front of her and leaned against the table to try and lessen the aching. When the waitress brought Annabelle's water and Sunny's beer to the table, Cassia ordered another Long Island ice tea. With two more sips of her second drink, Cassia's pain subsided to only about a 9.5 on a scale of 10.

Cassia could not tell if Annabelle was happy about the baby or not. It was obvious that Annabelle had been crying. The dark circles under her eyes and absence of any eye makeup suggested that's probably what she was doing when Cassia spoke to her earlier. Unable to decipher Annabelle's true feelings about the baby, Cassia said, "Congratulations?" Annabelle buried her face in Sunny's chest.

Sunny stroked Annabelle's hair and kissed her gently. Within a few seconds, Annabelle raised her head and addressed Cassia, "Cass, I am happy about the baby, but this really complicates things. Robert is a lawyer first and foremost. All of his life, that's what he has been groomed to be. His father would never have it any other way. And his mentality is that he does not lose at anything. If this baby turns out to be his, I will be fighting with him for the rest of my life." Annabelle shook her head. "I really made a mess of things. I don't want to even think about what my father will say."

Cassia wanted to scold Annabelle for being so irresponsible. She did not understand how a well-educated woman could be so stupid—sleeping with two men and not using protection. However, this was not the time for a lecture. Cassia then thought about that night with Ollie. She was too drunk to insist that he use a condom. She remembered how relieved she was when her period came that month. Cassia softened her thinking and said, "Belle, it will all work out, and I'm sure your father will come around eventually, especially when he sees his grandchild."

Sunny was quiet. He seemed awkward trying to console Annabelle. Cassia thought perhaps he was uncomfortable being affectionate with Annabelle in public fearing that someone who might know Robert would see them. Annabelle did not seem to care despite so much riding on their secrecy. Finally, Sunny spoke, "Annabelle, you know that we have always had a plan. We just have to accelerate it a bit. And even if this baby is not mine, I will love it like my own because it is a part of you."

Annabelle kissed Sunny and then turned to Cassia. "I love Sunny, and I have to stay with Robert and the firm for at least another week, maybe two. The last phase of the merger should be finalized by then. This has to happen because my father's company is in trouble with the IRS. This merger will save his company and my father's reputation. I can't shake things up right now. I need to do this for my father."

Cassia said, "Why didn't Uncle Charles help your father with his money problems?"

"My father has too much pride to ask anybody for money. I think that he was too embarrassed to let anybody know that he was so easily swindled."

"Swindled? Belle, what happened?"

Annabelle said, "My father hired a payroll company named Levy and Stone. They turned out not to be as reputable as he was led to believe. They were sending partial payments to the IRS and pocketing the bulk of the payroll tax money. When the IRS notices started coming in the mail, they were set up to go directly to the payroll company. By the time my father finally saw the notices, the IRS was already threatening to take everything. He met with the owner of the payroll company. Mr. Stone said that he would have a full disclosure of all allocated funds on my father's desk by the next morning. He never showed up. When my father went to the office of Levy and Stone, it was empty. He reported all this to the police. Levy and Stone and all my father's money were gone. They were out of the country before the district attorney could file a formal indictment. The new firm is willing to absorb his losses as part of the deal because of my father's good reputation and elite clientele. It really is a win-win situation. The firm gets to make a lot of money off his filthy rich clients, and my father gets to keep his good reputation intact. He will have plenty of money once again after the merger is finalized. That is the only way he can recover."

Cassia said, "Wow, your father has a lot on his plate right now. I guess you do too. So, how far along do you think you are?"

"We just took the test this evening." Annabelle counted the days since her last period in her head and said, "I would say just a few weeks."

"Does Robert suspect that anything is amiss?"

"No, he has been working on a new case right now, so he is distracted. He thinks everything is fine. I do not plan on telling him that I am pregnant. I will just end the engagement that evening after all the papers are signed for the merger." Annabelle laughed. "I should do it at a board meeting. I still can't believe how he put me on the spot in front of our fathers and all of our colleagues."

Cassia said, "That had to be embarrassing."

"If everything works out, he will never have to know because I have been planning to leave my job here in Richmond. In fact, I am in negotiations with a law firm in Virginia Beach right now. If they accept my counteroffer, I will be giving my resignation at the board meeting in two weeks. Sunny is ready to move his business too."

The waitress came back to the table and asked if they would like another round of drinks or anything else. Annabelle ordered another water. Cassia ordered her third Long Island ice tea. When the waitress returned with the drinks, Sunny asked for the check. Cassia placed her purse on the table. She reached inside for her wallet. Sunny said, "I got this." Cassia was thankful.

Annabelle stared at the ladybug brooch that Cassia attached to her purse earlier. Sometimes Cassia wore the brooch, but most of the time she carried it in her purse or attached it to her purse, especially on days when she needed her mother. Today was one of those days.

Annabelle said, "Cass, may I see that ladybug pin on your purse?"

Cassia removed the brooch and handed it to Annabelle.

"This is beautiful. It looks familiar. I think I've seen this brooch somewhere. Where did you get it?"

Cassia did not tell Annabelle that Peaches Winchester gave it to her mother nor did she say that Peaches was wearing it on her dress in the portrait hanging on the wall in the den. She said, "It was my mother's."

When handing the brooch across the table to Cassia, Annabelle accidentally dropped it into Cassia's full glass of her Long Island ice tea. Annabelle apologized.

Cassia laughed while retrieving the ladybug with her spoon. "Well, I guess we now know that ladybugs cannot swim. I better get this sucker out before it gets drunk."

Annabelle and Sunny laughed. Cassia looked down at her drink. There were now many UFOs (unidentified floating objects) floating to the top of her glass—particles of crud that had been jolted loose from the ladybug after twenty years of wearing and handling. Cassia could not remember ever having this piece of jewelry cleaned. She moved her drink away from her.

Cassia then dipped the ladybug into her glass of water. She said, "Time for another swim." When Cassia removed the brooch from the water and dried it with a napkin, the black and red colors of the ladybug were deeper and brighter than she had ever seen them. The six diamonds that dotted the top of the ladybug's red shell sparkled in a way that she had never seen either. Instead of reattaching the ladybug onto her purse again, Cassia tossed it inside.

Sunny paid the check. All three walked out of the restaurant to the parking lot. Annabelle hugged Cassia goodbye. Sunny kept his distance but nodded his head before taking Annabelle's hand and walking across the parking lot toward his truck. None of them saw the black Hummer parked under a tree at the farthermost end of the lot.

CHAPTER THIRTY

CASSIA STARTED HER CAR AND headed south on West Broad Street toward Ashby House. She turned up the radio. While gripping the steering wheel with both hands, one at 10 and the other at 2, she found herself tapping along to the thumping sounds of an upbeat tune that she had never heard before. The news of Annabelle's pregnancy did not sting as much as when she first heard the announcement. Cassia did not know if it was because the circumstances surrounding Annabelle's pregnancy were so complicated that she was glad *not* to be in Annabelle's shoes. And just for a few minutes, she was able to push Jewel and Mitch out of her thoughts too.

Cassia continued driving another mile down West Broad Street. She began imagining what Annabelle's baby might look like if the father is Robert. She then imagined what the baby might look like if the father is Sunny. She chuckled aloud. "For that child's sake, I hope that his or her father is Sunny." Cassia's thoughts then turned to her own baby, and her heart ached again. She tried to push the pictures of Elizabeth out of her thoughts. Part of her regretted saying yes to the doctor that she wanted to see and hold her dead baby after she was delivered. Mitch stood at her bedside, but she never knew if he looked down or away at their baby in her arms nestled in a pink receiving blanket. They never talked about that moment ever. Cassia was haunted by the images of how perfect she looked with her tiny fingers and toes. She reached for a napkin from the console and wiped her tears. Cassia glimpsed in her rearview mirror to see if her eye makeup was streaming down her face along with her tears. In addition to seeing her own reflection in the mirror, she saw flashing lights. She had been so engrossed in her thoughts that she had

145

no idea how long they had been blinking behind her. Cassia pulled onto the right shoulder of the highway to allow the patrol car to pass. She was immediately panic-stricken when the police car did not go around her but instead slowed down until it stopped directly behind her Prius. Cassia thought about her friend Trisha, who recently went on and on about her experience of being pulled over for speeding one night. She explained to Cassia a feeling of having your stomach bottoming out when those lights are blinking behind your vehicle. Cassia understood that feeling now.

Cassia immediately put her two front windows down hoping to release any odor of alcohol from her vehicle. She began frantically searching through the console for a piece of gum. Cassia finally located a piece and put it in her mouth. The officer was already standing at her opened passenger window.

"Ma'am, do you know why I pulled you over?" the policeman asked Cassia.

Cassia's voice cracked when she responded, "No…sir, I have no idea." She was certain that he had witnessed her putting the piece of gum in her mouth. She wanted to kick herself for being so stupid. Cassia had never been pulled over in all her years of driving, not even for speeding, which she was guilty of many times.

The officer asked to see her license and registration. She nervously fumbled for the documents in her glove box and handed them over. The officer returned to his vehicle. In her head, Cassia began bargaining with God, *If you get me out of this, I swear that I will never drink again.* She then reconsidered her original promise and made a slight change, *I mean that I will never have a drink and then drive—I mean that I will never have two drinks and then drive.*

The police officer returned to Cassia's car. "Please step out of the vehicle."

The police officer motioned for Cassia to stand in front of his car. Cassia was not aware that while in his car running her license through the computer, the police officer had turned off the front emergency lights on his vehicle because he was planning to perform a series of tests to determine if she was too impaired to drive. He kept the back emergency lights on for safety reasons. Because of his years of experience, the police officer knew that having the front emergency lights on could compromise the results of the first test that he was going to perform. The officer had made that mistake once when he was new to the force. It was his first DWI arrest, and the defendant was clearly intoxicated, but her attorney challenged the results of the test. The judge agreed that the lights could very well have interfered with the validity of the test. The case was thrown out. The same woman was arrested for DWI three weeks later. This time she killed a high school girl on her way to school. The officer swore that he would never make that mistake again.

Cassia obeyed his command and stood next to the vehicle. The headlights shining from the officer's patrol car provided enough light for Cassia to get a good look at the officer. In another situation, Cassia would have noticed that he was not wearing a wedding ring. She also would have noticed his blue eyes and handsome face—a face that resembled Christopher Meloni of the TV show *Law and Order*. However, Cassia stood with her arms folded in front of her, disregarding any thought to the storm clouds moving quickly overhead or the handsomeness of the officer. Instead, her eyes became glued to his name tag—MARRON. She called him Officer *Moron*, but only in her head.

Officer Marron got Cassia's attention when he said, "Ma'am, I will be performing a series of tests to determine if you are too intoxicated to drive. Please lean against the car while I ask you a few questions before I begin the tests."

Cassia once again obeyed his command.

"Ms. Burns, have you had any alcohol this evening?"

"Yes, sir, two drinks," Cassia replied thinking that is probably what everybody who has been drinking says.

Officer Marron was not surprised by Cassia's answer. He said, "Are you currently under the care of a doctor, dentist, or psychiatrist?"

Cassia was not sure how to answer about her therapist because she had not seen her in a while, so she said, "No."

"Do you normally wear contact lenses or glasses?"

"No."

"Do you have trouble seeing light?"

"No."

Officer Marron began explaining the first test to Cassia. Before beginning, he repeatedly asked her if she understood the test as he explained it.

The officer held up his right index finger. He said, "Ms. Burns, follow my finger with your eyes only—no head movements. Do you understand?"

"Yes." Cassia followed the officer's finger movements for what felt like forever although it was only eight different passes at various speeds—up and down, left to right. Cassia did not fully understand the purpose of the test but was too afraid to ask questions. She was not aware that the officer was looking for various indicators signaling failure such as involuntary jerking, inability to smoothly follow the stimulus, and comments from the test taker indicating difficulty with the test like the ones he had heard before such as feeling like eyes are bouncing or frustration with the test itself.

Officer Marron saw the first red flag when Cassia asked if the test was almost complete. She asked because it was starting to rain and she was getting cold. To him, it was a sign of Cassia somewhat struggling to stay focused. However, Officer Marron was somewhat struggling too. Cassia's beautiful green eyes made it hard for him to stay focused, but nonetheless he stayed professional throughout the entire administering of the test. Despite Cassia not failing (looking for four or six indicators), the officer continued on with the next test.

"Ms. Burns, please stand in front of the car about two feet away from it. I will explain the next test to you. Put your feet together, arms to your side until I tell you to move." He told her to walk nine steps down an imaginary line, keeping her arms to her side, count the steps out loud, and then turn around and repeat the same steps coming back.

Officer Marron once again asked Cassia if she understood the instructions. She responded that she understood. She was trying to keep her cool because she was tired of him asking that question and she was now dripping wet. She wanted to scream out that she was no friggin' dummy and that he was a moron. Cassia completed the test without difficulty. Officer Marron was now comfortable with Cassia's driving abilities.

Officer Marron explained that he stopped her because her taillight was out. He did lecture her on the dangers of drinking and driving. He was getting ready to write her a repair ticket, but a call came on his radio that there had been a hit-and-run accident about two miles from where he was standing with Cassia. Officer Marron listened intently to the dispatcher announcing the description of the vehicle that left the scene of the accident. Suddenly, that vehicle flew past his patrol car. Officer Marron ripped up the ticket and told Cassia before getting into his car, "Get that taillight fixed."

Officer Marron then sped off with his police lights flashing and siren screaming after the black Hummer. Heading back to the highway, Cassia admitted that Officer Marron wasn't such a bad guy after all. He was just doing his job. She felt a pang of guilt for calling him a moron, even if it was only in her head.

CHAPTER THIRTY-ONE

CASSIA SIGHED WITH RELIEF AS she parked her car in the circular driveway of Ashby House. She turned the car engine off and turned on the inside lights. She began feeling around at the bottom of her purse for her house keys but pulled her hand out quickly when she felt something pierce her skin. She yelled out, "Ouch!" Cassia reached for the napkin that had earlier dried her tears. The blood oozing from her pricked finger formed a small drop that began slowly trickling down her finger. Catching the drop in the napkin before it dripped onto her seat, Cassia cursed herself for forgetting to latch the ladybug pin when she put it in her purse at the restaurant. She opened her purse as wide as she could and spotted the brooch. She then dug back into it with her uninjured hand and carefully removed the open brooch. Cassia closed the clasp and cradled the brooch in her hand. She thought about how close she had come to getting arrested. If the brooch had not fallen into her third Long Island ice tea, making it undrinkable, she surely would be in jail right now. Cassia held the brooch tightly in her hand, closed her eyes, and said, "Thank you, Mom." When she opened her eyes and unclenched her hand, she traced the indentations that the brooch left. It did not spell out M-O-M this time. Instead it said, L-O-V-E.

Cassia entered the house without looking up at the chandelier or acknowledging Uncle Charles or any other entity(ies) that might be in the house. It was only nine thirty, but after her ordeal with Officer Marron, Cassia was wet, cold, and tired—too tired to deal with ghosts, Mitch, or anybody else. She proceeded directly up to her bedroom longing for a hot shower and the comfort of her favorite soft robe. With a towel wrapped around her wet hair and comfortably swathed in her pajamas and robe, Cassia sat on the edge of the bed. She checked her cell phone. As promised, Maddie had called and left a message inquiring about her health status. Cassia did not call Maddie. Instead, acknowledged the message with a text thanking Maddie for her concern and wrote that she was feeling better and would call her tomorrow. She wanted to tell Maddie about Annabelle and the baby, but not tonight. She ended her text, "Give my love to George and the family."

The shower gave Cassia a second wind. Not ready for sleep but not wanting to engage in any "ghost hunting" like she had originally planned earlier that evening, Cassia decided that watching television was the only thing that she wanted to do. And it has to be a show with mindless humor, like *The Office* or *The New Adventures of the Old Christine*. On her way downstairs, Cassia daydreamed about keeping Ashby House. She decided that there needed to be more than one television in the house and that it had to be bigger than the old twelve-inch on the wall in the den. She imagined a huge flat-screen TV in the living room, and she had already decided on the wall where it was to hang. She brought herself back to reality, now smiling and shaking her head remembering the $50 in her wallet, her maxed-out credit cards, and the five dollars and twenty-seven cents left in her checking account once her bills cleared.

The clock on the wall was at 10:10 p.m. when Cassia entered the den. She knew that the ten o'clock news would be on. Feeling disconnected from the outside world events since her three days at Ashby House, Cassia changed her mind about watching a comedy and decided to catch up on the news instead. Raymond had left the TV remote on the desk when he was at Ashby House earlier. Cassia picked up the remote and turned on the television. Instantly, the DVD player started too. To her surprise, a man—a man whose voice sounded familiar—began speaking. Still holding the remote in her hand, Cassia began repeating, "Oh my god, oh my god, oh my god." She walked toward the television until she was within inches of it. The man on the TV looked a lot older than she remembered, and instead of the huge presence that she once compared to a king sitting on his massive throne at the dining room table, Cassia saw a sickly shell of the man he once was. Because of the commotion with Cassia passing out and rushing to her aid, Raymond forgot to remove from the player Uncle Charles's video message to Cassia that he had set up to begin playing with one push of a button.

Uncle Charles began his message to Cassia with an apology, "My little Cassia—all grown up now. I am sorry that you have to see your old Uncle Charles in such a state. Raymond encouraged me to make this video months ago, but I kept putting it off. Time is running out, so I must begin. As far as the matters of money and the paperwork involved with the inheritance of Ashby House, I have instructed Raymond to arrange a time to sit with you and explain all that legal mumbo-jumbo. The sole purpose of this video is to explain to you many things and to make just as many apologies."

Raymond Oates had never mentioned anything about a video message from Uncle Charles. Cassia believed that her meeting with Raymond would include going over and signing documents. Cassia reversed the video until it reached the beginning again. She hit the stop button. She moved away from the television and pulled the wing-back chair, the one next to the table with the Bible, closer to the TV. Cassia held the remote in her hand, took a long deep breath, and sunk into the chair.

Cassia thought, this time, when the tape started again, that she would be prepared for Uncle Charles's gaunt appearance. However, she was still uncertain what he would say beyond the small intro that she had already heard. She was not sure if he would be providing answers to the questions that she had compiled in her head. She worried that he would just be giving her tidbits of information to make her continue playing detective like Will Smith's character, Detective Spooner, in her favorite movie, *I, Robot*. Cassia thought about the hologram video message that Dr. Alfred Lanning left after his death for his friend Detective Spooner, which gave him only jumbled clues to help him figure out if Lanning's death was truly a suicide like it appeared or was it a homicide like Spooner suspected. In the hologram, whenever Detective Spooner asked Dr. Lanning a straightforward question, he kept replying, "I'm sorry, my responses are limited. You must ask the right questions." In the end, Spooner asked the right question that unraveled the secret of Lanning's death, which led to a snowballing of bigger secrets revealed. Cassia hoped that the questions in her head were the right ones and that Uncle Charles's video would provide a cascade of answers so she could solve the mysteries of Number Six Ashby House. She pressed the start button.

CHAPTER THIRTY-TWO

Uncle Charles began speaking. Cassia studied his face. This time she saw through his gaunt appearance and recognized more of the man that she remembered. His voice was still strong but splintered in parts. His hair was thinner and almost all gray now, but he still wore it in the same slicked-back style as before. Instead of his cowboy attire, he wore a brown robe. His eyes did not glisten like they once did, but they were still the same emerald green. They were her eyes.

Uncle Charles began with the story about Cassia's mother and father, "Your parents were my best friends. They were so much in love. It broke my heart because they wanted to have a baby, but it just wasn't in the cards. One day, your mother and father came to me and asked for my help. Our hearts almost burst with joy when your mother announced that she was pregnant with you. Cassia, you were always *their* baby. It was our secret. We told no one."

Cassia pressed the pause button. She thought about what Uncle Charles said. She believed him—believed that he had no idea that her mother told Grandma B about her conception. A dying man has no reason to lie. Cassia did not understand after all these years of keeping the secret, why tell her now. The sweet smell of cherry tobacco filled the room. Cassia breathed in the aroma. She began the tape again.

"I'm sorry, my Cassia, that I let your grandmother keep me from you after your father died. Since you were a minor child, she had the power to dictate who you could see. I guess she had her own reasons to keep me out of your life. I kept tabs on you by hiring a private investigator to occasionally snap pictures of you and to inquire about your life from time to time. I was so proud when you graduated from college. You were a beautiful bride. Forgive me for being sneaky. When you were grown, I did not contact you because I did not want to complicate your life. I was afraid that you would see the family resemblance and ask questions. I knew that financially your father had taken care of you because Raymond set up your trust, naming your grandmother as trustee. Your father never imagined that something would happen to him at such a young age. God rest his soul."

Cassia hit the pause button again. She shouted, "What trust? Grandma, you and I are going to have a long talk when you get back from your trip to the Caribbean. Shit, she's probably there spending my money while I struggle my ass off to get by." Cassia shook her head. She hit the start button hard this time.

Uncle Charles continued, "I tell you the truth now because I am leaving you my home—Ashby House. I leave it to you because I know you see what I see. When you were a little girl, I know you saw me dancing with Elizabeth. I know that you have the gift. And it is because of your biological connection to me that you see them. Let me introduce my friends to you."

Uncle Charles was taping his message to Cassia while sitting at the desk in the den where she was watching it. He reached inside the desk and pulled out a manila folder. He opened the folder and held up an old yellowed black-and-white picture. It was hard to make out the image, but when Cassia got out of the chair and looked closer, she saw that it was Elizabeth.

He began, "Cassia, meet Elizabeth. She is one of the daughters of the original owners of this house. She is sad most of the time, and I don't know why. You might have heard her crying in the night. I cheer her up sometimes by dancing with her."

Cassia was familiar with Elizabeth already. Uncle Charles held up the next two pictures.

"Cassia, this is Frederick and his wife, whose name I never knew. They were house slaves here at Ashby House. They never had children of their own. That is all I know about them. Frederick likes to play checkers in the attic. His wife sits on the bed and knits. She taps her feet when I play my music. I think Frederick steals my pipe tobacco sometimes. He just smiles when I ask him."

Cassia listened while Uncle Charles's voice cracked. He coughed more and more. She watched him as he looked directly into the camera. He removed his reading glasses. He leaned in closer to the camera like he did when he told stories to Cassia when she was a child. With a quizzical look in his eyes, he said, "There is one more ghost to tell you about. I believe that he is the black overseer that I told you about when you were little. I do not have a picture. He is a bit scary, but he has never come into the house. He walks the grounds day and night. I think he is searching for something or someone. Most of the time, he can be seen by the weeping willow tree staring at the house. I know that he is scary, but he has never harmed anyone."

Cassia stopped the video again. She knew that the last slave that Uncle Charles talked about was Jonathan Welts. He was right about Jonathan being scary. And he was right about him looking for someone—his mother. Cassia thought about Jonathan's reunion with his mother. Since that event, he had not been seen on the grounds of Ashby House again. Cassia smiled thinking about how Jonathan hid the bouquet of fresh flowers behind his back and then pulled them around and presented them to his mother like he did when he was a child. Her eyes swelled with tears remembering them holding each other so tight and then walking hand in hand into the woods. Cassia wondered if she would ever get that kind of reunion with her own mother.

Cassia wiped the tears that escaped from her eyes with the back of her hand. She listened to the last part of the video. "I am sorry to leave you with such a *ghostly* and *ghastly* mess." Uncle Charles chuckled just a little. "My time is short. My mother hired a lady many years ago who claimed that she could remove the spirits from the house. She walked around from room to room burning sage and chanting." He laughed and said, "She was scarier than the ghosts. She said that the spirits needed to get to the other side but offered no clues about how to make that happen. So, here they stay. Cassia, please take care of yourself, take care of my friends, and take care of Ashby House. I will tell your mother and father what a fine young woman you have become, but I think they already know." White noise replaced the image of Uncle Charles on the screen.

Cassia sank deeper into the chair. She was angry at Grandma B for keeping her from having any relationship with Uncle Charles. She tried to understand his reasoning for staying out of her life, but she felt cheated. It would have been nice having family around her growing up, other than her grandmother. And the trust money, where is it? Cassia pulled out the paper from her purse, the one with Grandma B's name on the top. She wrote, "Trust fund?" Cassia already knew why her grandmother kept Uncle Charles from being part of her life.

Cassia was baffled by Uncle Charles's omission of the spirit who came rushing through her—the one that frightened her when she was standing at the attic door with Maddie yesterday.

If Jonathan Welts never came into the house, who was this unexplained spirit? Perhaps this was the one time that he came into the house. She folded her arms tightly in front of her to make it clear to any spirits that she wanted to be left alone. She hoped that the entities in the house, especially the mysterious one, understood body language. Cassia was jarred out of her thoughts by the ringing of her cell phone. She glanced at the clock on the desk—11:30. Cassia was excited thinking perhaps Mitch was calling from London. Then she thought maybe Grandma B was checking in while on vacation, but that would be so uncharacteristic of her because she never called when she was away. Cassia picked up her phone. She was surprised to see that the call coming through so late was Annabelle's number. She was even more surprised to hear Sunny's voice on the line.

CHAPTER THIRTY-THREE

SUNNY'S ANGRY WORDS ECHOED IN Cassia's ears, "If she doesn't make it, I'm going to kill him." Cassia quickly got dressed. Before heading out the door, Cassia stopped in the den to get the hospital's address—the one where the ambulance took Annabelle. Not familiar with the area, Cassia typed the information into her car's GPS before speeding down the driveway onto the highway. From what Cassia could make out from Sunny's jumbled words, Robert deliberately ran his vehicle into Annabelle and Sunny while they were talking in Sunny's truck in the parking lot of Friday's. It must have happened just after Cassia drove away. Robert was now in police custody, and apparently Annabelle sustained most of the impact of the accident. Her condition was serious. Sunny did not mention anything about the baby.

Cassia glanced over at the parking lot of the TGIF as she drove down West Broad Street toward the hospital. About a half dozen police cars with lights flashing were still blocking the parking lot entrance. Cassia guessed that they were collecting evidence from the accident scene. About a mile after passing the restaurant, Cassia saw one more police car with flashing lights. It was racing up behind her. She pulled over onto the right shoulder of the highway to allow it to pass her by. Once again, the police car stopped behind her. This time she did not search for gum in her purse but had her license and registration ready for the officer by the time he got to her window.

In a familiar voice, she heard, "Ms. Burns, do you know why I pulled you over *this* time?" He took her license and registration.

Cassia got a good look at the policeman's face. She could not believe that her luck could be so bad. Officer Marron was about to end his shift when he saw Cassia's car racing down the highway. Cassia knew exactly why she was being stopped this time but responded, "My taillight again?"

Officer Marron could not definitely say how fast Cassia was going because he did not have a radar gun clocking her speed. However, because of his years of experience as a police officer, he guessed that she was probably going at least twenty miles over the posted speed limit of 50 mph. Officer Marron shook his head. "No, Ms. Burns, do you know how fast you were going?"

Cassia began explaining that her friend was just seriously injured in an accident at the TGIF parking lot. She was on her way to the hospital. Officer Marron was familiar with the accident because he was the one who chased down Robert's vehicle and arrested him two hours ago. He knew from speaking to the other officers that the victim sustained some serious injuries.

He told Cassia to slow it down. He let her go.

Cassia drove her car slowly back onto the highway. She thought about the awkward scene facing her at the hospital and knew exactly why Sunny called her—not because she and Annabelle were best friends even though she did care about her. It was because he needed an ally. She pictured Sunny sitting in a small waiting room with Annabelle's father and mother throwing nasty looks at him every now and then. Cassia knew that Annabelle never told her father about her relationship with Sunny or about the baby. She had no idea if Annabelle shared that information with her mother. Sunny surely needed her.

Cassia followed the signs that pointed to the emergency entrance of the hospital. She came through the automatic doors and stopped at the front desk to get a pass to enter the waiting room. Immediately she saw Annabelle's mother, looking older but still recognizable. The man sitting next to her was holding her hand. Cassia assumed that he was her husband. Neither Sunny nor Raymond were anywhere in sight. Annabelle's mother stood up when Cassia came closer. "Cassia, thank you for coming," she said while hugging her. "Annabelle has been talking nonstop about you since you two got together the other night. I asked Sunny to call you because I thought you would want to know since you were with Sunny and Annabelle right before it happened. I never liked Robert, but I never thought that he would be capable of such a thing."

Cassia shook her head. "How is Annabelle doing?"

"She is getting prepped for surgery right now. I just came back out from seeing her. She is alert but in a lot of pain. Her left arm is badly broken and needs to be set. She has a couple broken ribs. The doctors are considering putting her into a coma and on a ventilator because of the swelling in her brain."

Annabelle's mother could no longer keep in her tears. Though they were never introduced, Cassia was now certain that the man sitting next to Annabelle's mother was her husband because he stood up and held her tenderly while she sobbed into his chest.

Cassia had no idea if Annabelle's mother knew about the baby. It was apparent that she knew about Sunny. Cassia asked, "Where is Sunny?"

Just as Annabelle's mother began telling Cassia that Sunny and Raymond were with Annabelle, they came through the door back into the waiting room. Sunny immediately came over to Cassia. He hugged her. It was a hug that screamed "thank you for being here because I really could use a friend." Raymond went directly over to his ex-wife. He was talking in a quiet manner. Cassia could not hear what he was saying.

Cassia held on to Sunny's arm. They moved to the far end of the waiting room—away from Annabelle's parents. She said, "How is she?"

"They are preparing her for surgery to fix her broken arm. The bastard broke it in several places. When she first got here, they talked about placing her in a drug-induced coma until the swelling in her brain subsides. The doctors are going to reevaluate her after she comes out of the surgery. She's in a lot of pain, but I think she's going to be all right."

Cassia whispered, "What about the baby?"

Sunny let out a long breath. "So far, everything is fine there. Did the police talk to you?"

Cassia thought about her two encounters with Officer Marron. She said, "About the accident?"

"Yes."

"I didn't see anything. I was already on my way back to Ashby House when all this was happening. Sunny, what happened with Robert?"

Sunny ran his hands through his hair. He leaned back into the chair and began his story, "We left the restaurant and walked over to my truck. Annabelle started crying. I was holding her. She then got into the passenger seat, and I got into the driver's side. We talked for a few minutes. She was feeling better. I told her that the beers gave me a headache and asked her if she would mind driving. The rain started coming down really hard, so we switched position without getting out of the truck. We were even laughing when she finally positioned herself in the driver's seat. I guess Robert thought that I was still in the driver's seat because he came at us full speed on the driver's side just as we started out of the parking space." Sunny looked down at the floor and once again brushed his hair back with his fingers. "If only I had not asked her to drive."

CHAPTER THIRTY-FOUR

It was 3:15 a.m. when Cassia left the hospital. Annabelle was out of surgery. The doctors were growing more and more optimistic about her head injury healing without putting her into a drug-induced coma. The broken bones in her arm were set, and her ribs would heal in time. Cassia was not able to visit Annabelle in the recovery room but left her good wishes with the family before leaving the hospital. She promised to return when Annabelle would be up for visitors. Annabelle's mother told Cassia that she was certain that Annabelle would love that. Raymond shook Cassia's hand. He said that he would call her later in the day with a new time to meet. Cassia wanted to tell Raymond about watching the tape of Uncle Charles that he left in the video player but knew that it was neither the time nor the place to discuss it. Sunny offered to walk Cassia to her car, but she assured him that she would be fine on her own.

Cassia exited the emergency room door. Officer Marron was leaning against his cruiser.

Cassia said, "I guess you're here to ask me about the accident."

"No."

Cassia smiled. "Well, I'm not speeding." She then turned her head around as far as it would go. Looking down at her butt, Cassia laughed. "Is my taillight out again?"

Officer Marron smiled. This was the first time that Cassia noticed his slight resemblance to Christopher Meloni—his deep-set blue eyes, bushy brows, and that smile was a close match. Cassia was amused because his first name was *Christopher*, though he introduced himself as Chris.

"How is your friend doing?"

Cassia took a deep breath, then exhaled. "Annabelle is going to be okay. She just got out of surgery. Only family can visit tonight, so I'll come back later when she is awake and in her room."

Chris replied that he was glad to hear that Annabelle would be fine. He said, "You left in such a hurry when I pulled you over that I did not have time to give you back your license and registration. The way you drive, you'll probably need it again."

Cassia laughed. "I hope not." She took the documents from Chris's hand. There was an awkward moment of silence. Cassia noticed that the man who emanated such authoritative power earlier in the evening was really quite shy in a casual social situation. Cassia thanked him for his concern but felt like he wanted to say something else. Too tired to wait for his next words, she smiled and waved a huge goodbye with her right hand like a fan moving from left to right. She turned around and started walking to her car. She felt his eyes on her as she walked away. Cassia stopped and turned around. She said, "You're not going to pull me over again, are you?"

Chris smiled even wider this time. He said, "I got off duty a couple of hours ago." The laugh lines in Officer Marron's face—the ones that grew more prominent since he turned forty, three years ago—added a desirable quality to his smile. Chris chuckled. "You were my last stop for the night—the second time I pulled you over." Chris's smile was gone. He took in a deep breath. "I came here to return your license and registration and to see if you might like to go for a coffee or breakfast. How about it?"

Chris did not tell Cassia until years later that he had planned on pulling her over again as part of a ruse in asking her out. He was glad that Cassia turned around again. She saved him from making a lame move like using his police muscle to get a date. He felt so out of practice in the dating game since the death of his wife eighteen months ago. His friends encouraged him to join an Internet dating website. One evening about two months ago after a long shift, he was feeling especially lonely, so he checked out eHarmony.com. Chris started filling out the questionnaire to begin building his profile. He never finished. A week later when his friend Mark asked how the Internet dating was going, Chris jokingly told him that he was too exhausted to date after filling out all those questions. The truth was that Chris got through a few items in the profile process and decided that the questions were too intrusive. He was the kind of guy who was willing to bare his soul at some point in a relationship but not to someone he just met and certainly not to a computer. He worried that his personal information—not his birth date or social security number, but the information that involved his feelings and desires would be etched not only on his computer hard drive but stored somewhere out in cyberspace for eternity. He felt silly believing that dating websites were set up in such a way that he could simply check a few boxes indicating his preferences, and then hundreds of women who matched those preferences would come up on the screen with one click of his mouse. Chris decided that he would stick with the old-fashioned method for finding a date. His faith was renewed when Cassia agreed to follow him to the Denny's about a mile down the road. On the way to Denny's, Cassia smiled because she was now following the police cruiser instead of it following her with its blaring sirens and lights shining in her rearview mirror like they did earlier— twice. She was also smiling because while he was not "*GQ*-fine" or "blue-collar chic," there was something very appealing about Chris Marron. She wanted to get to know him better.

Christopher Joseph Marron summed up his life to Cassia in a nutshell, "I grew up in the Richmond area. My father, now retired, was a police officer. I followed in his footsteps right out of college. I married the 'girl next store' that same year that I graduated from the police academy. We have one daughter, Amanda, who is in her freshman year at Florida State University." He shook his head and said, "And she has changed her major three times already. Amanda left for college about a month after her mother passed away from her three-year battle with breast cancer."

Cassia was very guarded about revealing too much information about her life. What she did tell Chris, she carefully worded. Cassia was sure that he was schooled in how to tell if someone was lying. She saw him as a human lie detector who could instantly ascertain if a person was lying just by reading the cues that one's body language put forth. Why not? He probably dealt with liars on a day-to-day basis.

Cassia told Chris that she lived in Baltimore, she was divorced, and she was in town because an old uncle had passed away—all truths. For now, she would not tell him about the circumstances surrounding her inheritance, the sordid details of her family tree, and there was no way in hell would she tell him about the ghosts.

Cassia did not have the same comfort level with Chris that she had when dining with Mitch. She scolded herself for once again comparing this new guy, just like every other guy she dated since her divorce, to Mitch. And of course, she knew that the comfort level that she had with Mitch took years to build. She just met this guy. One aspect that was starting to build, one that she hadn't felt in a long time, was excitement. Cassia then reminded herself that sitting across the table from her was a guy who was probably still mourning the loss of his wife.

The next hour of conversation between Chris and Cassia consisted of talking about the accident, her work, his work, his daughter, and once in a while something about his deceased wife, Angelina, would come into the conversation. Cassia was not surprised that Chris painted a perfect picture of his late wife because that's what people do when someone they love dies. The dead person's faults seem to disappear from their memory. Cassia knew firsthand about this syndrome. She was guilty of it too. And she was happy keeping her mother in a saintly form that she conjured up in her mind while growing up. Grandma B was hell-bent on making sure that Marianne's halo stayed intact.

Chris again mentioned something about his *perfect* life with Angelina. Cassia hated herself at that moment because she was a little jealous of this dead woman—she even had a beautiful name. Cassia wished her name was *Agatha, Morgana,* or some other witchy name that she remembered from reading books about ghoulish tales when she was younger.

It was 5:00 a.m. when Cassia and Chris said their goodbyes. There was no hug or kiss, but Chris took Cassia's hand before opening the car door for her. He placed his business card in her palm and said, "Call me later if you would like to get together for dinner."

Cassia looked into his blue eyes. "Okay."

Driving toward Ashby House, Cassia thought about Chris's dating approach. She liked that he did not put her on the spot for an immediate response about meeting for dinner, even though she would have said yes. Doing it that way allowed him to keep his pride in tact if she rejected his offer. Cassia especially liked the little spark that she felt when he touched her hand.

CHAPTER THIRTY-FIVE

Day 4—June 15, 2006

Cassia got into bed and wanted to sleep, but the morning sun, too much caffeine, and Chris Marron swirling in her thoughts kept her eyes from closing. She sat up in bed, and immediately the aroma of Uncle Charles's cherry tobacco filled the air, but no sounds could be heard. Cassia appreciated the silence of Ashby House for a few seconds before going back downstairs. She had a full day's itinerary in her mind and believed that she might be able to rest if the thoughts in her head were transferred onto paper. In the kitchen, she removed a page from the to-do list that was still attached to the refrigerator. While she knew that it was impossible to control every aspect of her life, Cassia craved some semblance of order for this day. She did not want to repeat the cluttered chaos and surprises of yesterday. And she did not want to deprive herself of the satisfaction that she always felt when putting a line through a completed task. Cassia wrote:

> Call Maddie
> Call Peaches Winchester
> Call Annabelle
> Email Mitch
> Meet with Raymond
> Call Chris?

Cassia gave up on the idea of going back upstairs to sleep. The ladybugs on the sheer curtains in her room already proved that they could not prevent the morning sun from barreling in. She went to the den, grabbed the shawl from the back of the wing-back chair, and carried it to the living room. Stretching out on the couch, covering only her legs, she closed her eyes and fell into a much-needed dreamless sleep. When Cassia awoke, her eyes searched the room for a clock. There were none around to even hint that the eleven o'clock hour had already struck some time ago. She added another item to the cerebral list that she had going in her head. Next to "the addition of more TVs in the house," she added "a timepiece for each room." Before getting up from the couch, Cassia imagined a Victorian-style *grand* grandfather clock standing in the corner of the room—the kind so large that one would believe that it could wake a village but instead chimed softly on the hour. She thought some more, perhaps the room could be an exception and have two clocks. In addition to the grandfather clock, there should also be an old-fashioned mantel clock that ticked and ticked so loud that it would draw some of the attention away from the striking grandfather clock in the corner.

In the kitchen, Cassia was shocked that the time on the microwave showed 11:45. Her to-do list now sat on the kitchen table with not one line drawn through any of the six items. Cassia picked up the list. She almost drew a line through Chris's name but stopped herself. A loud growling in her stomach interrupted her thoughts. Her belly roared in dissatisfaction because of the copious amounts of coffee that she had earlier, so more coffee was out of the question. She poured herself a glass of milk. After taking a sip, Cassia dialed Maddie's number. An involuntary smile appeared on Cassia's lips upon hearing Maddie's voice. She drew a line through Maddie's name. Cassia gave Maddie a play-by-play of the previous night's events. Maddie interrupted Cassia's story every couple of minutes saying, "Oh Lord sweet Jesus," and repeated those words twice when Cassia told her about Annabelle's pregnancy. Cassia was still not able to discuss or even ask Maddie if she knew about the pact that her mother, father, and Uncle Charles made about keeping her paternity a secret. Cassia was about to tell Maddie about her encounter with Office Marron but instead announced to Maddie that she had to go because she had a visitor. Cassia did not tell her that it was the old house slave Frederick, the one who Uncle Charles told her about in his video message. It was the spirit she yelled at yesterday. He exited the den. She watched him make his way down the hall. Instead of coming into the kitchen where Cassia sat, he turned at the steps and began his ascent to the second floor. Cassia followed up the stairs behind him.

Frederick was close to the top of the attic stairs. Cassia stayed at his heels. He walked through the attic door. Cassia opened it and followed him in. He sat at the table where the checkers board was set up ready to play. Cassia sat in the chair opposite Frederick. She looked down at the board, but it was not a hard-type of board at all. Instead, it was a twenty-eight-inch square thin handwoven tapestry with a fringed border. There were thirty-two light-gray and thirty-two dark-gray staggered squares. The size of the plastic twelve black and twelve red checkers matched the equally large squares. Cassia at first believed that it had to be a very old version of the game but then decided that if the pawns were truly from an earlier time period, they would probably be made out of wood, not plastic. What confirmed her conclusion about the age of the board was when she saw the box on the floor that once housed the game. It was from the Cracker Barrel Country Store. She smiled noting the $15 price stamped on the box.

Cassia looked into the eyes of her somber opponent. She saw a kindness in his eyes but was unsure of his proficiency in the game of checkers. She wondered if her rusty skills would be a fair match for her opponent. She had not played checkers since her last visit with Uncle Charles just a few days before her father's death. It was Uncle Charles who introduced her to the game on a smaller board. He sometimes would have the game set up for them in the sunroom on a rainy day. Cassia made the first move because she was sitting on the side with the black checkers, and she remembered that black moves first. While Frederick contemplated his move, Cassia got up from her chair and turned on the record player. The vinyl album dropped onto the turntable. The music started. Cassia thought that it sounded lovely, but the only exposure even close to the genre was when she saw a Broadway production of *The Phantom of the Opera*, which Grandma B tricked her into attending.

Grandma B was always trying to immerse Cassia in the arts, dragging her in and out of museums on a regular basis. However, as Cassia got older, she rebelled more and more against anything that Grandma B suggested, like refusing to attend church. Grandma B came up with a plan that Cassia had no choice but to go along with. Grandma B's fifty-seventh birthday was approaching. She told Cassia that she wanted one gift in the world for her birthday, and that was for Cassia to spend an evening with her at the theater. Up until that moment, the only theater that Cassia had been to was the movie theater with her friends. Cassia was not made aware that the show playing was *The Phantom of the Opera* until they arrived at the Lyric Opera House. Cassia yawned and yawned during the show not wanting to give her grandmother the satisfaction that she loved the theatricality of it all. And Cassia was not going to admit that the music and singing charged right through the tough exterior that she put up like a shield whenever she was with her grandmother. She never told her grandmother from that day on she was hooked on the theater—not exactly operas, but mostly modern musicals. While Cassia could not afford the larger productions at the Lyric or Hippodrome, she attended smaller venues and community college programs. Mitch surprised her a few times with tickets, and they would make a date night out of it by first going to a two-for-one dinner special and then the show. Once in a while they would eat at the more elegant restaurants because Mitch often made friends with some of the owners of the fancier restaurants when photographing a family member's wedding. He would sometimes be asked to shoot some promotional pictures for their advertising brochures. They often paid him with a free dinner certificate for two. Mitch always ordered filet mignon topped with crabmeat whenever it was free and on the menu. He often commented that he could learn to like living the good life.

Cassia thought about the money that her father left to her—the money that Grandma B withheld from her all these years. She desperately wanted to speak to her, but it would have to wait until she returned from her cruise. Grandma B never gave Cassia any information about how to reach her whenever she went on vacations, and she went away quite frequently. The only reason that Cassia even knew that Grandma B was on vacation this time was because when she called her house the day before she found out about inheriting Ashby House, Grandma B's friend Gladys answered the phone and told Cassia that her grandmother was out getting a few last-minute items for their trip to the Caribbean. They would be flying to New York and meeting the cruise ship on Monday morning. Cassia swore that she would never go away without leaving her itinerary with her child, if she ever had one. She believed that Grandma B was missing the "maternal instinct" gene because she fluttered around in life without any thought or consideration about anyone else's feelings—especially Cassia's. Cassia returned to her seat, and it was again her turn to make the next move.

Cassia distractedly made her move. Her thoughts were still on Grandma B. It was early in the game, so she was not upset when her lack of concentration cost her first pawn to be captured. She smiled at the old man but got no response in return. Before making her next move, from the corner of her eye, Cassia spotted an old black woman sitting on the edge of the straw bed. She was knitting. Her feet were dangling over the side, silently tapping to the beat of the music. Cassia recognized the woman from the picture that Uncle Charles showed her in the video. She was Frederick's wife. Unlike Frederick, who never smiled, she was beaming. Cassia rose from her seat and started toward the woman. Frederick rose from his seat too, blocking Cassia from going any further. While she was not happy that Frederick would not allow her near his wife, she was pleased that there was finally some form of communication going on.

Cassia returned to her seat and made her next move. Frederick contemplated his countermove. Cassia studied the old woman. Because she was sitting down, Cassia could not determine her exact size but guessed that she was probably less than five feet tall. Her kinky hair was short and graying. Her smile exposed a mouth full of eggshell-white teeth between large brown lips. She never fully looked up from her knitting, so Cassia could not see her eyes, but from her side view, Cassia was able to analyze her pronounced cheekbones and the creases and lines near her eyes and mouth on her round face. Cassia guessed that the woman had a kind heart but was given no concrete reason to back up her belief. She wanted to get closer to the woman but obeyed Frederick's unspoken request.

Cassia was not sure of the time but believed that it was probably close to three o'clock. She had only one item crossed off of her to-do list on the table downstairs. She rose up from her seat. The woman on the bed still did not look up from her knitting. Cassia explained to Frederick that she would be back later to finish the game. He nodded his head. Cassia was excited. She was finally communicating with one of the ghosts at Ashby House. She did not count the communication with any of the spirits in her dreams.

CHAPTER THIRTY-SIX

CASSIA STOOD IN THE KITCHEN. She picked up her cell phone from the counter. The ladybugs in her stomach fluttered. She was apprehensive about calling Peaches Winchester. Cassia wondered if her call would be met with a warm reception or if Peaches would not be interested in meeting with her at all. Cassia had no idea how much information Uncle Charles had shared with his mother. Did she know that Cassia was biologically her granddaughter? Did she know that Cassia's mother, Marianne, was the product of the affair between Cassia's grandmother and her husband? Would she consider Cassia an outsider, and would she be upset that Charles left her Ashby House? And what secrets, if any, would she reveal about the ghosts who roam Ashby House? Cassia took a deep breath and scrolled through her contacts. She located the number that Annabelle gave her for Peaches Winchester. She pressed the send button. After a few rings, a soft-spoken voice on the other line said, "Hello."

Cassia was somewhat relieved when Peaches Winchester seemed happy to hear from her.

She immediately checked any formality and told Cassia that all her friends call her Peaches and Cassia should do the same. Cassia expressed her condolences about the death of her son. Peaches thanked Cassia. Cassia wanted Peaches to come to Ashby House so maybe she could clarify some of the information that Cassia found in the Bible. Before Cassia could invite her to Ashby House, Peaches offered to host a lunch for them at her home the next day at noon. After giving Cassia her address, Peaches assured her that it was only a twenty-minute drive from Ashby House. Cassia became very optimistic about the meeting because of the cordiality of Peaches's tone, and before hanging up the phone, she said, "I'm so looking forward to tomorrow, dear." Despite the lady's pleasant disposition on the phone, Cassia wondered if that fuzzy feeling would continue when she reveals all that she knows to Peaches.

Cassia sighed with relief when she hit the end-call button on her phone. However, that moment of respite did not last long because so many questions flooded her brain like a tidal wave. How much information *should* she share with Peaches Winchester—about her mother, grandmother, and should she tell Peaches about her paternity? Should she take the ladybug brooch with her, or would the sight of it just open old wounds for Peaches? Cassia surely did not want to hurt the lady or offend her. She wanted to take the Lawson family Bible and Elizabeth's letter so Peaches could go over the family tree with her because Cassia believed that the letter and the information in the Bible might be the key to unraveling the secrets at Ashby House. However, Cassia feared that Peaches might want to keep the Bible and the letter for sentimental reasons. Then she might never get the answers that she so desperately wanted. The ringing of the phone stopped Cassia's brain overload. The familiar Richmond number on her caller ID was Raymond's. Cassia answered the call on the third ring. Raymond wanted to come to Ashby House at six o'clock. Cassia froze when she heard the time. She asked Raymond if he could make it by five thirty. He agreed. Cassia asked for an update on Annabelle's condition. He stated that she was doing well and had been moved into a room. Cassia promised to visit Annabelle the next day.

After hanging up from her call with Raymond, Cassia tore a fresh sheet from the to-do tablet and started her schedule for the next day. She wrote, "12 o'clock, Peaches Winchester." Cassia was uncertain how much time to allocate for her lunch with Peaches. She decided a half hour for the worst-case scenario, and maybe two hours if things went really well. She wrote, "2 o'clock, Annabelle." She set down her paper and returned to today's to-do list. Cassia smiled because four out of six items were crossed off her list. She stared at Mitch's name. She checked the time on the microwave. It was now four o'clock. Cassia struggled with either finishing her game of checkers in the attic with Frederick (even though he was not on

174

the list) or e-mailing Mitch. She opened her laptop and pulled up Mitch's e-mail. After a few minutes of blankly staring at the screen, Cassia could not come up with the words for Mitch. She closed her laptop.

Cassia glanced at Chris's name with a question mark next to it. She still felt unsure, but the tingling in her right hand where he placed his business card gave her courage. She wondered if it was too late to call him about having dinner that evening. Perhaps he had already made other plans. And how could she lock in a time when she had no idea how long her meeting with Raymond would last? Cassia dialed the number before she could make any more excuses. She was taken aback when Chris answered on the first ring. While he played it cool, Cassia could tell from the tone in his voice that he was happy that she had called. Cassia apologized for calling so close to dinner about wanting to get together and she understood if he already had plans.

Chris laughed. "Well, my cat LuLu might be a little disappointed because now I have to break our dinner date. She'll just have to get over it."

Cassia appreciated a man with a sense of humor. That personality trait was way up there on her list of must-haves in a partner. Cassia told Chris that she had an appointment at five thirty but hoped to be done no later than seven. She would call him if it ran any later. Chris said that he would pick her up at seven, unless he hears otherwise. He also told her to dress casually, jeans or something like that, because he was taking her to his favorite restaurant. He assured her that she would love it.

Cassia hung up the call. She counted the same $50 in her wallet. Chris paid for Denny's that morning. Without discussion, he just did it—like Mitch. She was sure that he was the kind of guy who always paid—at least she hoped.

CHAPTER THIRTY-SEVEN

THE CLOCK ON THE MICROWAVE showed that Cassia had an hour and a half before Raymond was due to arrive at Ashby House. She was already dressed casually for her dinner date just in case her meeting with Raymond ran late. She hoped to have time to freshen up a bit before Chris's arrival. Cassia opened her laptop to Mitch's e-mail. Wanting to read again his latest e-mail where he confessed his knowledge of Grandma B's affair with Uncle Charles's father—the one that produced her mother, she instead accidentally opened the e-mail prior to that. One part of the e-mail caught her eye, "I wish that I was a list-maker like you. That way I could argue the pros and cons on this decision." Cassia believed that her life ran more smoothly when she made her to-do lists. Like today for example, there were only a few items on her list, but so far, her day was proceeding right on schedule.

Cassia wondered if using a logical approach, like the pros and cons list that she would sometimes use to solve problems, would help her with the ghosts. Cassia thought about how Uncle Charles described each ghost at Ashby House and how he believed that they were hanging around because of some unfinished business. Cassia played in her mind everything that happened that had resulted in Jonathan Welts and his mother's departure from Ashby House. Cassia knew that Uncle Charles was right about how to rid the house of its ghosts even though she believed that she had accidentally stumbled on what was needed to reconcile Jonathan and his mother. Was it pure luck, or did the ghosts themselves have to aid in their own settlement of affairs? If help from each ghost was needed, how would she get Elizabeth, Frederick, and Frederick's wife to lead her in the right direction?

Cassia got up from her chair. She went into the den and began searching through the desk for something with more writing space than a page from the notepad on the refrigerator could provide. Finding nothing but a few sticky notes, Cassia leaned back into the chair while her eyes scanned the room. Leaning against the credenza in the corner of the room was a rolled-up white poster board. A green rubber band kept it from unraveling. Cassia rolled down the rubber band and unwounded the blank poster board. She rewound the poster board in the opposite way so it would uncurl enough for it to lie almost flat on the desk. Removing a black Sharpie from the desk drawer, Cassia centered and underlined two words at the top of the poster board: Ghost Busting.

Cassia sat back in the desk chair. She studied the two words and shook her head because of her choice of title. Since she had written the words with a permanent marker, they could not be erased. She pictured herself standing side by side with Dan Aykroyd and Bill Murray. All three dressed in tan overalls holding their ghost-busting equipment and taking down the Stay Puft Marshmallow Man like the 1984 movie *Ghostbusters*. Was Jeff Goldblum in that movie? No, he was in *Independence Day*. Cassia chewed on the end of the marker and thought. There was something very appealing about that man. Maybe it was because he resembled Mitch when he wore those black-frame glasses in some of his movies. She shrugged her shoulders. She then drew a small picture in the corner of the poster board—a silly-looking ghost popping out of a "no symbol," just like in the advertisement for the *Ghostbusters* movie.

Cassia never considered herself an artist, but she thought her drawing looked pretty good. It sure was better than the stupid stick figures that Mitch would always draw whenever they played *Pictionary* with their friends. Well, it wasn't officially *Pictionary* because they made up their own rules and played their own version of the game. It consisted of only identifying famous characters. Maybe Mitch's stick figures weren't too bad because she always guessed who they were. Cassia and Mitch were always partners. She thought about it and decided to give him an A+ for effort at least. Cassia smiled thinking about just how funny Mitch could be. If his stick person was a female, he would give her huge breasts. If his stick person was a male, his penis would be like a third leg. He always had everyone laughing because of his creativity when drawing male/female protruding body parts. One time he drew a stick female, of course, with breasts. She was holding a large snake in her stick figure hands. The snake was wrapped around her neck. He then drew a headset around her head with a microphone that covered the dot that represented her mouth. Cassia immediately guessed correctly that the person was Britney Spears. They had just watched her on TV at the 2001 MTV Video Awards. Mitch laughed at Cassia because she freaked out during the entire performance, certain that Britney Spears was going to be attacked or perhaps eaten by the snake. In another game, Mitch drew the same figure with a snake, but this time it had a penis. Cassia guessed that it was Alice Cooper. She wondered if Jewel ever guessed Mitch's bad drawings.

Cassia returned to her task. Under the words *Ghost Busting*, Cassia wrote Elizabeth's name in large all-capital letters on the far-left side of the page. She then underlined it. Cassia did the same for Frederick and his wife but placed them in the middle. Jonathan and Lily Roberts' names were printed on the farthest right side of the board. Underneath each of the names, she wrote numbers one through six, leaving a space between each number. Cassia was going to use the method that she learned in her Journalism 101 class to try and get a better story about each entity at Ashby House—the five *W*s and one *H*—who, what, when, where, why, and how. Cassia finished the template to begin her detective work. She then heard the familiar sound of gravel crunching. Raymond was coming up the driveway.

CHAPTER THIRTY-EIGHT

CASSIA QUICKLY ROLLED UP THE poster board. She secured it with a rubber band and hid it in one of the lower credenza cabinets before Raymond made it to the top of the driveway. She opened the door just before he knocked. Raymond once again offered Cassia his right hand and a polite smile. And he held tightly onto his briefcase with his left hand, just like he did in his earlier visit to Ashby House.

Cassia said, "Would you like some coffee?"

Raymond replied, "No," and then added, "thank you."

Cassia led the way to the den with Raymond not far behind. Once in the den, Cassia began a series of questions about Annabelle.

"How is Annabelle doing?"

Raymond said, "Better."

Cassia shook her head. "Good. Is she up for visitors because I would like to stop by tomorrow afternoon?"

"She has her cell phone. Call first."

Cassia finished with her questions about Annabelle. She realized that Raymond was an attorney who practiced what he preached—never offer more information than what is necessary to answer a question. She wanted an update on Robert, the baby, and what was going to happen with the merger between the two law firms, but those questions would have to wait until her visit with Annabelle.

Raymond placed his locked briefcase on the desk. He rolled the correct combination of numbers on the briefcase lock until they clicked. This process seemed so familiar to him. He did it with such ease that Cassia was sure that his procedure had become more habitual than necessary. If she were a gambler, she would bet that he kept his briefcase locked even when he was at home and probably unlocked it every time he needed something and then relocked it again. She wondered how many times a day he went through this process. Cassia smiled as she counted "thirty-one" in her head when the tumblers clicked. Raymond opened his briefcase, pulled out a manila folder, and immediately locked it. He again sent the tumblers into a clicking frenzy when he went to retrieve another piece of paper—"thirty-two."

Cassia watched the color drain from Raymond's face when he saw the empty sleeve for Uncle Charles's DVD. He had no idea until now that he had left Charles's video letter to Cassia in the DVD player at Ashby House during his earlier visit. Cassia was now sure that Raymond was the kind of guy who rarely made mistakes, and he would surely feel better if Cassia pretended that she had not seen the video. That's what she wanted to do. However, "I already saw it," spewed from her mouth.

Cassia explained, "I wanted to watch the news last night. I turned on the TV, and much to my surprise, the video came on."

Raymond said, "I wanted to give you some warning before you viewed the video. Charles's health was deteriorating very rapidly by the time he got around to making it. How much do you remember about him?"

"I remembered a little. As soon as I arrived at Ashby House, a flood of memories about my summer visits here came to me—mostly in bits and pieces. And when I saw his face again"—Cassia pointed to Charles's portrait—"it summoned even more recollections."

Raymond did not mention the shocking revelation about Charles's part in Cassia's beginning. He just handed Cassia a copy of Charles's last will and testament. "This is your copy. I have taken the liberty of highlighting a few important items. I will give you a few minutes to read over the document. We can then talk, and I will answer any questions when you are done. May I wait in the kitchen?"

Raymond smiled when he saw the puzzled look on Cassia's face. He said, "It is not done like in the movies where the attorney reads the entire will to the beneficiaries. That is just theatricality." Raymond cocked his head to the left. "Long ago, wills were read aloud by an attorney because many people were illiterate." Raymond then smiled again. "I don't believe that is the case here." Raymond picked up his briefcase, checked to see if he remembered to lock it, and excused himself from the room. He closed the door behind him.

Cassia sat at the desk holding the document in her hand. She had never seen a will before. She studied the bold writing on the front of the trifolded document—**LAST WILL AND TESTAMENT— CHARLES ALLEN WINCHESTER III**. Cassia fanned the document back and forth in her hand, creating a cool breeze. She then unfolded the document. She was expecting at least ten or twelve pages of legal mumbo-jumbo. Cassia was surprised to find only a cover page and two full typewritten pages. Cassia also thought that a "legal document" had to be on longer paper, hence the term *legal paper*, but Uncle Charles's will was written on standard 8½" x 11" white business paper. At the top of the first page was written the same declaration attesting that this document was Uncle Charles's last will and testament.

Cassia read the first paragraph to herself:

> *I, CHARLES ALLEN WINCHESTER III,*
> *of the City of Richmond in the Commonwealth of*
> *Virginia, being of sound and disposing mind, mem-*
> *ory, and understanding, do hereby make, publish*
> *and declare this to be my Last Will and Testament,*
> *hereby revoking all former Wills and Codicils here-*
> *tofore made by me.*

Cassia read aloud the second paragraph:

> <u>*ITEM FIRST:*</u> *I direct that my Personal*
> *Representative, hereinafter named, pay all my just*
> *debts and funeral expenses*

Cassia stopped reading the words and replaced them with blah, blah, blah. Cassia knew that Raymond was named Uncle Charles's personal representative without seeing it in writing in the document. She was thankful that Raymond was the personal representative because he had the job of taking care of property transfers and paying all taxes.

Cassia read the next section—the one Raymond highlighted:

> *ITEM SECOND: To my dear friend MADELINE DENISE YOUNG, I bequeath the sum of fifty thousand dollars ($50,000.00).*

Cassia smiled and thought she now understood why Maddie was so happy when she left Ashby House. She continued reading:

> *I give, devise, and bequeath all the rest, residue and remainder of my estate, that I may die possessed of, whether real, personal, or mixed and including any property over which I may have power of testamentary disposition, unto my dearly departed best friends MICHAEL AND MARIANNE WESTFIELD'S child CASSIA MARIE WESTFIELD BURNS, or to her descendants, per stirpes.*

Cassia had never been named in a will before but thought that there was some strange wording in the document. It wasn't the legal mumbo-jumbo (as Uncle Charles described it) that annoyed her, though the words "per stirpes" were foreign to her. It was the way the items were listed: ITEM FIRST AND ITEM SECOND. Why not, "Item #1, Item #2"? And she was puzzled by the way she was named in the will: "dearly departed best friends MICHAEL AND MARIANNE WESTFIELD'S child CASSIA WESTFIELD BURNS." She then just shrugged it off as Uncle Charles's way of paying tribute to her mother and father. She thought again and decided that it was his way of assuring her that her mother and father were her *only* parents.

The next part of the document named Annabelle as the "runner-up" if her father was unable to perform the duties as set forth in the document. The rest of the document included the date and signatures of Uncle Charles, Raymond Oates, and a witness named Alice Long. Cassia folded the document closed. She was confused because the only dollar amount stated in the will was the $50,000 that was left to Maddie. While she understood that she would be receiving the remainder of the estate, Cassia still had no idea what that meant in dollars. Before she could get Raymond from the kitchen to clarify what "everything else" meant, he was knocking on the door. Cassia invited him in. She said, "I have lots of questions."

Raymond anticipated that Cassia would have a flood of questions. While in the kitchen waiting for Cassia to finish reading Charles's will, he pulled from his briefcase financial statements and other pertinent documents relating to Charles's estate. They were already spread out on the table waiting for Cassia's perusal. Raymond led Cassia down the hall from the den to the kitchen.

Raymond pulled a chair away from the table and motioned for Cassia to take a seat next to him. Before Cassia could ask one of her many questions, Raymond began, "Charles left you Number Six Ashby House and everything in it." He shuffled through the papers on the table pulling out the last sheet from the bottom of the stack. Raymond continued, "He also left you a large sum of money." Raymond pointed to the last figure on the spreadsheet. "After taxes and other property transfer fees, this is a close estimate of what Charles was worth at the time of his passing." Cassia read the amount on the bottom of the paper, "$32,167,013.67." Cassia read the amount over again, "$32,167,013.67."

Raymond continued, "More than seventy-five percent of this money is tied up in stocks, bonds, and various holdings, some overseas. I can continue managing these accounts for you, or you can hire someone else if you wish. If you choose to have me continue on, it might be in your best interest to hire an independent consultant to verify the records. Just an idea so there is complete transparency. Tomorrow morning, we can meet at the bank to put your name on the checking and savings accounts. The bank can then issue you a check card so you can begin accessing your money. I will let you know when the papers are ready to transfer the title of the house to you."

Cassia leaned back in her chair. She stared down at the paper. She could not close her mouth. Two words kept swirling around in her brain—*your money*. The questions in her head that she so methodically gathered and cerebrally listed over the last few days were now a muddled mess. Cassia could not think or speak.

Raymond continued, "Charles's mother, Peaches, has not been named in her son's will. I suggest as a courtesy that she be allowed to go through the house and claim any family pictures, heirlooms, or anything within reason, if she so desires. I have not been in touch with her regarding this subject. I wanted to consult with you before I approach this matter with her. Of course, you have the right to say no."

Cassia stuttered one word, "Yeah."

Raymond collected and packed up the papers from the table and placed them in his briefcase. He told Cassia that he would be providing her with a copy of all documents when they meet at the bank in the morning. He closed the briefcase. His fingers quickly scrambled the numbers on the tumblers. He took Cassia's hand and placed his business card in her palm, just like Chris did the night before. This time she felt nothing. Raymond told Cassia that the card contained the bank's number and address on the back. Raymond looked into Cassia's blank stare and said, "Meet me at nine o'clock. And be prepared to do a lot of signing of your name. You will need your driver's license for identification." Without exchanging any other words, Raymond started down the hall and let himself out the front door. Cassia was not aware that he left until the pinging of the gravel against his tires startled her out of her coma-like state.

Still somewhat disoriented, Cassia pushed both hands down on the table and pulled herself up out of the chair. With her legs still a little shaky, she staggered the short distance to the counter like she had had too much to drink. Cassia picked up her open wallet and slowly counted the same fifty dollars that she counted earlier. She then dumped all the change out of the zippered compartment. She counted the coins one by one until all monies were counted. The total was $51.67.

Cassia reached for a page from the notepad on the refrigerator and began making a list of all her debts. Since her divorce, Cassia had developed a weakness for designer clothes, shoes, and handbags. She reasoned that she needed to look professional for her job as a wedding planner. On the first line, she wrote, "Car." She estimated that she owed $10,000. On the next line, she wrote, "Visa #1." Cassia knew that her credit limit was $5,000, and that was what she owed. The next line, she wrote, "Visa #2." That card was maxed out too, but only had a $2,000 credit limit. She then wrote three store credit cards on the next three lines: Macy's, Nordstrom's, and Neiman Marcus—all about $4,500 each.

Cassia began her love for designer fashion after receiving a Prada handbag from a client whose very expensive wedding she had planned. It was about a month before her breakup with Mitch. It was not unusual for Cassia to receive a small token gift or monetary tip from a client after a successful wedding. She always preferred cash but was nonetheless appreciative whenever she received the occasional gift certificate for a day at a spa or for a very nice downtown Baltimore restaurant. Cassia cringed every time she received flowers, which usually died within a few days. Regardless of the gift, Cassia always sent her usual thank-you note, "Thank you for your thoughtful gift. It brightened my day." She even wrote that same thank-you note to the bride who handed her one of the table centerpieces from the wedding party table as a thank-you. It was a small fishbowl with a live goldfish in it.

The goldfish was certainly an odd gift. It was right up there with the gift she received after the "Thing 1 and Thing 2" themed wedding. The bride was obsessed with the characters Thing 1 and Thing 2 from Dr. Seuss's *Cat in the Hat*. Cassia tried to dissuade the bride from having such a theme take over the entire wedding. She tried to compromise with the bride and suggested that they put on matching Thing 1 and Thing 2 T-shirts before leaving for their honeymoon. The bride insisted that she wanted things done her way. In order not to lose her commission, Cassia went along with the bride's ideas. There was a Thing 1 and Thing 2 cake, decorations, and during the reception (it was when Cassia felt that she had lost control of the entire party, so she removed her headset and sat down and ate two pieces of cake), the entire wedding party put their Thing

1 and Thing 2 T-shirts over their formal attire. The bride insisted that a group picture be taken. When Cassia returned home that evening with the red bucket containing two bottles of champagne—one labeled Thing 1 and the other Thing 2 clenched under her arm—Mitch shot her a quizzical look. She kicked off her shoes and shot him back a look that said, "I'm not ready to talk about it yet." After a ten-minute quick chill in the freezer of the Thing 1 bottle, Mitch first removed the blue tufts of hair made of yarn from the top of the bottle. He held a kitchen towel over the official seal so it would not become a projectile and cause any damage. He learned this trick after opening his first bottle of champagne, which resulted in a fairly deep indentation in the ceiling of his old girlfriend's apartment.

Cassia kicked off her shoes, sank into the couch, and began telling the story of the groom's toast where he made a surprise announcement that his new bride was pregnant with two babies. He jokingly called them Thing 1 and Thing 2. By the time the bottle was empty, Cassia was not sure if they were laughing at Mitch's rendition of pretending to be a teacher calling on his students Thing 1 and Thing 2 during the morning attendance count or from the bubbly, but it turned out to be a memorable night. A smile always came to Cassia whenever she reached inside her refrigerator and caught a glimpse of the blue yarn from the top of the Thing 2 bottle of champagne that over the years got pushed to the wayback. She drank it the day Mitch moved out of the apartment.

Now alone, Cassia stared into the noticeably emptier closet. She shifted her clothes, belts, scarves, shoes, and other accessory items in an attempt to make the closet look full again. In doing so, Cassia found the large box that contained the Prada purse given to her the prior month. She had not paid much attention to it when she brought it home. She even forgot what it looked like until she opened the box again. It was pretty—burgundy color but somewhat larger than Cassia usually had for a purse. The price had been removed from the tag, but the gift receipt was in the bottom of the box. Cassia contemplated returning the purse but decided to try it out for a couple of days first, careful not to put anything in it but her wallet. Cassia beamed at every compliment about her bag from people she knew, and sometimes even strangers on the street complimented her good taste. Mostly women, but even one guy gave her the thumbs-up. Not 100 percent sure his gesture was about the bag, but she smiled and pulled her purse closer to her. After that, she could not bring herself to return the purse to Neiman Marcus. She transferred the entire contents from her label-less purse to the Prada purse.

The following week, Cassia met with a female client at Neiman Marcus. She wanted Cassia's input on a table setting that she was adding to her wedding registry. Once hired as a wedding planner, Cassia worked closely with each and every giddy bride on matters that sometimes took her outside the realm of her duties. She had met this particular bride just once when she and her groom signed their contract. Cassia remembered only two things about the couple—their English accent and the bride saying that the wedding was going to be a small affair with about fifty of their closest friends and family members.

Cassia was surprised when the bride chose a table setting costing an average of $152 for each piece. Cassia's math skills were not great, but she knew that an eight-piece service would cost more than anything she owned. Cassia thought about how Grandma B would get so crazy when the table was cleared when using her prized Lenox butterfly china that did not cost anywhere near what the English setting cost. The pattern depicted English country life. It was crafted by Juliska and called "Country Estate" Dinnerware. The bride hugged Cassia when she enthusiastically complimented her exquisite taste. Later when Cassia began writing the invitations, the guest list was a who's who of British royalty. While the Queen was not on the list, many royal family members were. Cassia later found out that the groom was a polo player and old friend of Prince Charles and other family members. This was the first time that Cassia stressed about writing invitations. She worried that she might offend someone by making a mistake because the regal titles were so foreign to her. She had the bride and groom review each invitation and then reviewed them herself again before mailing them. While Prince Charles did not attend the wedding, he did send a small note stating his regrets.

He had a mandatory royal engagement the same day. After the wedding, the bride hinted that he sent a large check.

Cassia had about an hour to kill before meeting with her next client about a mile from the mall, so she walked to the expensive store after she and her client parted. In the shoe department, Cassia fondled a pair of shoes that she felt matched her purse perfectly. A salesclerk approached her and asked if she would like to try them on. Cassia had never been so enthusiastically pursued by a saleswoman before. She attributed it to the purse. Cassia thought only for another second before saying yes. She would try them on for fun knowing that she could not afford the $850 Prada floral-print ankle-wrap pumps. The salesclerk was good at her job. She told Cassia that she had never seen anyone look better in that shoe—like it was custom-made for her. The salesclerk continually gushed over Cassia's bag and her exquisite taste in pairing of the shoes. The next thing that Cassia remembered was that she was signing the sales receipt after the lady opened an account for her with a $5,000 credit limit. Cassia was in shock for two reasons when she left the store. One, how the hell did she get approved for a Neiman Marcus card with a $5,000 credit limit? And two, she just bought a pair of shoes that costs the same as her month's rent. Cassia became hooked on designer fashions though she learned to bargain basement shop after nearly maxing out her Neiman Marcus credit card within that first month. She also opened and carried high balances on Macy's and Nordstrom's cards. Cassia started another list. At the top, she wrote, "MUST HAVES." She thought for a moment. She wrote one word: "BABY." That was all she really wanted.

CHAPTER THIRTY-NINE

CASSIA WAS THANKFUL FOR THE hour that she had before Chris was due to pick her up for their date. Everything that Raymond told her was finally sinking in. She now believed that it was true—she really was the owner of Ashby House. She no longer had to stress about the costs associated with keeping up the house. Cassia had no money worries. She could now afford the $1,000 Jimmy Choo black tall boots that she had her eye on since forever. She could now take vacations like Grandma B took frequently (probably using Cassia's money). She was still angry about that. And she could now afford a baby on her own. Cassia instructed her mind to slow down a bit, but it would not listen.

Cassia wanted to talk to Mitch and tell him her good news. Cassia dialed his cell phone number. It went directly into voice mail. Maybe he was in the middle of getting married to Je-wel, a fact that she had placed in her "ignore file." It was the one she kept way back in her mind where all her hurt and pain were stored. Cassia smacked her forehead with the palm of her hand to try and keep the folder from surfacing, but it flew open. That knot in her stomach turned and turned like it did that day when she walked in on Mitch and Jewel.

Cassia searched the cabinets for a paper bag because she was sure that she would need one, but she managed to use a technique that her psychiatrist recommended. She slowed down her breathing on her own this time. She then did something that her psychiatrist would not recommend. Cassia closed her eyes and imagined a vault in her mind with tumblers like the one on Raymond's briefcase. For just this evening, she would stuff all hurtful items back into that folder, lock it away, and pretend that the combination was lost.

*****

Cassia climbed the stairs to freshen up a little for her date with Chris. However, instead of going into her room, she wanted a good look at what was now *hers*. At first, Cassia wanted to be just a visitor, fighting to keep from getting attached to Ashby House. Now, she no longer had to keep her heart at a distance.

Cassia had already been in Maddie's room. She walked down the hall to what were always called by Uncle Charles and Maddie, the guest rooms. Though she was sure that she had been in those two bedrooms a long time ago, Cassia was surprised that they were larger than her own. Maybe they appeared that way because of the two single beds in her own room. Each contained a queen-size bed with matching dresser and makeup vanity. Cassia giggled realizing that she could sleep in any one of the five bedrooms that night. She then came to Uncle Charles's bedroom. It was the first time that she had seen it since she was a child. The room looked almost the same as she remembered. It was the largest bedroom in the house. The bedding was different.

It had been changed from a regal red-and-gold trimmed comforter to a black-and-white quilt set, but it had the same impressive king-size bed with prominent hand-carved posts and newel tops with acanthus leaf carving accents. And there were two matching dressers—a five drawer and a dresser/mirror combination. On the far end of the bedroom was a library wall filled with books. Cassia ran her finger across the first row of books. She had forgotten how much Uncle Charles loved to read—mostly books about the history of the Civil War.

Cassia never spent much time in Uncle Charles's bedroom. She occasionally went in with Maddie to hug him goodnight. He was usually sitting in one of his two accent chairs. Most of the time he would stop in her room to say goodnight. He would stand in the doorway to her room while Maddie was tucking her in. He usually blew her a kiss. Cassia smiled remembering how he would pretend to catch her kiss and place it on his cheek when she blew one back. Uncle Charles was never super affectionate with her. She never remembered him saying "I love you." Perhaps he kept his distance to protect himself from feeling that biological connection. Tears welled up in Cassia's eyes. Her heart was breaking because she never told him she loved him. The only comfort that she could muster to pacify her aching core was hoping that Uncle Charles probably knew.

Cassia continued into her bathroom. She brushed her teeth and hair. She washed her face, reapplied her makeup, and once again scrutinized her green eyes in the mirror. The storm that she once saw was gone. Even the house was quiet and peaceful. For the time being, she put Elizabeth, Frederick and his wife, and Jonathan Roberts (Welts) out of her mind. A loud knocking at the door interrupted her stare.

CHAPTER FORTY

CHRIS STOOD OUTSIDE OF ASHBY House with one long-stem yellow rose in his hand. He was regretting listening to his friend Maura, who advised him to give Cassia a yellow rose instead of a red one, he thought as he waited for Cassia to come to the door. He always gave his wife red roses. She loved them, which led to an assumption that he felt all women preferred red. Earlier in the day, Maura told Chris that a red rose would be too personal for a first date. Chris had no idea that the recently-divorced, beautiful but slightly older, Irish-Catholic redheaded dispatcher at his work had purposely given him some bad advice, knowing well that a yellow rose is a symbol of friendship. Chris was oblivious to Maura's hinting for the last few months about her new status and availability. She was ready to ask him out and spill her guts about her feelings for him, when he called her for dating advice. He told her that he had met someone and she was incredible. Her name was Cassia.

Cassia answered the door with her Prada purse in her hand. She was ready to go. Chris complimented her on how great she looked and how impressed he was with Ashby House. She did not invite Chris in. Cassia was not ready to invite him into her personal world just yet. She thanked Chris for the rose. She thought about Mitch. He would have given her a sunflower—he knew her so well. Cassia scolded herself because she had no right to expect Chris to know her favorite flower.

This was the first time that she had been given a yellow rose and gave no credence to the symbolism associated with the color. She had no idea the story behind the decision of getting her a yellow rose versus getting a red one. As Chris opened the car door for Cassia, she again thanked him for his thoughtfulness. She liked that he showed up with a flower.

"So, where are we going?" Cassia asked as Chris "fired up his eight-horse team," a term he used when he started up his "baby," a pristine raven-black '69 375hp Ford Mustang Boss 429. He had purchased the car from a collector who gave him a good deal after Chris saved his life when he pulled him from his burning car following a collision with an eighteen-wheeler truck. While waiting for the helicopter to transport the man to a trauma center, Chris stayed with him and started a conversation to distract the man from the pain of his injuries. He found out that the older gentleman was a classic-car collector. Chris shared with him his love for the '69 Mustang. After the man recovered from his injuries, he got in touch with Chris and offered him a really sweet deal on one of his Mustangs. Chris's wife had just passed away a few months prior. The car provided a much need distraction. After purchasing the car, his daughter commented to her grandmother that watching her father washing his car earlier that day was the first time she had seen him smile since her mother passed away. Chris smiled at Cassia as he easily shifted the gears of the manual transmission on the Mustang. Chris explained, "The place where we are going is really just a little hole in the wall, but it serves the best steaks. I must admit that I am now second-guessing my choice. I am a little concerned that this place might not be up to your standards after seeing that huge house where you are staying."

Cassia was not ready to reveal to Chris that she was the owner of Ashby House. She laughed and said in her best hillbilly accent, "I is just simple folk, so don't you git your tail feathers ruffled."

Chris laughed. "That's right. For God sakes, you drive a Prius."

Cassia laughed, but then wondered, *What the hell does he mean by that comment?* She was pretty sure that it was an insult. Not having a clue about the value of Chris's classic car, she thought, "Well, at least my car is not old."

Cassia brushed off the Prius comment. The rest of the conversation on the way to the restaurant stayed friendly and light. Chris talked more about his daughter and her struggles with sticking with a major in her college studies. Cassia commented about her decision to major in psychology and how she wished that she had instead majored in business when she started her career as a wedding planner. But she admitted that her study of people and how they thought and reacted had been helpful in her work sometimes. Cassia thought about Robert and his ideas for turning Ashby House into a wedding venue. She said, "I might go back to school to get my business degree because I have been thinking about starting my own wedding planning business one day."

Chris parked the Mustang in a spot as far away from the other cars as was available. Chris turned off the engine. The loud engine noise was now replaced by the sound of country music roaring out of the restaurant/bar every time someone entered or existed. Chris opened Cassia's car door and said, "That sounds like a good idea. I'm sure you'll be successful." Cassia was not sure about getting a good steak when she saw the name of the restaurant/bar, "The Road Kill Bar and Grill." She now knew why Chris neglected telling her exactly where he was taking her to dinner.

CHAPTER FORTY-ONE

THE ODOR OF TOO MANY people in a small place perspiring alcohol from their pores hit Cassia as soon as Chris led her into the bar. It was like the day when her stomach became queasy by the smell of too many flowers mixed with the smell of too many colognes and perfumes along with the stench of an embalmed decomposing body at the funeral home where her father was laid out. Cassia quickly erased that thought from her mind, but she could not keep the ladybugs from taking flight in her stomach. Chris took her hand. The band was announcing its plan to take a short intermission and reassured the crowd that it would return in about fifteen minutes. Cassia was thankful because she did not relish the idea of screaming over the band in order to engage in any conversation with Chris. Cassia was even more thankful when Chris led her to an upstairs room where a handful of tables and booths were set up. On the way up to the restaurant area, Chris waved hello to a few people at the bar. Cassia was not aware that the men were his coworkers, and the only female in the group was Maura.

Chris did not wait to be seated and escorted Cassia to the last empty booth. The table contained a small clear vase with artificial daisies and a battery-operated candle. As soon as they sat down, Chris immediately picked up the flameless candle and blew it out like a real one to show Cassia how it worked. He then turned it back on for her so she could take a turn. Before Cassia could blow out the candle, a much older woman—whom Chris later told Cassia had been employed at the Road Kill as long as there had been the Road Kill—was standing at their table. She laughed and said, "Chris, you playing with them damn candles again?"

Chris got up from his seat, and the tiny woman almost disappeared into Chris's bear hug. She had her gray hair tied up in a bun and was full of energy and spunk. He smiled and replied, "Josie, you know I can't help myself." Chris then pointed to Cassia. "This is my friend Cassia. She is visiting from Baltimore and staying at Ashby House."

Josie addressed Cassia with a puckered brow, "The Winchester place?"

Cassia replied, "Yes, did you know Charles Winchester?"

"He and his lawyer friend come in here a couple times a month. Good tippers. Heard about his passing." With a knowing-all look, Josie leaned in closer to Cassia and whispered, "You staying at *that* house all by yourself, young lady?" Cassia locked eyes with Josie. The once friendly waitress now had a worried look. Cassia was not aware that Josie was the medium Josephina that Peaches Winchester hired to cleanse Ashby House many years ago.

Josephina Long was born with the gift. Well, that's what her mother told her because from little-up, she was a very intuitive person. At a very young age, Josie's vision came mostly in her dreams and then in what she called daydreams that she later recognized as visions. As she got older, Josie began experiencing a heightened awareness of her senses, sometimes becoming nauseous when smells and sounds became magnified and overwhelming. This time, when meeting Cassia, Josephina "felt" an overwhelming sense of sadness and loss. She was not sure if Ashby House was the reason for her sadness, or was it already in the girl before she came. She also knew that Cassia had the gift too when a blue "spirit orb" flew by Cassia's head. Neither woman acknowledged it, but they slightly ducked at the same time. Josie was certain that Cassia saw it too. She was puzzled by Cassia's lack of ownership of her gift. Perhaps nobody took the time to help her hone her unique skills like her mother helped her.

Josie handed menus to Chris and Cassia. She took their drink orders and asked if they needed time to look at the menu. Chris told Josie that he wanted his usual of—Josie interrupted, "I know. Steak, cooked medium, fries, and the vegetable of the day." Chris added, "Rolls and butter too." Cassia ordered the same. Josie briskly walked

196

away from their table. Cassia ignored Josie's earlier odd behavior and brushed it off when Chris commented that he has known Josie for a long time and has never seen her behave so strangely.

The music at the bar began again, but Chris and Cassia hardly noticed. The floor that divided the bar and restaurant muffled most of the sound except for the bass's bong-bong vibration that pulsated through the floor and through their seats. Cassia was determined not to reveal too much about Ashby House just yet, but Chris managed to pull a few tidbits out of her during their dinner conversation. Cassia knew it was the wine—her truth serum as she called it. It always made her talk too much. By the end of the night, she regretted that second glass.

Chris inquired, "You told me earlier that Charles Winchester was your uncle. How come you had not seen him for many years?"

Cassia took a long breath and began, "Charles Winchester was not my biological uncle. He was my—" Cassia stopped before saying that he was her biological father. It was too soon. Telling Chris would open the door to so many more questions that she was not willing to answer just yet. Cassia continued, "Charles was my parents' best friend. My mother died when I was born. My father passed away when I was six years old. My grandmother no longer allowed me to visit Ashby House." Cassia guessed the next question even before Chris asked.

"Why?"

Cassia took another long breath. "She never liked Charles Winchester. It's too complicated for me to go into that right now. All I can say is that Grandma B is not a very nice person. It's part of her character to not like somebody for no good reason." Cassia thought again. Maybe she did have a good reason to not like the Winchester family. Cassia said, "Sometimes I don't think she even likes me." Cassia regretted her words. The last thing that she wanted to do was come off as sounding pitiful. Chris stared into space not knowing what to say next. Cassia chugged down her last sip of wine from her second glass. She took Chris's hands into hers. "Listen, I didn't mean to incite any pity from you. I know it's hard for you to understand my life when yours is so different. Your parents live next door to you, and you have a great relationship with them. You have brothers and sisters who get together on a regular basis. I think it's wonderful that you have such a close family. I am not going to lie and say that I don't envy you because I really do. But this is my life, and I'm really okay with it."

Chris smiled at Cassia. "Good. Now let me get the check and we can get out of here." Cassia nodded and smiled back at Chris. He summoned for Josie by waving his hand. She came to the table after making a trip into the back room. She handed Chris the check and a candle in a box. All three laughed as Chris pretended to hide it under his jacket. Josie slipped Cassia a folded piece of paper while shaking her hand and saying how nice it was to see Chris out with such a lovely lady. Cassia was surprised to feel the paper in the palm of her hand when Josie let it go. Having no idea what was on the note and not wanting to be bombarded with a million questions from Chris, Cassia quickly slid the paper down into her purse.

Chris once again led Cassia through the bar on their way out. The band was playing a slow song, "Feels So Right" by the country group Alabama. Cassia was unprepared when Chris turned around and took her in his arms. They began slow dancing. Cassia was not sure if it was the wine or the heat from Chris's body that made her begin sweating like most of the other bar patrons. She buried her nose deep into Chris's neck, inhaling his naked scent, never noticing the woman on the other side of the bar staring them down. The once nauseating smells from the bar disappeared. The intensity of the heat between Cassia and Chris sat simmering like a pot of water on a stove at the brink of boiling. When the song was over, Chris held her hand until they got to the car. On the ride home, every smile and touch from Chris increased the riotous fluttering of the ladybugs in her stomach. In the last few years, Cassia grew tired of the awkwardness of dating and longed for the comfort of familiarity. Tonight, she looked for the passion that came with someone new—someone who was a mystery. Someone she could fantasize about. Someone who could provide a much-needed jumpstart to her lifeless love life.

Cassia was puzzled when Chris did not turn off the engine to the Mustang when he got out of the car. He walked her to the front door of Ashby House. Cassia had already made up her mind on the ride home that she was *again* willing to throw out her three-date rule. Perhaps Chris was not. He gave her a gentle kiss on her lips. It was not just a tiny peck but long enough to weaken Cassia at the knees. He said that he would call her tomorrow.

Cassia closed the door. She stood there and listened to the Mustang's roar and gravel pinging until she heard nothing but silence. In the kitchen, she threw her purse down onto the table. Its contents spilled out and spread across the table. Some of the items fell off of the table. Luckily, she caught her cell phone before it plunged to the floor. She tried to fight back the angry thoughts running through her head. She lost the battle. They came through like a swollen dam bursting through the floodgates—if I was as pretty as Annabelle, maybe he would have stayed. And if I was a slut like Je-wel, maybe he would have stayed. And if he knew how rich I now am, maybe he would have stayed. Cassia shook her head as if her efforts could disarrange the nasty thoughts and rearrange them into more pleasant ones. She knew that her irrational thinking was so unfair to Chris. He was a nice guy who probably didn't sleep with a girl on the first date. Maybe she was his first date since the death of his wife. Cassia's cell phone began vibrating on the table. It continued its mini spasm as it made its way off the table to the floor. She was glad that she had spent the few extra dollars on the protective case. She picked up the undamaged phone from the floor. The call was short. Chris informed Cassia that it was 12:01 a.m., already the next day. He was calling to invite her out for a second date.

Chris made a second call. It was to Maura. He gushed about his date with Cassia and thanked her for her earlier advice. He did admit that he was a little disappointed that Cassia did not seem impressed about his "very cool" car. Maura did not really want to hear about how great Chris's date went but was happy when he remembered how she drooled over his Mustang the first time that she saw it. She made a mental note to find out more about the car so that she could start an intelligent technical conversation about his "baby" the next time she made an excuse about needing a ride. She decided to never pretend that her car was broken down again because the last time she did, Chris got to her house and insisted on checking out the car. Her face was redder than her crimson-colored hair when the car's engine turned over. She told Chris that she had no idea why it did not start for her. Chris was clueless to Maura's lie. He suggested that perhaps she had gotten some bad gas and for her to add a bottle of gas treatment to the tank the next time she filled up. Before they hung up, Chris commented that he was looking forward to his second date with Cassia. Maura threw her cell phone across the room. It shattered the screen.

CHAPTER FORTY-TWO

Day 5—June 16, 2006

SINCE CASSIA'S PHONE CONVERSATION WITH Chris, her anger was replaced with a moment of serenity. She closed her eyes and inhaled the cherry tobacco aroma that had been hovering like a thin mist in the air since she walked into Ashby House. Chills ran through her body. Her lips still tingled on the spot where Chris tenderly placed his earlier. Every tiny sound resonated through her—the swishing of the blades on the ceiling fan above her head, the hum of the refrigerator's compressor, and the echoes from the crashes of the distant thunder of an impending storm rolling in.

Cassia ignored the spilled contents of her purse on the kitchen table, forgetting about the note that the waitress Josie slipped to her at the restaurant. It was now tangled in the scattered mess on the table. She was happy but tired. Cassia picked up her cell phone and a flashlight. She climbed the stairs to the second floor. Standing in the doorway looking into her bedroom, she contemplated moving all her things into one of the guest rooms. Sleeping on a queen-size bed would be nice. When she went into the bathroom, she saw her many toiletry items lined up on the sink and decided to stay put. Cassia positioned a headband in her hair to keep it from getting wet while she washed her face. Leaning over the sink, she avoided eye contact with the mirror. After washing the day off her face, she put on her pajamas. The thunder and lightning were now upon Ashby House. Cassia looked out the window toward the weeping willow tree. Every few seconds, the flashes of light illuminated the grounds of Ashby House, enabling the blackness of night to disappear and let daylight return for just a few seconds at a time with each burst. Jonathan Welts was nowhere in sight. Cassia could not understand why the once excited ladybugs in her stomach were now causing a disturbing sensation, close to nausea.

Before getting into bed, Cassia positioned her cell phone and flashlight within arm's reach on the table next to her bed. Despite the crashing of thunder and blazes of relentless lightning, she fell asleep. Her peaceful sleep was immediately violated. A nightmare began—only this one was new. Cassia was called to the stage as a contestant on the game show *The Price Is Right*. Cassia rushed excitedly toward the stage until the host, Bob Barker, introduced the other three contestants—Jewel, Annabelle, and a beautiful woman wearing a sign that said, "Chris' perfect wife." They are all dressed in stilettos and sexy black lingerie. Bob Barker ignores Cassia. He showers all his attention on the other three ladies, sometimes becoming a little too friendly. The three women laughed at his advances all the while smirking at Cassia. Bob Barker then announced, "It's time for the Showcase Showdown." A huge multicolored wheel is pushed onto the stage by Grandma B. She too is wearing stilettos and sexy lingerie. Her face is the same, but her body is that of an extremely endowed younger woman. The wheel contained slots with various dollar amounts ranging from one penny to one dollar. Bob Barker patted Grandma B on the butt. She laughed and left the stage.

Annabelle spun the wheel. The *boop, boop, boop, boop* sound of the wheel spinning seemed to go on forever. Finally, the large red arrow stopped on a $1 slot. Annabelle stepped aside. Jewel stepped up for the next turn spinning the wheel. It quickly stopped on $1. And Chris's wife stepped up, spun the wheel, and the red arrow stopped on $1. Cassia ran toward the wheel and lost her balance and tripped over her black floppy clown shoes. She fell into the wheel causing it to spin. All of the amounts on the wheel became penny amounts. Bob Barker, Annabelle, Jewel, Chris's wife, and the entire audience laughed and pointed at Cassia while she made several attempts to get up from the floor.

Chris appeared from behind curtain number one. He was escorted offstage before he could reach Cassia. Bob Barker yelled that he was disqualified from the game. Mitch then came out from behind curtain number two. He too is escorted offstage before he could reach Cassia. Cassia was still on the floor. She looked up, and Mitch was wearing a tuxedo and standing next to Jewel. Her outfit was now a sexy white nightie with a white bridal veil over her face. She was holding a bouquet of sunflowers in her hand. Bob Barker began performing their wedding ceremony. Uncle Charles entered the stage from door number three. He helped Cassia to her feet. When Cassia turned around to thank him, he was laid out in a coffin that appeared on stage. Raymond came out next. He was holding his briefcase rapidly turning the tumblers until it unlocked. When it opened, a dozen while gloved hands emerged. Raymond and the hands hoisted the coffin into the air and carried it off the stage.

Cassia's attention returned to Bob Barker, who began announcing, "If anyone can show just cause why these two lovely people should not be wed, speak now or never." A weeping willow tree started slithering onto the stage. It picked up speed and began crawling up Cassia's body. It covered her mouth. Bob Barker stopped the ceremony and looked at Cassia. "Aww, the clown can't speak. Poor clown." Everyone on stage and in the audience laughed and pointed at Cassia. Cassia was unable to break the branches to free herself from the tree. After pronouncing that Mitch and Jewel were husband and wife, Bob Barker began lecturing the crowd on spaying and neutering pets before he waved goodbye to the crowd. An unseen audience member shouted, "When are you getting neutered, Bob Barker?" He ignored the comment and left the stage. The "Macarena" song began playing. Grandma B, Jewel, Annabelle, and Chris's wife formed a line on stage and invited Cassia to dance with them. The tree branches disappeared. Cassia moved toward the women. She did not join them in their line but stood facing them. They started dancing, each exposing their pregnant bellies to her. Cassia was startled out of her nightmare by a knocking sound.

Cassia sat up in her bed. The knocking sound started again. It was coming from inside the "munchkin" closet. Cassia placed her hands on the doorknob. The nauseous feeling started getting worse. Cassia had believed that Jonathan Welts was gone, but the sickening feeling told her that something evil was still around. She closed her eyes and asked her mother to please not let him be in the closet. Cassia turned the handle.

At first Cassia saw nothing but darkness when she opened the door. She reached over to the nightstand for the flashlight and shined it into the closet. The beam from the flashlight illuminated three figures huddled in the backend corner of the closet—a black man and woman holding onto a black little girl about five or six years old. They were shoeless and dressed in dirty tattered clothing. The little girl whispered, "We need to get to the basement, but he's down there."

Cassia no longer felt ladybugs in her gut but now trembled all over. She said, "Who is in the basement?"

"Mista Jonathan."

Cassia did not want to believe that Jonathan Welts was in the basement. Besides, even when he was here, he never came into the house. Cassia offered to escort them to the basement after several attempts to convince them to go down on their own. They agreed. Cassia put on her robe and slippers and slowly moved down the stairs. She stood for a few seconds outside the basement door before opening it. She flicked on the light switch and slowly stepped onto the first step. She stopped and turned around. The man, woman, and little girl were still behind her with the same frightened look on their faces.

Cassia took a long breath. She slowly moved down the remainder of the steps. As they reached the last step, a shadowy figure emerged from behind the wine rack. The little girl screamed. Her mother and father took hold of her and ran toward the back wall of the basement. They vanished. Cassia stood frozen for a second looking into the angry eyes of Jonathan Welts. She turned away from him. Now gasping for air, she struggled to climb the stairs. Cassia felt his coldness closely behind her, but she never turned around. When Cassia reached the top of the stairs, Frederick was standing at the basement door with his arms folded in front of him. She ran past him and then stopped to catch her breath. She slowly turned around. Frederick stood at the basement door with his arms folded in front of him just like he did when Cassia attempted to approach his wife. Jonathan turned around and headed back down the basement stairs.

Cassia had seen enough. She ran up the stairs to her bedroom and locked the door knowing well that would not keep any spirits from entering the room, but it gave her some security nonetheless. With shaking hands, Cassia removed her mother's brooch from her purse. She held it tightly for about a minute. When she released the brooch from her grasp, it left a message in the palm of her hand—S-A-F-E.

Cassia sat on the bed rocking back and forth like she always did whenever she had a nightmare even though she was fully awake during her latest encounter with Jonathan Welts. She was worried. She was not sure her mother could protect her anymore. Maybe it was her mother who sent Frederick to help her. She started rethinking her plan of keeping Ashby House. Cassia checked the time on her cell phone. It was three o'clock in the morning. She considered calling Chris but once again felt that it was not the right time to let him in on all her secrets. Besides, he might think she was crazy. Sometimes she too wondered if she was. Cassia turned on every light in the room. She hoped the glow would keep her from falling asleep again. She was not sure what was worse—being awake and facing the demon Jonathan Welts or falling asleep and perhaps facing more demons in her nightmares. Within a short period of time, despite the lights on in the room, Cassia lost her battle with the conscious world and faced Lily Roberts in another dream. They walked side by side through a green meadow.

"Miss Roberts, why won't Jonathan leave Ashby House?"

Lily Roberts picked up a blade of grass and rubbed it between her fingers. She said, "My boy is scared. He done so many bad things in his life. He afraid to go toward the light."

Cassia woke to the beeping of her cell phone alarm. The sun was shining in her eyes. It was a welcomed sight.

CHAPTER FORTY-THREE

CASSIA'S EYES SCANNED THE ROOM before getting out of bed. She did not go downstairs for coffee but instead got into the shower. She then dressed for her nine o'clock appointment at the bank with Raymond. When coming down the stairs, she stared at the basement door and cautiously walked into the kitchen. She gathered up the contents of her purse. The plain white piece of folded paper that Josie had slipped to Cassia the night before at the bar lay next to her wallet. Cassia opened and read the note, "Call me if you need help. Josephina 804-555-1666." Cassia wondered, *Help with what?* Did she have something to say about Chris? Cassia shook her head. She had enough mysteries to solve and did not have time to try and decipher this cryptic message right now. She folded up the note and stuffed it into her purse.

Driving to the bank, Cassia made several changes to her to-do list in her head. She would stop at the hospital to see Annabelle before her lunch with Peaches. In front of the bank while waiting for Raymond, Cassia took her pen out of her purse and began writing her day's activities.

She always felt better seeing her schedule in ink. Cassia then pulled out the folded note from Josie. She read it again. Looking up from the paper, Raymond was standing by her window with his briefcase in his hand.

The bank manager shook Raymond's hand. He extended his hand out to Cassia introducing himself as Mr. Winters. He led them to his office and motioned for them to sit down. He was ready with all the papers necessary to transfer Uncle Charles's accounts to Cassia's control. Mr. Winters was a talker, so the hour of business turned into two hours. Cassia was surprised to hear Raymond converse so easily with Mr. Winters since he always appeared disinterested and closed-mouth whenever she tried to engage him in any small talk. She guessed talking business was easier for him but was confused because within the business talk, there was also a fair amount of personal conversation between him and Mr. Winters. She then realized that the personal conversation taking place was mostly one-sided only—Raymond listened while Mr. Winters talked about his family and his life. Raymond shook Mr. Winters's hand before leaving the bank. Cassia did the same with her right hand while her left hand held onto an overstuffed large envelope with copies of everything that she signed. Leaving the bank, Cassia thought that maybe it was time to approach Raymond about what he knew about her paternity, but he hurried to his car before Cassia could start the conversation.

Cassia waved to Raymond as his car exited the bank parking lot. She was not sure if he waved back because of his dark tinted windows. She started the engine to her car. The mall across the street was calling to her. Besides, she had to try out her new debit card. She would visit Annabelle later.

Cassia placed three items totaling nine hundred dollars in purchases in the back of her car. As usual, she pulled the shield over the items like she always did whenever she had things of value in her car. Cassia scolded herself for walking through the baby department on the way out of the store. She looked at the baby clothes lined up in neat rows. As usual, a salesperson asked if she needed any help. And as usual, she fought back tears and said, "No, thank you."

Cassia started her car and worked at shifting the gears in her head to place herself in another frame of mind to prepare for whatever might happen with Peaches Winchester. Mild nervousness turned into panic when Cassia realized that she had forgotten her list of the questions that she wanted to ask Peaches. Not accustomed to just winging it, for the next ten minutes left on her ride, Cassia rewrote most of the questions on her mental tablet in her head. She would first express again her condolences for the loss of her son. Then let Peaches begin the conversation hoping that whatever Peaches might say offers her an easy segue into her questions about Ashby House,

Uncle Charles, her mother, and her paternity. Cassia believed that Peaches Winchester could hold the answers to all of her questions. She was not aware that Peaches would let a skeleton out of her closet that would change everything.

CHAPTER FORTY-FOUR

Peaches Winchester answered the door looking very much like she did in her portrait hanging on the wall in the den at Ashby House. She was just a little older and grayer. Cassia studied her face. Like in the portrait, Peaches's eyes matched Cassia's. Now up close, Cassia saw matching high cheekbones and identical puny lips—well, that's what Cassia called them. Cassia's lips were average by all standards, but she was always searching for the newest lip-pumping product on the market. Peaches smiled while removing a gardening glove from her right hand. She extended her right hand to Cassia. She smiled. Cassia smiled back, lowering her eyes to keep Peaches from noticing any familiarity in them. She anticipated that Peaches would be "dressed to the nines" like Grandma B did whenever someone came for lunch. Much to Cassia's surprise, Peaches's petite frame was dressed in khaki-colored capri pants, a bright-yellow blouse, and white tennis shoes. No jewelry. Cassia felt appropriately dressed in her black pants and mint-green belted blouse.

"Please come in," Peaches said while moving aside to let Cassia enter. Her quiet voice fit her tiny frame. Her house was nowhere near as grand as Ashby House, but Cassia could see an Ashby House–like style, like the bookshelf full of books that covered the entire wall in the room and the Bible on the coffee table where Peaches led her to be seated. It was *her* Bible—well, not hers, but it looked the same as the one in the den at Ashby House. Was it the one from Ashby House? If it was, how did it get here? Peaches excused herself to retrieve the drinks and sandwiches that she had prepared earlier. As soon as she was out of sight, Cassia opened the Bible, looking for Elizabeth's letter. The letter was not there, but the Bible was the one from Ashby House. As Cassia was closing the book, Peaches entered the room carrying a tray with their lunch. She said, "You've probably seen Charlie's Bible in the den at Ashby House. Everyone in the family has their own. Come, let's go out to the terrace. It is a beautiful day."

Cassia immediately felt bad about forgetting the first item on her list—expressing her condolences to Peaches. She was puzzled. Peaches seemed so upbeat considering that her son had been gone for only two weeks. She decided that people grieved in their own way. Perhaps Peaches was a private person, and inside she was really a wreck. Cassia helped Peaches remove the items from the tray to the table. She motioned for Cassia to take a seat. She sat across the small round table and poured their ice tea from the tall pitcher.

Cassia took the glass of tea from Peaches. "I am so sorry for your loss, Mrs. Winchester."

"Thank you, my dear. Please call me Peaches."

"Okay, I will." Peaches handed Cassia a plate for her to begin choosing from the variety of sandwiches that were prepared. The items on the table—finger sandwiches, scones, jellies, and creams—reminded Cassia of the tea parties that Grandma B would have when Cassia was a child. Cassia finished her first sandwich. She waited for Peaches to begin just as she had planned.

Peaches said, "Raymond tells me that you are a wedding planner in Baltimore. How did you get involved with the business?"

"When I finished college with a degree in psychology, I had no idea what I was going to do with it. Then, I was invited to a friend's wedding. Up until then, I had never been to a wedding where everything was precisely planned and applied so meticulously. The bride later told me that because the planning was left to a professional, she and everyone else were able to relax and enjoy the wedding. I got in touch with the wedding planner and shadowed her through the process. After a couple of weddings, she hired me."

Peaches said, "Will you be going back to your job in Baltimore?"

Cassia answered as honestly as she could at that moment, "I'm not sure."

Peaches then asked about her family back in Baltimore. Cassia answered without giving too many details except to say that she did not have much family except for a grandmother who lived in a retirement village not far from where she lived. The remainder of the conversation during lunch included small talk about the weather and the wicked thunderstorms that had been rolling in through the area almost every day lately. It seemed that today would not be any different. The white puffy clouds that were overhead when Cassia first arrived were now being replaced with dark ominous storm clouds. Perhaps they followed Cassia from Ashby House. Cassia finished her last bite of scone. She placed her napkin down on her plate. At once, the wind increased, lifting Cassia's napkin from her plate. It landed on the grassy area. While Cassia chased the napkin, Peaches gathered everything else onto the tray and said, "Let's go inside."

In the kitchen, Peaches told Cassia that she would take care of the dishes after the storm. Peaches led the way back to the sitting area where they were before lunch. Cassia tried to muster any remnants that she could remember from her psychology lessons to help with an analysis of this woman, but she had trouble reading Peaches so far. She seemed nice enough, but Cassia was not sure how she would react to talk about Ashby House and the other hard topics that she wanted to cover.

When they reached the sitting area, Peaches sat in the spot where Cassia was earlier. She patted her hand on the space next to her. "Come sit next to me."

Peaches picked up the Bible from the table. She opened it to the pages that listed the family tree. She pointed to the title on the first page. "This is not the Winchester family Bible. This Bible belongs to me and the Lawson family—my family." Peaches turned the page that listed the family tree.

Lawson Family

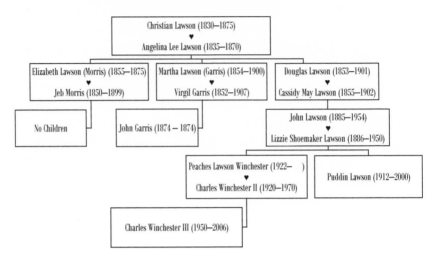

Peaches said, "Ashby House was once called Lawson Estates. My late husband changed the name in 1951. He was a good businessman but not a very good family man. Charles had a mean streak. It came to the surface whenever things did not go his way. Charlie and I walked on eggshells around him especially when he had a bad day at work. I wanted to sell the house when it was passed down to me by my father. Charlie's father was hell-bent on us staying there. He was all about status. As soon as he passed away, I was out of there."

"Don't you like the house?" Cassia asked.

Peaches closed the Bible and placed it back onto the table. She turned and faced Cassia, looking into her eyes while taking both of her hands. Peaches leaned in closer to Cassia like Uncle Charles did when he told her a story. Peaches whispered, "Those ghosts in that house scare the shit out of me."

Peaches abruptly let go of Cassia's hands. She got up from the couch. She began pacing back and forth across the room. Cassia was not sure if looking into Cassia's eyes had anything to do with her sudden agitation. Peaches continued, "I turned the house over to Charlie. I moved into this place where I have peace and quiet. I have probably been back to Ashby House only about a half dozen times since I moved out. Charlie has always loved Ashby House, and he has always seen them, even when he was a child. My son is brilliant. I love him, but he is an odd sort of fellow. And I don't mean anything negative when I say that. You see, the truth is Charlie never had many friends, so he saw the ghosts as playmates, even when he got older."

Cassia said, "I see them too." It was the perfect time for Cassia to begin telling her own truths.

CHAPTER FORTY-FIVE

Cassia was ready to begin her story about Uncles Charles's relationship with her parents, and of course Grandma B's relationship with Peaches's husband. However, before she could say a word, Peaches opened the Bible again. She pulled out an envelope. She once again sat next to Cassia. In the envelope were about a dozen pictures. She said, "Cassia, my great-great-granddaddy Christian used slaves to build what you know as Number Six Ashby House. Many renovations and additions had been made since its initial construction." Peaches showed Cassia the first seven pictures. They were old, yellowed, and faded, showing Ashby House during different phases throughout the years. Cassia knew that they were all of Ashby House because she recognized the unmistakable six columns standing tall at the entrance of the house. Peaches handed Cassia another picture. It was a white man standing next to a black man. Though she had never seen the white man before, Cassia recognized the black man.

Peaches continued, "I believe that around the time this photo was taken, ideas about slavery were changing in many people's minds. My great-great-grandparents Christian and Angelina Lawson owned slaves but offered them protection. Sure, they worked hard, but they were treated like people, not property. They were provided for better than many slaves on other plantations. Eventually, Christian and Angelina joined the abolitionist movement, hiding slaves in a secret room in the basement. In the dark of night, they transported slaves to the north. They even offered freedom to their own slaves. Some went north, and others stayed because they were afraid of the unknown. Many stayed just to keep their families together."

Cassia pointed to the black man in the picture. She said, "I've seen this man and his wife at Ashby House. I believe his name is Frederick."

Peaches replied, "Yes, the man standing next to my great-great-granddaddy Christian is Frederick. He and his wife were house slaves. They were bought together at auction. When Christian discovered that Frederick had been educated by his previous owner who passed away, he was given the job as tutor for his three children. His wife became their mammy. The story that has been handed down from generation to generation was that Angelina and Christian were gone from the plantation so often that their three children Elizabeth, Martha, and Douglas became more attached to their black mammy and less to their own mother. Angelina became so jealous of her children's desire to be with this black woman over her. After the signing of the Emancipation Proclamation, Angelina sent her children away to stay with a family member for a few months. When the children returned, Frederick and his wife were gone. They were released from service. They never got the chance to say goodbye to the children. They never saw them again."

Peaches showed Cassia the next picture. It was a faded picture of a black man chopping wood. Cassia could not make out his face on the old photo but believed that it was a picture of Jonathan.

Cassia inhaled and exhaled. "Is that Jonathan Welts?"

Peaches nodded. "Yes, my great-great-granddaddy Christian heard stories about the famous—or should I say infamous slave Jonathan (Roberts) Welts. He had been purchased by a neighboring plantation owner and had run away three time. Every time he was caught, he was beaten so severely. Christian offered to buy him for the same amount that was paid for him at auction. Wanting to get rid of the unruly slave, the plantation owner agreed. Jonathan was delivered to what is now called Number Six Ashby House. He was about as broken as a man could be. After healing from his beatings, Christian made a deal with him. He would put him in charge of planting and harvesting that year's crop. If he did a good job as overseer, Christian would help him to freedom by the following spring. Jonathan agreed."

Cassia said, "What about the stories that Uncle Charles told me about Jonathan beating other slaves in the barn. Were they true?"

"Unfortunately, they were. When he was a young child, Jonathan saw his mother as she was being repeatedly raped and beaten and left for dead by her boyfriend and his friends after he was told that she had been having sex with another black slave. When Jonathan got older, any black man who reminded him of those men, he would beat to a pulp. So, when Christian and Angelina were out on their runs to the north, Jonathan would routinely beat other slaves in the barn. He threatened to kill their families if they told on him."

Cassia sank back into the chair. "It now makes sense. I could not figure out why Jonathan beat other black slaves." Peaches handed Cassia another picture. She recognized one of the women in the picture. It was Elizabeth as a young girl. The other girl was about the same age. Cassia had never seen her before.

Pointing to the girl on the right in the picture, Peaches said, "This one is Elizabeth, and the girl on the left is her sister, Martha. Frederick and his wife were put in charge of the two girls and their brother, Douglas."

Cassia told Peaches about her encounters with Elizabeth and about finding a letter tucked inside the Bible at Ashby House. Cassia shook her head. "I wish I could find out why Elizabeth is so unhappy. And I think Frederick and his wife want out of Ashby House now that Uncle Charles is gone. I just don't know how to help them."

Peaches said, "Many years ago, I hired a local woman who claimed that she had some type of sixth sense and she could help me. She came and walked around the house burning sage. She claimed that smudging the house would rid it of its spirits. I can't remember her name, but I think I still have her card with her number in the kitchen somewhere. Let me get it for you." As she was in the kitchen, she said, "Oh yeah, her name was Josephina."

The storm that quickly came through with such vengeance pretty much exited with the same speed. However, Cassia still heard low grumblings of thunder far off somewhere in the distance. The noise muffled Peaches's last words. Cassia said, "Did you say that the woman's name was Josephina?" Cassia dug the note that Josie had slip into Cassia's hand at the restaurant. Peaches returned to the room and handed Cassia the card with Josephina's name and number. Cassia held the note and card side by side in her hand. They matched.

Cassia folded the paper and returned both the card and paper to her purse. She believed that it was now time to find out how much Peaches really knew about her family's connection to the Winchesters. Cassia took a deep breath and exhaled as much air that her lungs would release. She said, "Peaches, do you know why your son named me in his will to inherit Ashby House?"

Peaches replied with certainty, "Yes, you are his heir."

CHAPTER FORTY-SIX

FROM THE MOMENT THAT CASSIA arrived for lunch, Peaches longed to embrace her—her granddaughter. Now that the secret of Cassia's paternity was out in the open, Peaches reached out to her granddaughter and hugged her for the first time. Both women were teary-eyed when they finished. They laughed while wiping their eyes. When Peaches finally composed herself, she said, "When Charlie told me a long time ago about your ability to see the ghosts, I was confused because up until that time, only those with Lawson blood running through them saw the spirits. I only found out about your paternity about a month ago when Charlie told me the story about your mother and father."

Cassia was still enjoying the remaining warmth from Peaches's embrace. She thought about the last time that Grandma B hugged her. It was when she lost the baby, but Cassia was too numb to feel anything during that time. Cassia did not want to spoil the moment, but her longing to get everything out on the table overrode her desire to keep her mouth shut.

"How much do you know about my mother?"

Peaches said, "I know that she wanted a baby so badly and that she and your father were heartbroken when they were unable to conceive. That's when they asked Charlie for his help."

Cassia pulled the ladybug brooch out of her purse. She handed it to Peaches. "There is more about my mother that I need you to know."

Peaches always wore her heart on her sleeve, and this time was no different. Her emerald-green eyes filled with tears at the sight of the brooch. Cassia immediately regretted causing her so much pain, but it was too late. Peaches took the brooch and held it in her hand. She said, "I gave this brooch to your mother." Peaches stared straight ahead. Her voice became fainter as if the words were not meant for Cassia to hear, "I remember that day like it was yesterday." Peaches did not go into the story that the brooch was an "I'm sorry" gift from her husband trying to cover up another one of his many affairs. Cassia saw the pain in Peaches's face. Cassia wanted to stop. She did not want to cause her anymore hurt, but once again her need to bring all the truths and all the lies to the surface overrode her desire to show any mercy.

Cassia said, "Do you know that my mother's maiden name was *Brittle*? Catherine Brittle was her mother and is my grandmother."

The brooch slid from Peaches's fingers and dropped to the floor. She said, "No, Charlie never told me. Then again, why would he?" Cassia reached down to retrieve the brooch from the floor.

Peaches said, "So, your mother was my husband's illegitimate child?" With her eyes now staring at the floor, she said, "I had no idea, Cassia." Peaches thought about the day when she received that phone call from Catherine Brittle blaming her family for Marianne's death. Peaches began speaking just as fast as her mind was racing, "Cassia, when did your grandmother find about Charlie donating his sperm so that your mother and father could have a child?"

"My mother told my grandmother when she was already three or four months pregnant. After my mother died giving me life, my grandmother believed that her daughter's death was her fault and her punishment for having the affair with your husband. When I became pregnant, she told my husband the entire story that she believed, and I think she convinced him too that I would die giving birth because of what she called her 'sins.' Instead, the baby died when I was six months along. My marriage died a short time later. My ex-husband just recently revealed all this to me."

Peaches once again took Cassia's hands. She smiled and said, "Your grandmother has it all wrong. After finding out about my husband's affair with her, I wanted revenge. So, I sought out a gentlemen friend of the family, and we had a one-night stand. When I got home, I flaunted the affair in Charles's face thinking that might cure him of his own cheating. It did not. A few weeks later I discovered that I was pregnant."

Peaches got up from the couch and filled two snifters with brandy. She kept one and handed the other to Cassia. Peaches continued her story while pacing back and forth in the room. "We both knew that the child was not Charles's because we were sleeping in separate bedrooms during that time. To protect my husband's career and our social status, we decided to raise Charlie as a Winchester. We never told anyone. And Charlie never questioned his paternity because I have shown him pictures of my father, and he is the spitting image of him. He always liked the idea of being more of a Lawson than a Winchester."

Cassia finished Peaches's next thought, "So Uncles Charles and my mother were never blood related." Cassia thought about how tormented her grandmother must have been all these years believing that in some twisted way, she was responsible for her own daughter's death and maybe her great-granddaughter's death too. Cassia felt a little guilty about thinking perhaps she deserved some of that torture but knew that she would tell her grandmother the truth—*eventually.*

Peaches shared with Cassia pictures of Charles and her father. The resemblance was uncanny. She then showed a picture of her mother, Lizzie, and her sister, Puddin', who died several years ago. Afterward, Peaches walked Cassia to the door. They hugged, and Peaches made Cassia promise that she would visit on Saturday. She had a few more things to share with her. Before leaving, Cassia turned to Peaches. "Why Ashby House? When your husband changed the name of the house from Lawson Estates, why Ashby House? Why not Winchester House or Winchester Estates?"

Peaches picked up a notepad and pen from the small table in the foyer. She said, "Charles changed the name as a punishment for my affair. He could not humiliate me publicly because it would also have brought him shame, so he found a way to hurt me. He knew how important my family name was to me." She wrote on the paper.

A=A
S=SHAMEFUL
H=HOUSE
B=BE
Y=YOURS

Cassia held the paper in her hand. "Why the number six?"

"Charles knew that I had this odd obsession with the number six. I believed then—and still believe today—that the number six is bad luck."

Cassia sat in her car playing over and over in her head Peaches's confession about Uncle Charles's paternity. She picked up her phone and dialed Mitch's number, but his phone was still turned off. While Cassia was trying to reach Mitch, Peaches was inside making a phone call too.

She said, "Yes, she just left. She is so sweet and beautiful." There was a pause, and then Peaches continued, "No, no, she doesn't suspect anything. Everything is fine on this end, but listen, my dear, I have to tell you something really important. First, I want to begin by saying how sorry I am to have kept this from you all these years."

CHAPTER FORTY-SEVEN

Cassia called Annabelle's phone. She asked if she was up for visitors because she was only twenty minutes away from the hospital. Annabelle excitedly said, "That would be great. I have so much to tell you." Cassia continued on the short drive toward the hospital. Her thoughts returned to her visit with Peaches. Would Peaches eventually ask Cassia to call her *Grandmother* or some other form of endearment? Could she ever think of Peaches as her grandmother? Cassia was not sure what constituted being a grandmother, but there was one thing she was sure about—Peaches was so much warmer than Grandma B.

Cassia drove by and eyed up the mall on the other side of the highway. She decided that she could be in and out in ten or fifteen minutes. At the next light, Cassia made a U-turn. She found a parking space close to the entrance. This time instead of shopping for clothes, Cassia's mission was to purchase her first clock for Ashby House. It would be a *grand* grandfather clock like the one she imagined in her daydreams. Before turning off her car's engine, Cassia received a call from Chris. He asked if she had any objections to having dinner at his parents' home that evening at seven. Objections—yes, she had lots of objections but did not express them to Chris. She thought about Mitch's parents and how much she liked seeing them—*yeah, about once or twice a year.* So instead of clock shopping, Cassia purchased a "meet the parents" new outfit and of course a new pair of shoes. Her phone indicated another text. Chris was sending Cassia his parents' home address and a "looking forward to seeing you later" message. She did not respond.

Cassia dialed Annabelle's phone from the hospital gift shop. She apologized for taking so long and assured her that she would be there in just a few minutes. Cassia placed the basket of daisies on the nightstand next to Annabelle's bed. She bent over and hugged her friend, careful not to disturb her injured arm. Annabelle said, "You just missed Sunny. He did not want to leave me alone, but I convinced him to go because you were on your way."

Cassia got a good look at Annabelle. Despite her injuries, she looked wonderful. Even without an ounce of makeup, Annabelle had a natural glow—the pregnancy glow.

Cassia quietly said, "Is the baby okay?"

Annabelle touched her stomach. "All is well so far." She shook her head and smiled. "And that was not the way that I wanted my parents to find out about their first grandchild, but it all worked out because they were too pissed off at Robert to be angry at me and Sunny."

Cassia did not ask Annabelle if she shared with her parents the possibility that the baby might be Robert's. She let Annabelle do the talking. "I'm getting out of here tomorrow. Robert has been arraigned and held without bond pending a psych exam. I had no idea that he would ever try to kill me. Maybe he is crazy." Annabelle laughed. "At least I got a warning from this guy's wife who threatened to kill me if I didn't stop seeing her husband. That was a couple of years ago. Robert didn't even give me a warning."

Cassia and Annabelle looked at each other and burst into laughter. Annabelle cried out in pain holding her side but continued laughing. After a few seconds, she gained her composure. She then pressed her call button for the nurse and requested more pain medicine. There was something so out of control about Annabelle that Cassia could not help but love.

Cassia said, "Can you take pain medicine while pregnant? Is it safe for the baby?"

"My doctors discussed with me that there are a few meds that would not affect the baby, so I am given pain meds in moderation. I guess he or she will be getting happy pretty soon."

After Annabelle got a shot of pain medicine, she warned Cassia that she might fall asleep soon but asked her friend to stay and talk with her a little while longer. Cassia told Annabelle about her visit with Peaches but did not share any details about their conversation except to say that Peaches was a very nice lady. She would tell Annabelle another time because Cassia was still processing the information herself. Cassia did, however, elaborate on her story about meeting Chris. After filling Annabelle in on all the details of how they met, Cassia could not hide her uncertainty about continuing to see him. Cassia said, "He wants our third date to be a *family* dinner with parents. I am not up for that type of meeting just yet. When Mitch and I were together, it was just us—no family except once or twice a year. I liked it that way."

Annabelle's eyelids felt like weights were trying to close them. She fought hard to listen as intently as she could to Cassia's story. She finally chimed in, "Listen, Cass, you can't continue comparing every new relationship with the one you had with Mitch. You will never be able to move on that way. It sounds like you and Chris might have some heat between you. Give it a chance." Annabelle was beginning to slur her words a little. Cassia told Annabelle that she would think about what she just said and she would check back in with her soon. Cassia left the hospital remembering how Chris was standing outside when she left that night. She thought maybe there was something there worth exploring.

Cassia turned into the driveway of Ashby House. She craned her neck looking at the sign just like she did the first day that she arrived. Cassia smiled. Now that Ashby House was officially hers, she could change the name to whatever she wanted—Cassia's Castle? C's Mansion? Cassia Manor? Cassia began speaking as if she were an excited bride telling someone about where her wedding would take place, "We...we...are having our wedding at...at...the famous Cassia Manor, the greatest place ever." Cassia laughed. She knew that if she ever did change the name of Ashby House, she would check with Peaches before doing so, not because she had to, but because it would be the right thing to do. Cassia was so lost in thought that she did not see the car parked in the circular drive until she was almost completely down the driveway. She parked next to the unfamiliar vehicle.

Josie was standing on the step near the front door. She shouted to Cassia as she got out of her car, "Chris was at the Road Kill getting his afternoon coffee when he called you. When he got off the phone, he mentioned to me that you were on your way home, so I hope you don't mind that I just showed up."

Cassia removed her packages from the back of her vehicle. She said, "I saw Peaches Winchester this afternoon, and she told me about your earlier visit to Ashby House. I'm so glad to see you. I was going to call you this afternoon because I really do need some help."

Cassia opened the door. Josie followed her to the kitchen. It did not take long for Josie to transform into Josephina. Before Cassia could offer her a seat at the kitchen table, she turned around and saw that Josephina's eyes were closed. "I feel a tug-of-war going on with the spirits. While many of them want to go to the other side, something is keeping them here at Ashby House." Josephina opened her eyes and looked into Cassia's and said, "And there is one really nasty spirit here. He needs to go first."

Cassia told Josephina the story of Jonathan Roberts Welts and her most recent encounter with him in the basement. She continued, "His mother is the key to getting him to leave. She almost had him convinced, but he changed his mind at the last minute. Lily Roberts told me that her son is afraid of what might be waiting for him on the other side because of all the bad things he has done in his lifetime."

Josephina closed her eyes again and breathed in the cherry tobacco scent that hovered like a thick cloud over the kitchen. "There's someone here *very* protective of you."

Cassia said, "I think it's Frederick, the household slave who once lived here. He was standing at the top of the stairs and would not let Jonathan get by." Cassia thought again after being overwhelmed with the tobacco odor, "Or...maybe it's Uncle Charles protecting me."

Josephina opened her eyes again and assuredly said, "No, it's a female spirit."

Cassia thought about Elizabeth, or perhaps it was Frederick's wife, but she did not feel particularly close to either one of them. She then thought about Maddie's special bond with Elizabeth. It had to be Elizabeth. Cassia turned her thoughts back to Jonathan Welts. She was anxious to rid Ashby House of his spirit. As she asked Josephina where they should begin, the ladybugs began invading Cassia's stomach because she already knew the answer—the basement.

Josephina said, "If he's in the basement, that's where we need to go."

Cassia opened the basement door. She turned on the light and cautiously walked down the steps—one step, pause, one more step, pause. She continued this same motion for every step with Josephina mimicking her moves behind her. It was like they were trying to sneak up on Jonathan or perhaps trying to keep him from waking up. Josephina stopped on the next-to-the-last step and announced that he was indeed still in the basement, though she had not seen or heard him. She felt his presence.

Cassia moved off the last step. Jonathan came out from behind the wine rack like he did before. However, he did not look menacing like he did earlier. The anger that haunted every inch of his face was now replaced with resolve. Josephina said to him, "It's time for you to go."

Cassia added with a crackling voice, "Your mamma is waiting for you, Jonathan. There is nothing to be afraid of. She wants you to be with her."

A spirit came through the far wall, the same wall where the family disappeared into earlier. Lily walked over to Jonathan and took his hand. They disappeared through the wall together. Later, when Cassia and Josephina discussed the event, they could only agree on the fact that Lily came and got her son. What puzzled them both was that each recalled seeing something different during the event. Josephina saw a glowing Lily dressed in the usual white robe scenario that Hollywood has cashed in on as the look of people "going into the light." Cassia saw Lily like she had seen her at the graveyard and in her dreams, not in a glowing light but as a real person. The scar on her left cheek was gone. Cassia felt her happiness. She could not express or describe to Josephina how she knew that Lily was now happy, but something deep inside of Cassia just knew.

Before leaving, Josephina explained to Cassia that spirits stay in the place familiar to them. Sometimes they will return to a place where they were their happiest. Many will not go to the other side if they have unfinished business in this world. In Jonathan's case, he was afraid of what he might face on the other side. There is always a reason they stay. Cassia uncovered her ghost busting chart that had been partially covered up by her recent purchases. She took the chart off the table and headed to the den. Cassia opened the Bible. She removed Elizabeth's letter. From the desk, she removed Frederick's journal and the bag containing the needle guards. Cassia then placed the journal and the letter side by side on her chart. She was sure that the reason Frederick, his wife, and Elizabeth stayed at Ashby House had something to do with the items. There had to be a connection. Cassia carefully flipped through the old journal. She came to the last entry and read it aloud:

Summer, 1867

> *They are calling us freedmen. However, after initially rejoicing and celebrating this so-called freedom, I now have many fears. What was once some semblance of security where my former masters provided food and shelter, I am now faced with an uncertainty of survival as a free black southern man. I am trying to remain optimistic about the future. Today, there are two things that I am certain about. One, this new freedom comes with a price; and two, turning back is not an option.*
>
> *Without a place to live and without a job, every day is a struggle. I am grateful for the family that has taken us in. I'm willing to work but I've been offered only field work and very low wages. I am bitter. As my wife sits knitting, she tells me that bitterness is the work of the devil and the past cannot be changed. She says I should look to the future. Maybe she is right.*
>
> *I went into town today looking for work as a free black man but found many whites unfriendly and hostile toward me. I became afraid for my safety.*

Even though I gave them no reason to fear me, I sensed that some of them were afraid of me. Many would not make eye contact with me. Those who did gave me evil stares. Others just walked quickly away when I attempted to wish them good morning. I was angry at first until my wife reminded me that perhaps these changes are hard on them, too.

I am thankful to the person who secretly taught me the ABC's as a child while I was working for a master who was kind enough to look the other way. Well, at least for a while. This education has been a blessing and a curse. All of my life I have worked as a house servant and tutor and now I am offered only field work. At sixty-seven years old, I do not have the strong back needed to work the fields.

My wife refuses to go with me to ask our former master for help after the scene that the miss' caused before we left. I never knew the degree of jealousy this woman harbored against my wife because she believed that the children preferred her comforts over their own mother's. She provided care for the children, nursing them when they were sick, cooking meals, and knitting them socks and shawls to warm them in the winter; she loved them as her own. Maybe she loved them so much because she could not have children of her own. I've heard her cry in the night because she misses them. Her heart was broken because they never came down those steps to say goodbye. I could find peace in my heart if I knew that they had the same love for her.

Cassia looked up from her reading. Elizabeth was standing next to the wing-back chair. Frederick was standing in the doorway. His wife was standing behind him. Cassia had never seen the three spirits in such close proximity before. Cassia opened Elizabeth's letter. She scanned it for any clues connecting Frederick, his wife, and Elizabeth. She began reading the last paragraph of Elizabeth's letter.

> *I, too, my dearest sister am upset about the freeing of our black slaves, especially the loss of our Mammy. I cannot believe that she is gone. My heart is broken because she never said goodbye. Remember the beautiful shawls she knitted for us? Every time I look at mine I cry because I miss her so.*
>
> *Your loving sister,*
> *Elizabeth*

Cassia placed the letter back on the desk. She looked up and said, "Oh my god, Elizabeth, you have been heartbroken all these years thinking that your mammy did not care enough to stay or when she left to even say goodbye. It was your momma who made her leave." Cassia pointed to Frederick's wife, who was now inside the room. "And you never knew that Elizabeth's momma sent the children away so they could not say goodbye to you. She was so jealous of your relationship with her children."

Frederick smiled. He walked over to Elizabeth. He took her hand. Frederick's wife touched Elizabeth's face with her right hand. Elizabeth smiled at the woman. She held on tightly to the shawl that Frederick's wife had made for her many years ago. Cassia got up from the desk. She watched the three spirits walk arm in arm down the hallway as their essences became more and more translucent until they totally disappeared.

Cassia should have felt content, but instead she was confused. Were they really gone? It did not seem as final as when Jonathan exited with his mother through the basement wall. Maybe she did not want them gone. Cassia sat back at the desk. She looked down at her ghost busting chart. With a black Sharpie, she drew a huge X across the poster board. She sank into the large desk chair. The ladybugs, the ones in her stomach that always alerted her to either something really good or something really bad, were fluttering out of control. Cassia tried to ignore the chaos going on in her gut. She checked the time on her cell phone. "Oh shit, it's five thirty. I'm going to be late if I don't get ready now." Cassia got up from the chair. She felt weak. Cassia grabbed her stomach. She convinced herself that the idea of seeing Chris again had caused this latest trembling. While she was excited at the thought of seeing Chris, the thought of spending the evening with his family, a group of strangers when he was still a stranger too, lessened her excitement.

Cassia made her way to the wing-back chair. She gave herself permission to sit for just a couple more minutes. She closed her eyes. Lily Roberts took her hand. She was smiling. Cassia said, "Why are you still here? And why are you so happy?"

Cassia thought about what Josephina had told her that her protector was a female. Could it be that Lily Roberts was her protector? Lily said, "I have a gift for you—for helping me get back my son." Lily moved aside. Cassia saw a woman—it was someone she only saw in pictures. Cassia remembered the last message that appeared in her hand from the brooch—S-A-F-E. Her mother had been with her all along. She hugged her so tight.

CHAPTER FORTY-EIGHT

CASSIA WAS SOBBING WHEN SHE woke to the sound of her cell phone alarm. She had set it earlier as a reminder to get ready for her date with Chris. She looked around the room for any traces of her dream. The room was quiet. The stillness in the room made her sad, but she thought about what Josephina had said about how people from beyond reach out in various ways. Some find enough energy to actually appear like Elizabeth, Frederick, and his wife. Then there are some who reach out in dreams and even daydreams. Some reach out in less obvious ways like when a toy or music box starts playing in a quiet room without any prompting, or finding something that you are looking for in the exact place where you have looked a thousand times, or missing someone so much that you think you are going to die, then that person's favorite song comes on the radio, but instead of making you sadder, it brings comfort.

Cassia reached for a tissue from the box on the table. She dabbed her tears away and checked the time on her cell phone. It was 6:15. Cassia felt zapped of energy. She was sure that her tear-soaked face would not be presentable for any public viewing. She dialed Chris's number and apologized for cancelling on him at the last minute but she had a terrible headache. The truth was not too far off because all her crying did make her head ache, but it was her heart aching more. Even though Chris made her promise that she would reschedule the dinner with his family soon, Cassia was not sure if he was being polite and if he would ever call again.

Cassia got up from her chair. She went to the kitchen and made a snack of cheese and crackers. Cassia took a bottle of wine from the rack and looked at the label out of habit before opening it and pouring herself a glass. She was certain that Raymond got only the finest quality wines. She raised her glass and toasted Uncle Charles before taking a sip. She waited for a response, but not even the scent of Uncle Charles's cherry tobacco filled the air this time. Cassia was cautiously optimistic that the spirits had found their way home. But she was a little sad too because Ashby House was so dead now.

Cassia walked into the living room. She placed her wine and cheese and crackers on the table next to the couch. She started a list in her head of the changes that she would soon be making in the room. Again, clocks and a television were the first two items. Cassia took a second sip of wine and placed her glass back on the table. The silence in the room let in the far-off sound of gravel pinging against tires. She was expecting no one. Cassia got up from her seat and looked out the window. It was Chris's Mustang making its way down the drive. Cassia ran into the bathroom, splashed water on her face, and dried it with a towel before going to the door. She watched Chris exit his vehicle. He closed the car door with his elbow because his hands were full. He was carrying an aluminum foil–covered plate in each hand. He smiled a wide grin when he saw Cassia.

He shouted out while holding the plates tightly between his fingers and walking toward Cassia, "How are you feeling? I hope you don't mind, but since you could not come to dinner, dinner is coming to you." Before Cassia could answer, Chris was at the top of the step leaning in and kissed her on the lips. He then took turns lifting one plate higher than the other. "This was my mom's idea."

Cassia smiled. "Well, your mom has good ideas."

Cassia took one of the plates from Chris. She led him into the kitchen where Chris saw remnants of some sort of distress in Cassia's face. He placed the plate onto the table. "Are you okay?" Cassia had no intention of discussing the evening's events with him. She said, "I think the headache is almost gone. I'm hungry. Let's eat."

"Before we eat, I have a favor to ask." Chris continued, "It's about my car. I put a new windshield in it a couple of days ago, and I have to reseal it because I got a small leak going on. Can I put it in your garage just in case it rains?"

Cassia playfully handed Chris the garage remote. She pulled it back at the last minute and said, "We wouldn't want your *baby* to get wet, now would we?" Chris snatched the remote from Cassia and, throwing Cassia a fake smile, said, "Ha, ha, ha."

Cassia cleared the old to-do lists from the table. She made a neat pile on the far end of the counter. Chris returned from the garage. While Cassia retrieved her snacks from the living room, Chris already had the table set, candles lit, and two glasses of wine poured. When he saw Cassia's plate of cheese and crackers, he said, "Was that your dinner?"

Cassia looked at the plates on the table with stuffing peeking out from under slices of turkey smothered in gravy and mushrooms, mashed potatoes, and green beans with slithers of almonds throughout. Cassia crinkled her nose, looked at Chris, and said, "Cheese and crackers—*appetizers*." She smiled. "Now *this* is dinner. You must thank your mother for me." Ordinarily Cassia would have sent a thank-you note just like Grandma B taught her, but sending her thanks through Chris seemed appropriate this time even though she was sure that Grandma B would not have approved.

During their dinner, Chris did not question Cassia about her headache again. She looked better. Any traces of distress were now gone from her face. Cassia did most of the talking during dinner, filling Chris in on Annabelle's recovery and tidbits of her visit with Peaches Winchester, which led to her confessing her inheritance of Ashby House. Cassia realized that Chris was a good listener, never prying or making her disclose things that she was not ready to reveal. He just let her talk.

Cassia got up from the table and gathered the plates. She washed and dried them for Chris to return them to his mother. Chris cleared the remaining items from the table. He then finished his glass of wine and said, "How about a tour of your house?"

Cassia smiled. "Where would you like to start?"

She did not know Chris well enough to read his personal signals, but she was fairly certain she knew what he meant when he said, "How about starting upstairs?"

Cassia took Chris's hand, and they walked up the stairs. All thoughts of spirits and Mitch and Grandma B disappeared. She did, however, consciously pass up Uncle Charles's room and opted for one of the guest bedrooms. One day she might be able to stay in there, but not tonight.

There was not a "rip your clothes off" excitement like she experienced with Ollie. Instead it was a gentle gratifying experience. Cassia did not even try to compare it to her times with Mitch because she thought about what Annabelle had said to her earlier.

Chris held Cassia in his arms and kissed her forehead. She could sense that he had as much going through his mind as she did. He finally spoke, "I might have been a little rusty. This is the first time being with someone since my wife." Cassia could tell that he was uncomfortable after his confession. He then laughed. "Well, maybe it's like the bicycle thing—once you learn how to ride…" Cassia laughed. "Well, you're really good at bicycling." Chris held Cassia tightly. Within a few minutes, she felt his body relax and heard his shallow breathing that soon was replaced by light snoring. Cassia's mind did not allow her to fall asleep so quickly. She scolded herself for not having "the talk" with Chris about previous partners and birth control before they did anything. If Cassia had, it surely would have killed the mood. It was too late now. Cassia remembered a conversation that she had with Chris at the Road Kill where he stated that he and his wife did not want any more children after their daughter was born. Though he never said, Cassia convinced herself that Chris probably had a vasectomy after his daughter was born. That would have made sense. And he did confess that he had not been with anyone since his wife died, so she was sure that he was not the kind of guy that did a lot of sleeping around. She felt safe. Cassia drifted off to sleep without dreaming that night.

CHAPTER FORTY-NINE

Day 6—June 17, 2006

CASSIA WELCOMED THE MORNING SUNLIGHT. Her eyes shifted back and forth thoroughly examining the décor in the unfamiliar room as well as the unfamiliar curves of her lover's sleeping face. She smiled. Cassia contemplated pulling the top blanket off the bed to cover up her naked body but knew that type of jarring would definitely wake Chris, so she slipped out of bed and scurried like a jackrabbit across the room and out of the bedroom to retrieve her robe from her usual bedroom. Before going downstairs, Cassia peeked in on Chris. He was sitting up with his legs dangling over the side of the bed. He turned around when he heard the creaking of floorboards outside in the hall. "I once saw a streaker run across the field at a pro bowl game during halftime, and he was nowhere near as fast as you." They laughed.

Leaning against the doorway with her face a little rosy, Cassia said, "I was going to make you coffee and maybe even breakfast this morning, but after that remark, I'm not sure you deserve it."

Chris held out his hand to Cassia, and with a smile, he pulled her to him. "Can I make it up to you?"

Cassia stood in front of Chris. She untied her robe. Chris gently slipped it off her shoulders and watched it glide down her body until it hit the floor. He inhaled deeply. "You look a helluva lot better than any streaker I've ever seen." He pulled Cassia onto the bed and made love to her again.

Chris held onto Cassia. He wanted to tell her that he was falling for her but thought maybe it was too soon. The ringing of Cassia's cell phone downstairs distracted them from any type of serious conversation. Cassia sighed. "I need to get that. Whoever keeps calling is being very persistent." She slipped out of bed and whispered while putting on her robe, "Hope nothing happened to Grandma B."

Chris did not hear her last comment and did not attempt to cover up his naked body as he got out of bed. He began streaking across the room but not quickly like Cassia did earlier. He knew Cassia was watching, so he moved in a slow-motion run. When he got to the bathroom, he turned around and flashed her one last time. He said, "I'm getting a shower. I'll be down in a few minutes."

Cassia laughed. "There is something seriously wrong with you."

The phone started ringing again as Cassia made her way to the kitchen. The idea of something happening to Grandma B troubled her but not as bad as something happening to Mitch. It was the sixth month of the year and her sixth day at Number Six Ashby House. Cassia scolded herself for trying to connect the number six to everything bad that happens in her life.

Before she reached the phone, it stopped ringing. Her attention turned to a loud knocking at the door. Cassia opened the door. Mitch was standing with a bunch of sunflowers clenched in his right hand. He smiled that familiar toothy smile and said, "Jewel is really going to be pissed when she lands at Heathrow this morning."

Cassia pulled Mitch into the doorway. She held him tighter than she ever had before. The ladybugs in her stomach were now doing a happy dance. When Cassia let go of Mitch, he kissed her face all over and excitedly said, "I have been trying to call you all morning, sleepyhead." Cassia thought about Chris and froze. She had trouble concentrating. She heard Mitch's voice but only grasped tidbits of words like *love* and *baby* coming from his mouth. Cassia tried to come up with a way to get Mitch out of the house before Chris came down the stairs, but Chris was already halfway down the steps. It was now Mitch who stood frozen.

Cassia introduced Mitch to Chris. They did not shake hands but nodded their heads. There was an awkward silence that seemed to last for hours, when in fact it was just a few seconds. Mitch handed Cassia the sunflowers that were still in his right hand. "I have to go and umm…" Mitch did not finish his sentence but instead turned around and walked out the door. Cassia could not move, but the gravel pinging against Mitch's tires as he drove away from Ashby House amplified in her ears. Chris kissed Cassia on the cheek and said, "I'll call you later." Cassia continued standing motionless as Chris closed the front door behind him. Immediately, there was a knocking on the door. Cassia jumped out of her stupor. She opened the front door. Chris said, "Can you open the garage door so I can get my car out please?"

Cassia sat in the kitchen listening to the unmistakable rumbling muffler of Chris's Mustang moving farther away from Ashby House. When all sounds were gone, she thought about Annabelle— Annabelle would know what to do. She was probably in this sort of situation hundreds of times. Cassia picked up her phone and scrolled down to Annabelle's number. She stared at it for a few seconds and then placed the phone back on the table. She knew that no one except her could decide who she wanted to be with. Then the ladybugs took flight again after a most disturbing thought entered her head— maybe she had lost both of them. Cassia put her head down across her arms on the table. She closed her eyes and whispered, "Mama, what should I do?"

Birds were singing, and the sky was bright blue. Cassia walked arm in arm with her mother in the same green meadow where she had walked with Lily Roberts in an earlier dream. She knew it was the same field as before because she recognized the rows and rows of tall sunflowers growing high up on the hill. Marianne took her daughter's hand and led her to a blanket where they sat facing each other.

Marianne took her daughter's hands into hers and began, "My first love was a boy named Billy Gardner. We were high school sweethearts. When he left me for another girl, I went a little crazy. I took some pills and then told your grandmother." Marianne thought for a moment and then continued, "I was always so insecure even though I knew that your father loved me. I probably questioned his love for me on a daily basis. You see, Cassia, he needed reassurance every now and then too, but I did not see it because I was too caught up in my needs. You are a stronger person than I ever was."

"Mama, how come I feel like I want to crawl into a shell this time?"

Marianne placed her right hand under her daughter's chin. "Listen, you are a logical problem solver. You need to settle this in the same manner which you live by—list the pros and cons of each relationship, and you will come to the best decision for you."

Cassia looked up when she heard a giggling little girl. Her father was a few steps away from the running child. Before Cassia could rise from the blanket, the little girl's arms were wrapped around her neck.

Cassia fought to stay in her dream. She kept her eyes closed tightly, but the sounds from the singing birds were replaced by the refrigerator's hum and the *click click* of the ceiling fan above her head. Cassia rose from the chair and wiped her eyes. She pulled off two sheets of paper from the notepad attached to the refrigerator. On the first page, she wrote Mitch's name and ran a line down the middle dividing it. She then wrote the word *Pros* on the left side and the word *Cons* on the right side. She did the same for the second sheet, except she wrote Chris's name. Cassia started writing on the list with Chris's name first:

Pros:

1) nice
2) nice looking
3) good sense of humor

Cassia started with the cons:

1) loves his damn car too much
2) too close to his family and too many of them

Cassia felt guilty about putting Chris's family in the negative column, but she was not accustomed to a large family presence in her life nor did she believe that she could get used to that kind of smothering. The next item on Chris's list was the deal breaker:

3)   does not want any more children

Cassia began on Mitch's list. In the pros section, she wrote, "THE LOVE OF MY LIFE." Cassia picked up her phone and dialed Mitch's number. He did not answer on the first or second ring. For all she knew, he could be on a plane heading back to London.

CHAPTER FIFTY

CASSIA SIGHED WITH RELIEF WHEN Mitch answered his phone on the third ring. She was even more relieved when he told her he was still in the area—only twenty minutes away from Ashby House having coffee at a McDonald's. Cassia dressed quickly and drove to meet with him. Mitch waited about ten minutes and then ordered Cassia a cup of coffee with three creams and one extra on the side. Mitch then thought about how he felt seeing Cassia with another man. It hurt him.

He finally understood Cassia's pain. About ten minutes later, Cassia slid into the seat across from Mitch. Cassia looked up. "Mitch, I love you. I want to be with you."

"What about that other guy, Cassia?" Mitch said with his voice cracking.

Cassia thought about her mother's words about reassurance. She reached for Mitch's hands from across the table. She held them in hers and said, "I'm not in love with him. It's you and has always been you."

Mitch smiled. Cassia took her cup of coffee and motioned for Mitch to follow her to the booth near the window. Instead of sitting across from him, Cassia sat next to him. Mitch put his arm around Cassia and kissed her like it was the first kiss shared by new lovers. When they looked up, a lady cutting pancakes for her two small children shot them a look that said "get a room." Cassia and Mitch put the lids back on their coffees. They got up from the booth keeping their heads down as they walked hand in hand out of the McDonald's.

Mitch turned around when they got outside the door. "Let's get married when we get back to Baltimore."

Still holding onto Mitch's hand, Cassia led him to her car. "Mitch, I'm not going back to Baltimore. I want to live here. Ever since I came to Richmond—to Ashby House—I have been thinking about turning the mansion into a wedding venue. What do you think about that?"

Mitch's eyes were open wide. His eyebrows were raised. This caused his eyeglasses to slide halfway down his nose. He pushed them back up to the bridge of his nose. "Ashby House a wedding venue? Hmm…that might work. I never really got a good look at the place this morning for some reason." Mitch held his hand over his mouth and coughed out two words—*that guy.*

Cassia smiled. "Sorry. Okay. Follow me in your car, and I will give you an official tour."

Cassia said, "Oh, by the way, I am very rich now. Along with the house, Uncle Charles left me tons of money."

Mitch shook his head. "Damn, if I'd known that, I would have made you pay for the coffees."

They laughed. Mitch took Cassia in his arms and kissed her again. She gave into his kiss and then abruptly broke free. "Oh shit. I am meeting with Peaches Winchester at noon." Cassia did not search through her purse because she knew that Mitch always kept his phone in his pants pocket. She stood in front of Mitch and motioned anxiously for him to get his phone. "What time is it? What time is it?"

Mitch checked the time. "It's eleven forty-five."

Cassia sighed with relief. "Oh, good, I can still make it on time." She looked up at Mitch, and after thinking for a second, she said, "Come with me. I want you to meet my grandmother."

Mitch said, "Your grandmother? I've met Grandma B."

"No, not her. Peaches Winchester."

Mitch smiled and said in his best Cuban accent, "Okay, Lucy, you got some 'splaining to do."

Cassia laughed and said, "Just follow me, Ricky."

On the ten-minute drive to Peaches's house, Cassia made two mental notes in her head—her usual to-do list, which included a phone call to Chris (Cassia mentally wrote a question mark after *phone call* because she knew that she needed to tell Chris her plans in person), and another listing the things that she needed to tell Mitch, things that she had discovered and uncovered since arriving at Ashby House, like encounters with her mother, father, and most of all, their little girl, Elizabeth.

Cassia parked her car in the driveway at Peaches's house. Mitch parked behind her. They walked hand in hand to the front door. Before they could knock, Peaches flung open the door. She let out a half smile, not showing any surprise at seeing an uninvited person with Cassia. Just as Peaches wore her heart on her sleeve, she also could not hide the degree of anxiety on her face. Peaches moved inside motioning for them to come into the house. Cassia introduce Mitch to Peaches as her ex-husband. She pulled Mitch close and whispered that she did not want to go into any details about them just yet. Even though Cassia did not believe that showing up with Mitch was the cause of Peaches's agitation, she nonetheless apologized. Mitch did not say a word. His silence spoke loudly to his feelings of awkwardness.

Peaches was thrown off by Mitch accompanying Cassia. She wondered if Mitch being there would throw a wrench into her plan. Peaches saw the look of uneasiness on Mitch's and Cassia's faces. Her intentions were never to be rude to anyone, so she hugged Cassia and then Mitch. She said, "It is so nice to meet you, Mitch. I am so glad that Cassia has brought you here." She motioned to the couch where Cassia sat yesterday. "Please, please have a seat. I will get us some drinks."

Peaches disappeared into the kitchen. Cassia immediately said to Mitch, "I am so sorry. She is not acting like herself—well, not like she did yesterday. We will only stay a few minutes." Mitch smiled and patted Cassia's hand.

In the kitchen, Peaches placed a few ice cubes in a glass and poured a generous amount of scotch from the decanter on the counter. She guzzled down half the glass of liquid. Peaches placed the half-empty glass onto the counter. A hand gently touched hers. "Mother, everything will be fine."

CHAPTER FIFTY-ONE

PEACHES HANDED ONE GLASS OF tea to Mitch and the other to Cassia. She paced back and forth across the room and did not say a word. After a few seconds, Cassia broke the silence, "Peaches, are you okay?"

Peaches sat down on the only wing-back chair in the room just a few feet from where Mitch and Cassia were sitting. She leaned back in the chair and began, "Cassia, I asked you to come back today because I have something more to tell you. However, first, let me begin by telling you how happy I am that you are here. I realize that the circumstances behind your conception might keep you from considering me your grandmother." Peaches looked at Cassia and smiled. "Probably one of those gray areas, but I would really like to be part of your life."

Cassia stood up and hugged Peaches. She said, "I would be honored to call you my grandmother."

The women stood facing each other holding hands. Then Peaches turned and began pacing again. She said, "Cassia, you might want to sit back down." Cassia complied.

"About six months ago, Charlie got really sick. The video that Raymond showed you of Charlie's was taken right before his kidney transplant. He was close to death."

Cassia interrupted, "What do you mean? He *was* close to death?"

Uncle Charles entered the room from the kitchen. He did not look sickly like he did in the video, and he certainly wasn't dead. He looked healthy and older, but Cassia knew his face. He said, "It took being so close to death to make me realize my one biggest regret in life. I could not fight your grandmother to see you when you were younger, and I was afraid to get in touch with you later because you would see that you have Lawson eyes—my eyes. I planned to honor your parents' request and keep their secret, but for so many reasons, some truths need to be told." Charles looked at his mother. "Right, Mother?"

Peaches smiled and nodded. She knew that he was referring to her recent confession telling him about her affair and that he was not a Winchester.

The ladybugs in Cassia's stomach were panicked and confused. The urge to bolt out of the room came over Cassia like it did the day she found Mitch and Jewel locked in that kiss. Cassia stood up. She looked at Uncle Charles, who finally stopped pacing back and forth across the room. Through angry tears, she said, "I don't understand. Why the charade?"

"I know you are upset, but please stay and hear me out," Uncle Charles said while touching Cassia's arm. She stood with her eyes closed and arms folded in front of her for a few seconds. She then opened her eyes, took a deep breath, unfolded her arms, and sat down on the couch. Mitch moved closer to Cassia.

Charles began pacing again with his hands doing as much talking as his mouth. He continued, "While I was waiting for my kidney, not sure if I would get one in time, I told Raymond about all the regrets in my life and things that I would have changed. When I recovered, Raymond reminded me that I had been given a second chance for a reason—to make things right. Cassia, I am so sorry. When I came up with the plan, it seemed like a good idea, but now"—Charles shrugged his shoulders—"but now I wonder if I made a mistake. Perhaps I should have handled things differently."

"Why not just call me? I would have come to see you."

"Cassia, yes, I probably should have just called you, and I do believe you would have come to see me. However, there was something else that I wanted from you, and I wasn't sure you would or could do—I wanted you to fall in love with Ashby House like you did when you were a little girl. I needed you to care about the spirits in that house like I do."

"Is that the reason for the stipulation that I stay in the house for six days?"

"Yes, I was hoping that in that time you would remember why you loved Ashby House and my friends who occupy it. I knew that you had the gift that day when you saw me in the attic dancing with Elizabeth."

Cassia asked, "Why tell me not to say anything to anyone about what I saw?"

Uncle Charles shook his head. "Cassia, people can be so cruel. I did not want you to experience the ridicule that I had to deal with as a child when I told them about my friends at Ashby House."

"So, who all was in on this sham?" Cassia smiled.

"My mother and Raymond."

Cassia said, "What about Maddie?"

"No, I had no idea that she was still in touch with a gal that she befriended when she lived here. Well, this woman called her to tell her about my demise. She was not to find out. Raymond told Annabelle that he had already contacted Maddie. He didn't really, but she found out anyway. Of course, I had no idea that her mama had just died. I felt bad about deceiving her, so I decided to 'ease her pain' by enticing her here with the promise of an inheritance. I hope the fifty thousand dollars is enough of an 'I'm sorry' gift. I will call her...better have Raymond call her because she might have a heart attack if she hears my voice on the phone." Uncle Charles poured himself a drink from the carafe on the table. "I owe her a *big* apology,"

"Yes, you do." Cassia looked at Uncle Charles with a puzzled brow. "So...is Ashby House really mine?"

Uncle Charles hugged Cassia and laughed. "Yes, and so is the money. All that paperwork you signed was real."

With her face buried in Uncle Charles's shirt, Cassia took a deep breath. She then pulled away. "Tell me something, Uncle Charles, how did you get your tobacco scent to seem so strong at times in the house? Was there a diffuser or something that emitted that sweet cherry smell into the air every now and then?"

Uncle Charles's big-belly laugh brought back many good memories. After he recovered, he leaned in close to Cassia like he did when telling her his stories when she was a little girl. He said, "That Frederick! He loves my tobacco."

EPILOGUE

Six years later

"DID WE EVER FIGHT LIKE that, Cass?" Annabelle said while watching their two girls from the front porch screaming at each other.

Cassia laughed holding her six months pregnant belly. "No, Belle, we were *always* angels."

Annabelle called out, "Abigail! Emma! On the porch *now!*"

Cassia reached out for Abigail while Emma stood next to her mother. Cassia said, "Abigail, what is the problem?"

"I told Emma that I wanted to play with the little dark-skinned girl for a while and that I would play with her later. She said that I was making up the little girl because I didn't want to be her friend anymore." Cassia's eye scanned the property. She saw the face of a little black girl about Abigail's age peeking out from behind the weeping willow tree.

Annabelle said, "Okay. You girls have reached your VC (visiting capacity). Time to go. Emma, tell Abigail you are sorry."

"Say you're sorry too," Cassia said, nudging a stubborn Abigail closer to Emma.

*****

September 6

I am sitting on the front porch swing with Abigail sleeping next to me. She is leaning against me, and I am in awe of her sweet face. I know it is time to have the *talk* with my daughter. However, instead

247

of making her feel like a freak because she can communicate with the dead, I am going to teach her how to embrace her uniqueness and be proud of her gift, but for just a few minutes, I am going to let her dream peacefully.

With Peaches's approval, I changed the name of Ashby House to Elizabeth Manor (in honor of my daughter). I am pregnant with my third child—another girl. Mitch and I will be naming her Allison. When we named Abigail, a third person—Chris, her biological father—had input.

Chris and I share custody of Abigail. Mitch is daddy, and Chris is papa. Abigail has a wonderful extended family. Mitch and I have learned to embrace the idea of more people in our lives because it means more people loving our children. I suppose that I am keeping with family tradition by having a child with someone I am not married to. However, I am breaking away from part of that tradition because Abigail is growing up knowing who her biological father is— no secrets.

The merger between Raymond and Robert's father halted in light of what happened between Annabelle and Robert. Robert was paroled a few months ago after serving only five years for attempted murder (he had a great attorney). He told Annabelle that he will be taking a paternity test when he gets out of prison. Annabelle has never told me whether Robert is Emma's father, but the resemblance to Robert is unmistakable. If the paternity test confirms that Robert is Emma's father, he will be going for full custody.

Uncle Charles bailed out Raymond's law firm, and Annabelle stayed with him. Sunny and Annabelle got married here at Elizabeth Manor about a year ago. Sunny filed for divorce after six months. He caught Annabelle cheating with a much younger lawyer in her office. He is doing well and can be seen (just about all of him) in the Richmond Fireman's Calendar (he is Firefighter July).

My mother still comes to me in my dreams. She brings Elizabeth sometimes. I talked to Maddie last week. She has never had another nightmare about her ex-husband since Lily killed him in her dream. Uncle Charles stops by about once a week. He sometimes goes into the attic, and I don't see him for hours. He tells me that Frederick slips away from his wife once in a while (when she lets him) so they can play checkers, listen to music, and smoke. I don't like the smoking in the house but confess that I cannot control the smile that forms on my lips whenever I get a whiff of the aroma of the pipe tobacco meandering down the stairs. Elizabeth, Lily, and Jonathan have never appeared again. I guess they are really gone. However, there are others that come to me. I try to help them.

Mitch and I are doing great. Our wedding business has really taken off. On the sixth of June, which was six months ago, we threw ourselves a huge anniversary party. We called it our 6+6 (six years before and six more years now). I still try to "avoid" the number six in my life, but I don't get freaked out as much anymore because something good came of that night of "sixes." That was the night that Allison was conceived. Chris and his family came to the party along with Chris's new girlfriend Haley. (He had to get a restraining order against Maura after she broke into his house one night. He found her next to him when he woke up in the morning.)

Mitch's mother and father, Uncle Charles, Raymond, and Peaches came to the party. Oh yeah, Grandma B came too. She has turned over all of my mother's belongings to me including her journals. She told me the reason that she withheld those things from me was to protect me from finding out about my mother's mental health issues. I have forgiven her for spending the money that my father left for me in trust (but I made her turn over the Renoir to me). I refused to press charges. I could not send an eighty-four-year-old woman to jail, though sometimes she still makes me regret my decision.

Cassia put down her journal. She watched Mitch photographing a group of Girl Scouts. He was wearing the vampire teeth. They were laughing. Cassia smiled.

The End

ABOUT THE AUTHOR

Jo-Ann Pasternak Gilbert grew up in Baltimore, Maryland. Her grandchildren, her cat, Lulu, along with her writing keep her busy.